European Trash

DZANC BOOKS

www.dzancbooks.org

Originally published in Swedish as *Europeiskt skräp. Sexton sätt att minnas en pappa.*

First Edition: November 2013

ISBN: 978-1-938604-36-2

Translation of this novel was made possible by support from the Swedish Arts Council.

This project is supported in part by an award from the National Endowment for the Arts and the MCACA.

Cover and book design: Black Coffee Press

Printed in the United States of America

10 9 8 7 6 5 4 3 2 1

European Trash

Fourteen Ways to Remember a Father

Ulf Peter Hallberg

Translated by Erland Anderson and Ingrid Cassady

Ulf Hallberg
1919-2007
In memoriam

For the collector the world is present—even orderly arranged—in each and every item.
Walter Benjamin

To my sons,
Julian and Lenny

EUROPEAN TRASH

To Peter and Lena,

Remember that I will still exist in
a wider sense. Or rather, that any
inanimate object may be your father,
expecially if that object is older
than you. They all make memory of
me possible, so keep an eye on them
(every once in a while at least). I
will eventually lose track of the
them, like the rest of my baggage.

"RULES AND GUIDELINES"
Ulf Hallberg, black notebook

1. The Collector's Will

I open the door and walk into my father's empty apartment. Already in the hall I get the feeling that he is still in the kitchen making coffee, quickly turning around to look in my direction. In that unfamiliar silence, visions and memories are released: how he walked toward me with that gleam in his eye, how he pronounced my name, how he inspected me to check my level of fatigue. It's been a lifelong relationship from childhood to adulthood, his personality reflected in his slow movements, my impatience and joy. All that is overshadowed now by irretrievable silence and total darkness. All paintings and objects speak to me of him, of his sense of order, of his tender dedication as a collector. I know everything will soon be scattered about, but his objects are still resisting; they are still attached to him, even though he vanished and left them in the apartment. I stand by the rarely used fireplace, which once caused so much smoke, right next to his priceless Endre Nemes watercolor, which he sold against his will because we needed the money, to a teacher at the Mellanheden School who really didn't appreciate it enough. That four-edged *The Machine Man* set my imagination working because it didn't look like anything I'd seen before. My father's directorial hands made sure that Beauty had a place in our home in a miniature exhibit of everything created, like a mirror image of a grander scheme. That way he could love the universe and give it its own meaning. My glance meets the writing desk where he always used to sit. In front of that large oak desk, he held vigils long into the night, stooped over his books and clippings. He always had classical music playing directly from the radio, or from cassette tapes in frightfully bad conditions, which he got off the P1 radio station's classical recordings, filling two closets. And these things helped him rally his energy during the twelve years following my mother's death.

His place in front of his desk has become the axis my world revolves around; his glance has filled my life with meaning. His black notebooks are lying there on the desk stacked neatly together as if ready for mailing, some with beautiful elastic bands wrapped around certain important pages. I still don't dare to touch them, even though he often picked one up and read to me. One of the books is open right in the middle of a note. A foreign word translated: *"Erato = the Muse of Love."* I know that he jotted down his own and others' thoughts without bothering to differentiate whose they were. Everything became immersed in his grand structure, the collection that was his life's energy, and unusual defense against the world's entropy. Night after night he wrote with his thread-like style, going from one context to another, from one commentary to another fancy, from one fact into larger fictions. That was his encyclopedia—the words he had made his own, the energy he had mustered against the void. I hit upon another gem by chance: "Birds who are larger than wind itself don't know where to rest their wings." The words pull me toward him. I still feel his breath, though I just closed his eyes. I keep turning the pages, quickly and nervously: "The novel is usually the combination of two absolutes—absolute individuality and absolute universality." I am alone among his gifts. There is no real message, just this obvious pile of notebooks from the Local Swedish Agrarian Chapter in Hörby with the birth and death dates of my grandparents, Victor Hallberg 1885-1951, Hertha Hallberg 1890-1971, as well as a pink-dotted notebook with foreign words and a catalog of all the paintings stored in the kitchen cabinets. My glance falls on a note that, unusually enough, has been attributed to its source, "All creatures subject to emptiness" (Romans 8:20). The first words in the pink-dotted notebook are "redundancy = superfluous, excess information (which can be eliminated without any loss)."

> Comprendre ce qui est = to understand what is really happening.

It's a fictional world my father has passed on—all these quotations, directions, figures and stories that he left behind. The figures in his collection are messengers.

13

They stand out as in a mirror of a dream novel that will always join the two of us together. He has given me a new assignment. I will no longer take care of him, not make any phone calls, not listen to his rambling associations. Now I have to hold together everything that was ours. I am the last one who still remembers. All this miscellany that actually doesn't go together, but by dint of a unifying force—that strong interest and passion for beauty in all its details—is contained in this collection of notebooks. Our family memories connect to the objects in this collection. All these things belong to a parallel universe that for my father was always equal, if not greater than the real world. And what is "the real world" in the face of annihilation? Who can say anything about reality when faced with death? Who is strong enough to die without fear? Who can lift all sorrow from a son's chest faced with an empty chair at a deserted writing desk? Who can explain the real world when a son and a daughter will stand aghast before their father, who, bandaged around his head to keep his jaw from gaping wide, lies there like a worshipful astronaut gazing at heaven with perfect attention and waiting to be engulfed by the vast reaches of outer space. The great collection, worthless in the eyes of ordinary people and the market place, and the novel are all we have in the face of death. My father knew this and gave us that insight as his legacy. That was his big gamble on a blessing that would last. Perhaps just because of that he wrote on the

What are the possibilities in a world that has been transformed into a trap.

inside cover of his black notebook: "When I am laid in earth, remember me." And on page 145, the following: "From Peter I expect the most significant expansion of our reality." That's what a father does, because a father knows that his son's life needs that protection. That every life depends on strength and effort. That a father believes in his son or his daughter, and that his eyes watch over them. In that paternal care and responsibility there lies a pledge for our eternal salvation.

When my friends used to ask, "What does your Dad do?" I never knew how to answer. He was more than an art historian, more than a connoisseur of life, more than the one who vacuums and sits in the kitchen clipping out articles from Scandinavian newspapers, which, thanks to that noise, helped my sister and me fall asleep peacefully. He was the foremost purveyor of the European Trash and the connecting link to the past, a monk from distant times who had been given the task of uttering truth in an age dominated by lies. He clipped articles on nineteenth century Danish painters out of duty and joy; he read novels in order to become a better human being; he made notes in his black notebooks so that his "encyclopedia" might uncover everything that related to the human dilemma; his allusions both to art and to books were assertions that emptiness can be overcome, that light is greater than darkness. As he lay dying, having looked at me for the last time, as the pupils in his eyes wandered toward the place where my sister

> The mystery of the human being is the mystery of responsibility.

15

was sitting, and then back toward me and my eyes, and then burst and became one with me—right then, when his breathing ceased, I was still not certain he wouldn't rise up one last time and describe the serve in tennis, tell me how he took his stance, tossed up the ball a little more to the right and, by this crucial change, allowed it to get an extra punch from above the right shoulder, and then, so clearly triumphant: "What do you think of that, Peter?" Yes, now he had proved at last that one really could get enough power from the hip necessary to ace the most difficult opponent—something he had always recommended before. And therefore, there was nothing frightening about his death. He died as he lived with full concentration on the task at hand. He could have stood up and referred to the place where Endre Nemes' water color used to hang on the wall in the living room to the right of the open fireplace, and say: "I would never have sold Nemes if we hadn't needed the money, but it was still the wrong thing. The few times I tried to sell something I was never offered a sufficient sum. I was finagled or short changed. Now Endre Nemes' *The Machine Man* lives somewhere else. He is a refugee again."

In the year 1984, I was residing in La Maison Belgique at the Cité Universitaire in Paris and was making my living writing articles for the Helsingborg's Dagblad on the Solidarity intellectuals in Paris, Michel Foucault's and Jürgen Habermas' lectures at the College de France, and stories about the City of Lights' favorable influences on a young psyche. One spring day I walked along the book shelves at the Maison Heinrich Heine in Paris and took out books at random: Goethe, Schiller, Büchner, Wedekind,

Mann. Outside, in the park at the Cité Universitaire, the springtime sun was shining brightly, and young couples were fumbling for words that would ring fresh every time as long as they could believe in them. Inside in the library, I paused in front of two enormous volumes with the title *The Arcades Project* and began skimming through the pages. It was a labyrinth of entrances into the city outside, but also into its past, the innermost glowing cells in the City of Lights. I sat down at a table nearby and started to read. Suddenly I was in a passage, a little glass-domed street that for Walter Benjamin functions as a time machine and a short cut, the passageway between two house gates, two centuries and two Parises: the nineteenth century capital, and the twentieth century city of dreams. Baudelaire is the arch-witness: the secret spy of dissatisfaction with the supremacy of his own Middle Class, and the one who in his use of words catches the intimate connection between the mechanics of shock and the contact with the big city masses. Victor Hugo on the rolling balcony of the omnibus, Baudelaire strolling around the Île St. Louis in his indoor slippers and work shirt, the conspirator Blanqui with his quill pen in hand in his prison cell, the flâneur who saunters through the passage with a turtle on a leash, Balzac who lives his harried life constantly in haste and breaks down prematurely, the prostitute who is both the entrepreneur and the commodity, Dickens who can't write without street noise, the voyeur Saint-Simon

> In our Milky Way alone there are thirty to fifty billion stars. The number of Milky Way systems, "galaxies", visible to the best and strongest telescopes amount to a billion.

preparing to transform human society, the workers who stop shooting from the barricades in order to allow a wedding procession to pass through—all these things spoke to me intimately.

Above all, I saw the collector in my inner eye (as a starving student, and as a Hjalmar Branting scholar, sitting at a table in the National Library), my own father in front of his desk on Rönneholmsvägen in Malmö, writing in his notebooks, making an order out of the clippings from the newspapers, pasting those articles down, arranging postcard photographs in boxes and drawers, moving slowly among his beloved objects: porcelain Samurai warriors with drawn swords over the piano, an African wooden sculpture high atop the bookshelves, all the first purchases of paintings by Nyhavn in the blue afternoon light, Klenø's nude painting of Karen, his wife, still lifes that were sold before the paint was even dry and therefore stained the self portrait of the artist with brush in his hand—and finally over my father's desk a sunset over the Färö Islands, signed Frimod Jensen, 1972. Where is Klenø's wife today? Is the artist still alive and, if so, where? In France? Why did such a thought occur to me? What did all these paintings in my memory add up to, unexpectedly released by my work at the library in Paris?

It was a way to freeze historical time, just as in Malmö, where my father, behind closed Venetian blinds, devoted himself to Baudelaire's shady world and the Danish nineteenth century. He didn't have a particular purpose, no credit toward retirement, but a shining energy that successful people secretly envied.

Sitting there in the library I paid no notice of time's

passing. I noted down the names of the passages and set out into the city in order to find them. Passage du Caire, Passage des Panoramas, Passage de Jouffroy; I found them everywhere among houses and squares. A certain dim light, worn-away letters, a clock with hands that had stopped moving. I forgot all about the spring sunlight and stopped meeting with Heather and Moira, put off an advance by a seriously neurotic Egyptologist, and treaded instead through the pillars at the Palais Royal from nineteenth century Paris. I became acquainted not only with Baudelaire but also with coquettes and visionaries, writers and artists, flâneurs and collectors. Was this an escape or a homecoming? I saw my father's lifestyle as a painting in a frame, but nevertheless magically protected, kept secret, yes, mounted onto the softest of velvet borders. He took on a mission that he considered connected to the very core of existence.

> It is not difficult to age; that takes place automatically. What is hard is to get rid of the feeling of youth.

My father came to Mölle in the mid 1950s. Together with my mother, Eva, and me, we rented a small cottage, named Pyttebo. From the room with a window you could see the ocean and the Norra Strandvägen with the relief of Kullaberg Mountain in the background. My sister was born the following year and we spent every summer thereafter in Mölle. My mother was a teacher, which meant long summer vacations. In 1959 my parents were among those who started the Mölle Tennis Club. There was an old clay court up at the Garden Café, and they saw a possibility of constructing something worthwhile and also developing stronger ties with their friends. They all believed in sportsmanship, camaraderie, and physical exercise. My father was the coach of the junior level every summer. His salary was paid in cans of coffee and Magnusson's delicious Vienna pastries from the Garden Café. No one cared that he wasn't making any real money. Least of all himself.

In 2007 when the Mölle Tennis Club had its annual meeting—in the midst of the ongoing summer tournament—decisions were made about updating the language regarding certain rules; however, it was unanimously decided to keep the antiquated "mission statement": "The Club shall henceforth be dedicated to the members' spiritual and physical well being as well as to the promotion of their good fellowship and sportsmanship." All members of the board understood the original wording perfectly. It had a taste of everything that the Swedish Post Office and Television Networks had cast aside. It is reiterated in the statement from the regulations, "The Idea of a Sports Movement." It's a matter of honor, sportsmanship, and human values. It's about standing up for something, maturity in the face of situations that demand strength, concentration, bravery and endurance. It's about developing your instincts in order to connect mind and body, about doing your best so others can develop their own potential. When large organizations in society eliminate the need for personal responsibility and human values, the field of sports becomes the last playing field where values remain well defined—right over wrong—learning how to lose with grace, and win without boasting. You can't lower the standards of the game without a penalty because the opponent may shape up and improve at any time. Those who disdain sport, with their snide grimaces at soccer fans, tennis amateurs, swimmers, runners, and cyclists, miss out on the brilliant moments of demanding struggle and potential growth—the constant dose of wisdom out of wins and losses, the participants' playful and pleasurable challenges to themselves. The genius of sports is that it includes unexpected challenges in numerous abilities: timing, clever stratagems, and lightning-fast, difficult exertions for the psyche. The odd thing—and at the same time the opposite of sinking to the level of pathetic jokes, shaggy dog stories, and stereotypical characters on all the media channels—is that in the realm of sports no one ever tires of finding a better opponent. It's something you want to face up to. You long for the challenge! In this era of resounding big lies, it is a comfort to realize that no soccer or tennis player can talk or argue his or her way to victory. You can make moves of low cunning in tennis and hit lousy shots, but those who object to such moves are forced to control their emotions and strengthen their focus on the goal until next year, and thus they learn something essential. One shouldn't be the victim of a weak moral standard, a psychological warfare based on petty boredom. Instead, hit the ball even more forcefully and expel that corruption from the court by dint of one's skill. Don't crawl down into the abyss of self-pity. In sports, a victory is never unjust, but a defeat often delivers strengthening qualities with lightning-like insight into the nature of change, endurance, and continuing struggle. It's as in Cesar Vallejo's line: "I always want to be alive, even lying on my stomach." The ability to lose without succumbing to bitterness is the key for improving the game, and even life. We know that the game is an exceptional case of mercy—a shining light, the scent of fresh grass, the sound of the bouncing ball, the fans catching their breath—it is a place of dreams beyond death and the abyss. For my father, the collector, it was his point of concentration, his tennis swing was an art, and mental challenges were a matter of philosophy and inner strength.

Find the sounds
wait
listen to the rain
before it falls.

It was natural for my father to say "a healthy mind in a healthy body," and to teach his son how to keep his eye on the ball to outsmart his opponent. Later he searched in the Temple of Art and read little by little every line I wrote or translated as an adult. He often sat and read through *The Arcades Project*. No excuses, no stories, no deceptions—just that desire to be alone, to be absorbed into his own world, collecting things, writing down significant phrases and sentences. Yet these activities were provoking to others. "Who does he think he is? Oh, your Mom is supporting him? What does she think about that?" And all of these people working full time and discussing their salaries and pension systems. "I only have five weeks vacation so you can't expect me to flip through articles and clip them out, ask deep questions about the meaning of the universe. I need my vacation time to unwind. The alarm clock goes off every morning and then it is time to go to work, leaving no time for nineteenth century Danish art, Ulf! And no time for reading through all the different Scandinavian papers. Perhaps it is good that someone does such things. But then he had better have a sweet wife like you, Eva, who leaves him alone to his leisure activities." I never heard my mother raise any complaint about it. Never a dispute about money. Never an inquiry about his activities. Just loving respect. Perhaps she had gained that belief in art at school, where she sat at a green desk in that spacious library handing out books to children whose eyes gleamed with questions.

What is left of that world today? I see only children blinded by their cell phone displays. I have watched my father's peers become passive and lose their humanity despite their positions in society and a comfortable living in old age. I have seen them lose that energy despite new upgraded models of their fancy cars every other year, and taking several weeks of vacation in various European countries. That despite of or as a consequence of becoming executives or members of the judiciary. Their position, security, and material comfort didn't help to improve the condition of their souls. Their problem wasn't that they had closed their eyes. In fact, they kept a constant watch on everything, but they didn't have my father's passion, they were missing that special attachment to the European Trash. Important experiences from the past withered in the glare of their lifestyles, becoming a dead language. On vacation they were willing to cast a quick glance at that Trash, in order to be persuaded that in some strange way these things belonged there, things to be mentioned later in conversation. Cultural experiences were a kind of necessary burden that would allow you to unwind later with a clear conscience—just to lay back. In those moments, members of the male sex would always pour down a stiff drink. "It's vacation time." So when they became old and sick they were disarmed against Death. They often died fearful and embittered with the perception that some unknown, all-mighty, primordial force had extinguished their social network. Their last words were "Life is unfair. Look at what life's done to me!" Their machine-like contempt for the values that supported my father's life, as a single retiree on 59 crowns a day and careful shopping at the local market, led them to die shamefully—their well-aired, antiseptic retirement homes and hospital rooms reeked of a nauseous stench of machine angst. Their sons and daughters didn't find the time to visit them on their deathbeds. That was the collapse of their welfare system: a single-minded devotion to consumerism detached from any link to a solid culture. During their heyday as Machine Men the essential ingredients had been transformed into trash. My father's lonely fight to achieve the stature of a great collector, his apartment filled to the brim with miscellaneous paintings and other objets d'art, dragged home from the flee markets even when he didn't have enough money to buy them—all this was the work of a madman, an outsider's hobby, a fool's errand. The machine men were totally convinced that all this activity was some kind of cover up. My father had achieved nothing; he had no status, no position in society. But, really, my father was (and this was a convenient way for the machine men to categorize him) a pauper. Just look at our car. But, according to my father, his secret from the outside world—despite his utter ignorance of his poverty—had led him directly into the high Temple of Art.

I heard the tearing of magazine paper, the sound of scissors as my father cut out those extremely valuable collections of truths from the wide world, and it gave me the feeling that everything was as it should be. Then I would turn to my pillow and say to myself:

> Now I lay me down to sleep.
> I pray the Lord my soul to keep.
> If I should die before I wake,
> I pray the Lord my soul to take.

And then it might happen that I would go to my father to tell him that my pillow was too warm, asking him to stuff it in the refrigerator for a while. A few minutes later, up in my bunk bed, I would lay my head on a refrigerated pillow, light my flash light under the blanket and read about wild Indians, English boarding-school boys, David Copperfield, Sherlock Holmes and Dr. Watson. And always the sound of my sister's soft breathing and the tearing of magazine paper.

I was always reading in the corner of the living room, by the radio, because I didn't have my own room. My father sat at his nut-brown desk in the other corner and cut out those articles from Scandinavian newspapers. Then he glued them into binders, which were marked under different labels: Swedish collection exhibits, foreign exhibits, the Danish nineteenth century, twentieth century Swedish art, and so on. He gave me an inkling that the true knowledge of the world could be found right there on our bookshelves.

"Artistic values are the true ones," he would say.

"Money isn't interesting. You'll inherit these collections later."

I imagined how I, after his death, would donate all these pearls of knowledge to the great museums of the North.

A staff of attendants would give lectures and visitors would be directed to a certain room—Ulf Hallberg's Room—just like the one I had seen at Malmö's City Library for that "Son of Malmö," Hjalmar Gullberg, the poet.

> Not even death,
> whose name I am afraid
> to mention, can take
> beauty away from me.

But when I was thirteen years old, my father suddenly moved all of the folders down into the cellar.

When I asked him what had happened, he said, "We're in a new era. I'm going to start reading novels now, just like you." At the time I was reading André Gide's *The Counterfeiters* and Dostoevsky's *The Brothers Karamazov.*

Naturally I was proud I could influence my father. But it was my own life's darkest moment—an incredible undermining of his values—and I didn't dare ask any follow-up questions. How could he lower those files down to the cellar? What was to come of those collections now? Had he considered the problem of dampness and mildew, among other things?

Five years later our landlord, with the French-sounding name, Deros, took over some of our space in the cellar before my father had the time to empty out his things, so a large portion of the collection and a set of elegant furniture from Fammi, his mother, were lost.

This was among the things I never dared to ask my father about. It had its source in a certain kind of silence that would follow inadmissible questions, a silence which my sister and I perceived as a break down into some desolate, icy landscape. Some of the most important questions were the following: How could he suddenly lose interest in what he had labored at for thirteen years? Why could we never peer at a naked woman's body without embarrassment? Why did he hate his own father? How could he have forced us to move into our grandmother's old apartment on Rönneholmvägen just when my friend Gert Olle's father had offered me his one-bedroom apartment with full bathroom in the cellar only four houses away? I was sixteen-years-old and had felt the world grow during the year I lived in my own room of books and clippings. These questions remained unanswered.

The process of grief is affected by questions hanging in the air, conversations cut off in the middle, memories that can no longer be cross-examined. Thus, grief gets released in a process of reconstruction related to the griever's whole existence and world of thought. There's a creative element to the grief that is healing, a link to the past that revives all the schemes that are about to be lost.

Old photographs suddenly become sacred items. My own memories connect to an existence I know nothing about: my father's life before my birth. Notes appear in file folders and envelopes, creating pictures of the past. One envelope was labeled: "Our Dearly Departed and Our Not-So-Dearly Departed." My father's childhood had been filled with conflict and division. Each detail provides a new piece to the puzzle of the past. The Asp family's disappearance can be studied in the lives of the four daughters. Shady men in pursuit of money, not art, surround them.

On one of his pieces of paper, my father had written something about Fammi's sister: "One of Hertha's sisters, named Hildur, married a Danish jockey named Cocheron-Pay. Due to this marriage, the couple was shunned by the family, and had a daughter, Evy, who married Munther-Ingeman, lived at Amager in Copenhagen, but after a fall from a horse, became disabled." This whole past creates a serious background to life, expressing the bourgeois values of the era. My father's life as a reaction to his family's values and disciplines, an internecine struggle toward another way of living and a personal set of values taken right out of art and books that really didn't interest the bourgeoisie. Those black notebooks as a protection from instincts and impulses all men and women struggle with, a means to approach some kind of vision of love for the world—*la terre est si belle.* My mission is to save those stratagems from death, to translate the collector's vision into our present time that has become blind to those old values.

I will never narrate the last sixteen hours of my father's life. They will remain inside me as the final stories before the great loneliness, in a safe place no one can penetrate. I want to hold on to them, not write about them. I can write about the days just previous, which were also important. The most difficult thing to tolerate at that point was the idea that the scent of my father, his breathing, his profile, and his thoughts would soon disappear. Now, all that he was begins to merge with my own appearance. I look up at someone I have not seen for a long time, and the person smiles and says: "You are looking older. You look like Ulf." We grow into our parents' features, especially after they leave us. We locate the source of our movements and expressions. I advance in a desolate world without the protective eyes of a parent, and take on more and more of my parents' features. At least that's something.

I mourn among teeming crowds of people. They are all I have. That empathy for the passers-by, the homeless, the amorphous masses with individual complications, their smiles and grimaces, their illusions in response to life's frustrations. I watch sons and daughters laughing at their parents, and then I know that I have lived among those riches, those obvious joys, filled with irritation and complication—this chaos of Italian Neorealism called Happiness. The emotion in the crowd, that's what is left of my father's collection, the European Trash, and the last chosen objects in the cellar. Everything I have saved and refused to be separated from. I feel that some strangers on the street relieve my sorrow more than others. I walk on alone, surrounded by unknown fellow travelers, limited by the time still left for me and my reduced capacity. I revel in walking down the sidewalks, overcome by a communion that surpasses all understanding. It is my last defense against partaking in the Machine Man's fate and being turned into an automaton. My anonymity in the crowds of people saves me from alienation. The collector's task was to activate life's energy in his own heart. What he used as props didn't matter: photographs, small statues, objets d'art, and quotations—the main point was to convey a child's viewpoint. Always, I noticed him looking through binders and books, folders and newspapers in restless pursuit of answers to all life's questions. His entire collection should make us richer than millionaires at the Grand Hotel Excelsior in Interlaken—and I grew up into adulthood under this impression. Until Fatsy, who ran the local auction company, exposed all those "sacred things" as if to say: "It's mostly crap!" That cartoon character's snide glance at my father's things crushed the last of my childhood illusions of our boundless wealth. Although I was never shielded from the power of money and knew inside that we were people of little means due to my father's unreasonable refusal to adjust his dreams, illusions, and projects to practicality and business etiquette, I maintained that illusion until he actually died. From my early years I always heard how paintings were of a priceless value and that they would support us for generations to come after his death. Perhaps these illusions were the product of his bourgeois upbringing in Malmö. He never managed to sell anything to his advantage, but, nevertheless, he claimed that "priceless value" as a definite triumph over the future. He considered the economic aspect as a clear inconvenience that spoiled the true value of things, and when he realized he was mistaken, he was prepared to suffer ridicule and endure unfavorable situations rather than admit the triumph of Mammon. He was very naïve in that way and I pardon him for passing this inheritance down to me when I attempt to pull myself up by my bootstraps. I actually admire that he turned his back so completely on all things financial. That is the reason I turn my eyes, as a result of his parenting, toward the people on the sidewalk and see so clearly immense riches in gestures and expressions, which he still conveys in his notebooks even after his death. And I, despite his contrary stance, take pride in being the provider of a family.

After my father's funeral, I traveled to Istanbul, and was riding in a taxi next to my good friend's wife, Asu, who wanted to show me the café where Pierre Loti used to sit. She asked me quietly why I looked so sad. I told her about my father's death, our friendship, how long he had been ill, our troubles, and how much I still miss him.

"Not even the Bosphorus can cheer me up."

I told her about my father's last days in the Swedish hospice. Silence fell in the taxi while I sat there feeling sorry for myself. Suddenly I noticed that she was crying softly, inconsolably, without saying anything. I felt I had made a mistake. Had I gone on too long about my grief? She looked at me soberly.

"My parents disappeared in 1986. They were university professors. I don't know what happened to them. They were secretly rounded up and murdered."

An old man was steering a rowboat over to the other

side of the water. The Bosphorus lay still, spread out like a mirror. The boat's keel was breaking the water's mirror into different fragmented colors.

"Having no connection to their actual deaths, my life was exposed to the power of emptiness. I would give anything to have had your experience, your sorrow, and close relationship."

By night I walk along Istiklal Caddesi, the wide pedestrian street in Beyoglu, where a hundred thousand heads undulate simultaneously among the masses, like a wave above the ground, those lost souls in the evening. A friend says that in two hours everyone will have traded places. They take their proper places punctually at our spots on the sidewalk, those replacements. The thought that a double will walk here after me puts me in a good mood again. I feel some continuity in the flow. My father's belief in education and self-development is not dead but still lives on in our, and our replacements' movements, like a hint that you can change your own identity, that it is possible right here on the street to jump at the serve and reach the ball in flight at its highest point with a solid hit. I peer into unknown faces and eyes. Every blink of an eye, taken seriously, becomes a part of the phosphorescence of the sea, shimmering beautifully but quickly disappearing among the waves. Your moment, your choice, your footwork, your place in the masses transcends Power

> It is through its decency that literature compensates for life's total impudence and lack of principles.

and Indifference. Since the beginning of creation, billions of such meaningful moments have passed behind us, performed and lived by others, then later collected by my father in his neatly stacked black notebooks, with his annotations such as "Spec desperantium," "Comments on art," "Ulf Hallberg's pulpit," "la terre est si belle,"on the inside cover. When I found those black notebooks on his vacant writing desk, I knew they were his last gift to me. We would simply continue our dialogue into the darkness, beyond and through the experience of death. We would talk about everything on this beautiful and horrifying earth, where no one can be perfectly at home.

Those replacements give me a sense of an Istanbul Aesthetic, which doesn't just guide worried souls but also heals the worst of sorrows.

Why do people make collections? My father had one essential characteristic: a hunger for new acquisitions. The continuous search is the collector personality's most emphatic mission. Important features of the psychology of the collector are the rush of joy at finding longed-for gems and the black melancholy of missing out on another chance to acquire one. Even as a child I understood that my father's objects were an extension of his character. The fact that there were no empty spaces to reveal the pattern in the wallpaper, the fact that as many pictures as possible were jammed together and hung by hooks—these things defined our world and carried my father's signature. He was the apartment. Each figure in the painting had its unique history: Endre Nemes' *The Machine Man*, Klenø's naked ladies, wildly-dressed Italian jesters, and the love-seat couples from the nineteenth century Danish colorist

Erik Larsen's world—they were all messengers. Everything on our walls were expressions of something bigger, values that, with my love for chivalric romances, I called the Holy Grail for a time. I was the one who was summoned to pull Excalibur out of the stone. I was the one who was raised to become Sir Lancelot.

That little lamp from Istanbul, with its miniature piano on its wooden stand, shines on my new novel, which, unread, my father holds in his hand. It was just released, and he looks at it with pleasure without understanding its purpose. Before his condition got worse, he read my earlier books one last time. Some of them remain, bookmarked, lying under his pillow on Rönneholmsvägen. "I want to give them another try," he says. "To feel their weight."

Here at the care center he only has a few of his own possessions around him, carefully chosen by my sister Lena and me, but he doesn't ask about things anymore. They belong to another world. In his room on the third floor he had a quiet roommate, and sweet old ladies who secretly admired him in the hallway, but he was beyond these people. He had been removed from his home and his connections. He felt deceived and betrayed. His mind turned dark and desperate. I was afraid he might die right away, robbed of his links to life. But he survived, oddly enough, this dislocation from his normal environment. Perhaps it's his removal to this single room's light and tranquil atmosphere that held him there. He maintains his ability to concentrate; he keeps his eye on the ball. The large stained-glass window, and our deep friendship have a calming effect on his condition. I am allowed to stay over night here. We share our lives. Even at his worst he is aware of my presence. We breathe in the space. I wonder if he hasn't thought up a new stratagem that will revolutionize all maneuvers.

A fractured consciousness, exposed to attacks, mobilizing its basic knowledge. Unconscious clarity without limitations. Contracted skill in a well-defined danger zone.

"Mind the edge of that rug. It must lay straight. Look out for that edge! I have a new friend to comb my hair, so you don't need to any longer. The rug edge! It must be straightened, Peter!"

His breathing becomes irregular. I am lying on a cot next to him, holding his hand. The same hand—so often used to hold my little fist in his, carefully clipping my finger nails on the veranda in Mölle, while I couldn't wait to be turned loose—now so small and gray and lifeless. His hand trembles like a little sparrow in my big, warm hand. I huddle next to my father's shoulder. I take shelter there.

It is dark, and the seconds are measured in breaths, which sometimes turn into gasps and then almost cease.

The nurse comes in, adjusts the IV, and empties the urine pouch.

"Don't you want to go home for a few hours? At least during the night?"

"I want to be here."

"That's not typical, but your father is far from typical. He's a real sweetie. Did you hear that, Ulf! Yes, he perks up when he overhears such things. I know you are listening, Ulf! Watch out so you don't wear yourself down completely, my friend."

"It's unreal out there."

Ulf Peter Hallberg

"Yes, that's what many say. There is such confusion just struggling to live, your father used to instruct me. He is good at clear conclusions. He has really listened to life."

She walks away, and the light goes with her. We lie in the dark.

I want to bring time to a halt. This room is my only home. Here lies the only one who still keeps me together. This is the air I grew up in. Here lies everything I believe and depend on. Here lies my confidence and trust. I go on continuously about our lives. I am trying to keep him engaged in our stories, which nonetheless will vanish. I try to comfort both of us with memories. I want to shield us from destruction with everything we've experienced, everything we thought was impressive and important. I tell about Ulf's tennis matches with Arvid Ribbing, his mean backhand and how Ulf with his clever stratagems defeated that old fox. I tell about how I won the Men's singles open in 1972, and I tell about the time I first beat him—my own Father! His breathing increases, as if he is indicating that he remembers. I talk about Kullaberg mountain and the harbor, Fröken Jeppson and Olga's chess parties, that horrid Hugo and his hideous hound. I tell about the scent of the ocean at the beginning of summer and how the clear, starry sky brings Fasse's stories to my

> Heaven has that broad, blank straightforward Saturday tone from adolescence, when heaven every Saturday morning was an unwritten score board for a long game that was just about to start.

36

mind. We have kept all these meanings so dearly, these shared moments, our family's incomparable past, these valued experiences. We have been practicing throughout our lives, studied, thought, and felt, and now we shall endure this darkness together, the entire wasteland. I squeeze his hand hard, and he responds. He glances at me from the side.

"It is important that these people who come early in the morning, whom I hear now because they are so important, be included in our deliberations which we Swedes in our kingdom have managed to create as a defense against everything that falls apart, the forces of Evil. Our society must be prepared for the possibility of accepting those refugees, with their joy of merging into our constellations, which now need to be active so that these minorities aren't scorned by a few knuckleheads."

He looks at me, becoming alert and happy.

"I have studied the landowners and enjoyed the women dancing. There were different exhibits of my fiftieth birthday, all very successful. Everything was aimed at showing what a wonderful person I was. Do you understand?"

I nod and squeeze his hand.

"You cherish that social interaction. We have always had that. When you realize in your heart that two times two is seven, then don't forget to pay the bill. Look around! You must save this European Trash. You must keep it all together. Nobody else cares. Only you can make the connections. We must save all those lovely antiques. You explode your time with music, art, literature and languages. For art it is enough that it is true. Have I exploited my suffering, as a wise man should? Eighty-seven years, what's that, a moment, and it's gone!"

I eagerly nod in agreement, as if he was showing me for the last time how to raise my arm to serve.

Keep looking at me, I think to myself. Just keep looking at me! But his eyes are closing. He is breathing irregularly, with great effort.

I want to show him that I can jump with my left foot over the baseline for a hit in order to marshal the whole power of my body in the first serve.

He seems to smile. He whispers with great difficulty, but I can decipher his words.

"I can feel your grasp from inside."

My presence guarantees that the mission is accomplished.

Nothing can be carried over that border.

There is so much he wants to save.

We must look for new stratagems.

He has appointed me as his messenger.

If he can't communicate his commands clearly enough, then I am forced to decipher them from his cryptic reasoning.

It's about that rug and those refugees now.

I must depend on the bookmarks of our lives and letting my imagination go.

No piece of trash must be forgotten.

The key word is "constellations."

Help keep the constellations up in the sky!

It's the same strategy he had in his collections.

The world ever present, even well ordered.

Even in the final moment.

The most important thing is not to lose your faith.
His command is given, the messenger sets off.
Like a father, the son strokes his Dad's hair.
We're back where we began.

In reality, all art is devoted
to one thing: Love.

        "EPIPHANIC KNOWLEDGE"
    Ulf Hallberg, black notebook

2. On the Tracks of Neorealism

Fors was a tall beatnik who lived on Ryttmästaregatan in Malmö. He was at least seventeen-years-old, trying to act eighteen. Someone said he had taken part in stealing a car from rich people in Falsterbo. He always wore a large black leather jacket with enormous pockets, where he hid his threatening fists. One day he offered me a very fine piece of chocolate, a deliciously tempting one. It had soap for filling, so I spit it out quickly. I had to vomit it up into the sandbox.

That was the same week Bo beat me up for the third time in front of all the others, even though I was a year older and a head taller than he was. On our street, this was considered good entertainment. Because I had been raised as a "humanist," everyone knew how defenseless I was. Unable to retaliate, I retreated toward the door. They usually caught up with me there, but this time the door slammed shut behind me. I was safe, rescued. Phew! I stuck my hand in my pocket. There I could finger the little packet of movie star cards: Roy Rogers, Jayne Mansfield, Yul Brynner, Rita Hayworth, Burt Lancaster, Romy Schneider, Tony Curtis, and Gina Lollobrigida. The true movie star is the gods' answer to all evil and treachery. Gina Lollobrigida spoke to me of another world, how beauty in art does really exist—parallel to but yet beyond Fors and Bo, beyond the reach of their fists—and that it exists, that it is pure, was expressed in her body, in her manner, in her glances, and in her words—and all of that played itself out in a dream land—Italy—in the world's most beautiful language. Gina Lollobrigida was the promise of happiness.

In the 1950s Gina Lollobrigida became a big screen movie star. Policemen and bodyguards had to protect her from the surge of people wanting to throw themselves at her. The Roman cleaning businesses had to wash off obscene graffiti from the walls surrounding her villa on the Appian Way. At this point in time it was crucial for an actress to land a big role. Or in the words of Gina herself: "My life was all about insisting that I did not want to take off my clothes." Is the point of the movie star exclusively about sex and not about life itself? Someone is bigger and more beautiful—or yet more evil and thievish—than we are. Or is purity itself

How do you get a great tone? Through loving it.

about to dissolve completely? Walter Benjamin wrote about what he called "aura"—radiance, the essence, the magic—and how it collapses when the movie star's personality is based on artificial publicity beyond the movie studio. This new personality, he wrote, consists of a stale magic resulting from commercialized characters. But life is always full of exceptions. Gina Lollobrigida had many small roles in films that were labeled as "Pink Neorealism," a light variation of Roberto Rossellini's and Vittorio De Sica's recipe for connections to reality. After her big breakthrough in the historical-costume film *Fanfan la Tulipe* (1952) she became, in one hit, one of Italy's first and greatest post-war starlets. Her purity had to do with instilling a desire to live and the revelation of a true superiority. In King Vidor's last big film *Solomon and the Queen of Sheba (*1959) Gina Lollobrigida played the Queen of Sheba with Tyrone Power, but he died of a heart attack during the last full-body film shots in Spain. The director was not done with the close-ups, so the whole film had to be redone, with Yul Brynner in a blonde wig as the wise King Solomon. The biggest and most complicated mass scene was a dance honoring Dionysius. In a bikini top she had insisted on herself—not part of King Vidor's plan—and in an attempt to break away from the ordinary, Gina erupted with Lollobrigidan control like a volcano. The world trembled at the actress' honesty and pure sensuality, which always had something to do with finesse. But in that film the Lord throws lightning bolts at the temple of the gods, which collapses and is crushed down to dust and ash. Gina has gone too far. Her aura has become apocalyptic.

My father warned the kids on the street not to hit me again. He appealed to their sense of art and justice, looked with piercing eyes at one of the hoodlums who was holding me tightly in his grip.

"Haven't your parents talked to you about Humanism?"

Then he went back to his writing desk and continued snipping out his magazine articles while Oma bandaged me up and iced my bruises and bumps in the kitchen.

"Die bösen Jungs" she said. "Mein lieber Peterlein." During the holidays when the snow fell, my best friend in the neighborhood, Lars, got lured into putting his tongue on the iron rail leading down to the cellar. He was the one who teased the others the most, preferably behind our closed living room window facing the street. There his taunting celebrated its greatest triumphs. I received most of the punishment for our outsider status. Lars' tongue froze to the iron rail; it was his punishment from the others for his annoying statements. His mother Kirsten yelled:

"Now you see what all your chatter leads you to!"

Kirsten, while expressing her condemnation in damning words, used a damp and warm piece of cloth to loosen his tongue from the iron rail, as Lars squealed like a stuck pig.

From inside our kitchen window my mother called for me to come in. Everybody sat lined up in there as in a Fellini movie: Aunt Gullan, my grandmother Olga, Fammi, and Fasse, my other aunt Britt and her husband, the Hungarian-born doctor Sandor Pasternak, Aunt Sara, Uncle Mats, and my cousin Staffan. Out on the street we boys hadn't noticed how far into Christmas Eve time marched on. That tongue, frozen stuck there, caused time to stop.

Britt and Sandor Pasternak let us know of their early departure the next morning; they were traveling from Kastrup to the Canary Islands.

"The bartenders are very courteous." said Britt and glanced at her brother with diffidence.

Sandor and she rarely gave presents to us kids. They never had enough time, always in a hurry to their next destination.

I clearly remember Britt's gold rings and necklaces, the overwhelming scent of her sweet smelling perfume, and her attempts at pressing us up against her ample breasts.

She was colossal. Her enormous weight spurred me to fantasize about what really happened when, there in the Canary Islands, she dove into the swimming pool she always mentioned while we were having Christmas dinner.

She wore sunglasses even on Christmas Eve.

We all sat around expectantly waiting, as she was about to call the taxi.

As we ate rice pudding à la Malta, my Uncle Mats shoved it down into his mouth with a serving ladle, rolling his eyes. Aunt Gullan and Olga bent over with laughter, had another sherry, jumped up and down on the couch, and Fasse, a dwarf, called:

"Let's have a contest to see who is tallest!"

Viaggio in Italia is Rossellini's masterpiece about love and the struggle for the truth. The story is very simple, the screenplay bare bones. It's about the married couple Alex and Catherine Joyce, played by George Sanders and Ingrid Bergman. They are on their way to a house outside Naples, on the slopes of Mt. Vesuvius, owned by Alex's "Uncle Homer" who has recently died.

They journey to Italy to attend to the practical arrangements connected with the selling of the house— after eight years of marriage it is the first time Alex and Catherine are left alone together. With a sense of panic, they search for other people to interact with. But the outcome is always having to witness with surprise how the other develops some unexpected qualities or energies, mostly apparent in conversations with others. What is suspended is time, the chronology, and what is revolutionary about the film is that the main emphasis of action is on the sidelines: the field trips and discoveries. Rossellini and Neorealism view art as a cancellation of the differences between the living and the dead. If everything is life, then we must have respect for our incomplete love and the responsibilities of the moments of truth. The film is actually about the voyage inward, the neo-realistic journey toward regions of truth. Alex looks for this on the streets, in the bars, on Capri, but the other women are just as lonely as his wife, and in the end he does not choose infidelity. Catherine's inner journey takes her through Museo Nazionale, and the catacombs. It's always about a confrontation with the dead, with the beauty of statues, Art's respect for life and the common man's forgetfulness of it all. Everywhere in Naples she witnesses couples in love, women with baby strollers, the beaming faces of children and the intensity of life. But her own relationship is dead. Her epiphany takes place in Pompeii when a scientist pours plaster of Paris into a hole, creating a cast of a two-thousand-year-old human being at the moment of death. Catherine rushes away from this sight. As Alex drives her back to Naples, they talk about divorce, about life and death. Perhaps the problem is rooted in the fact they never had any children.

> It depends on art, in a secularized and materialistic culture, to act as a kind of replacement for the love of God that is present in a religious world.

Suddenly they are stuck in a procession. It's the holy Saint Gennaro, whose blood, which flows once a year, can heal the sick and save lost souls. Throngs of people push and shove, the couple loses sight of each other, terror grips them—but suddenly they find each other again. "I don't want to lose you!" Catherine says. As viewers, we do not know what will happen to them, but we are deeply involved in the process of how lives unfold.

As a boy I was struck by the strong, painful quality of Gina Lollobrigida's pure beauty, and the sudden feeling of imminent separation from that beauty one is unable or unwilling to accept. That feeling is like a lump in one's throat, a premonition of the terrible fact that we're all going to die. Looking at Gina Lollobrigida's color picture on the collector's card I held in my hand and, later on, watching her on the silver screen, was like getting injected with some magic drug, filling me full of the desire to live strong and long. And by the time I had to leave the theater because the movie was over and the lights were being turned off, I left completely drained by the rush of that rare, intense love for her and an obsessive urge to see her again soon.

People who are envious of beauty are fiends of life because beauty is a god-given gift of inspiration and a source of power despite whoever is endowed with it. We can't all be so lucky, and it's better to have bad luck than no luck at all, but best of all is that we all are lucky enough to be able to sense what is authentic for ourselves. We don't need to ask what that word means when we see a person like Gina Lollobrigida. Neither the owner nor the observer know what to do with that beauty—and this, of course, becomes Gina's fate as well. Her purity also has to do with a certain limit to her resources as an actress. It's not only that lack of diction is replaced by her looks, but it's also her expression that evokes strong feelings of sympathy in both male and female members of the audience. It's that lust for life, and for excellence. It's transcendental.

In 1947 the scriptwriter Zavattini and the director Vittorio De Sica picked up a novel, *The Bicycle Thief,* by Luigi Bartolini. Zavattini adapted it into a simple story about the unemployed Antonio Ricci who gets a job putting up billboards but fails because his bicycle gets stolen. A child, his son Bruno, experiences the consequence of the theft. Father and son travel to different locations in post-World War II Rome: a police station, a bicycle market, a church with a soup kitchen, and into an alley with some Mafia-type individuals. All those characters represent everything a person would collide against: harsh, illusionless reality; economic realities; elbows, knuckles and cold-hearted egotism. In the final scene, when the father sees an unguarded bicycle, he has some kind of lover's gleam in his eyes, and we see him fall for the temptation to steal it as a regression into the lower depths of his own character and his tarnished relationship with his wife, Maria. He is no longer trying to live up to anything. De Sica portrays the tendency in us to lose all ambition, with unrelenting consequences, and at the same time with an absence of judgment. In the film, it's the child's look that becomes the only tribunal. When the boy picks up his father's hat, in *The Bicycle Thief,* and brushes off the dust from the street where he's been chased as the thief of a bicycle, he is shaking off the dust of the entire human race.

The first time I ever heard Vittorio De Sica's name was in 1974 when I saw Ettore Scola's *We All Loved Each Other So Much,* a film about four friends from the Resistance Movement in post-war Italy. One married into wealth and became a landowner; the others come to visit him. They park their car in front of a luxurious villa outside Milan, and say: "Gianni can't possibly live here!" But they peek over the wall and see him jump into his swimming pool from a diving board. That frame freezes in the middle of his jump, and then the whole story unfolds: love, friendship, betrayal, treachery—changes that pull everyone along the stream of time, everything inexpressible and wondrous. Some hold on, and others vanish; some still laugh and some become solid citizens as if they had been cast in cement. At the time I saw that film, many people were obsessed with worshipping big words. It was the 1970s and the house walls echoed with slogans about working-class struggles, resistance and solidarity. Sometimes it felt like a smog of words covered up everything real, the concrete and inexplicable. That fleeting life so hard to get a handle on. All troubles and difficulties in one single incident. That's what Neorealism and *We All Loved Each Other So Much* was all about, how we are unfair and mean, self-serving and exploitive right in the midst of political grandstanding and idealization—but there was still something in Neorealism and Scola's film, an energy in the action, a laugh of liberation. An understanding that we are both weak and wonderful, both truthful and deceitful. "We all loved each other so much." To come up with such a title is to go beyond the scope of words. A hint of contradiction: things don't turn out the way one hoped for, like Antonio in the film, who introduces his loved one to his best friend, full of enthusiasm and love for life—but suddenly it's so quiet, and we as spectators get to hear their thoughts, like in a play by Pirandello and we suspect and fear that she has fallen in love with the friend. But Antonio won't admit to such a thing until he is told by the friend he introduced. We don't always know what causes us to act the way we do, who our true friends are—and for how long our lucky moments will last, if we really have any. Or if we even can make discoveries despite our troubles. That is the De Sica-problem, which influenced *We All Loved Each Other So*

> When you are mistaken with a face, it is because the real picture is being concealed by the illusion it feeds.

Much. A search for the genuine and true, because in Art even what seems false must ring true.

It is strange how Vittorio De Sica is mentioned in *We All Loved Each Other So Much.* In the film, a movie fanatic living in a small town with wife and kids is a member of a local film club. One beautiful day, after seeing De Sica's masterpiece, *The Bicycle Thief,* he left his little town and went to Rome to become a film critic. In Rome he becomes famous as a columnist for the cinema and an expert—wise, witty and lonely. One day he enters a game show as a specialist on Vittorio De Sica. He survives until the grand finale and all the locals from his hometown, who had previously regarded him as a piece of shit and an immoral egotist, show up at the TV studio to watch him win. Now he's a popular TV-personality they are proud to know. Finally he is given the $64,000 question that he has thirty seconds to answer: "In De Sica's film *The Bicycle Thief,* why does the boy start crying?" the game host asks. The critic looks happy, because he knows so much. "Yes, it's like this" he says "De Sica knew a lot about a child's psyche, so he used a little trick to get the boy to cry over a very abstract occurrence." The film critic laughs and gets tangled up in all his detailed knowledge of De Sica's mastery at directing children. "Dong!" the bell sounds, and time's up. He has not answered the simple question. "The boy cries because his father has betrayed himself by repeating the crime that started the search for the stolen bicycle in post-World War II Rome," the game show host declares with a sigh—"but at least you came in second." The film critic wins a little red Fiat instead of money, and those locals from his town, including his ex-wife and children, his grandparents, and the president of the film club, leave the studio muttering among themselves that they knew he was trying to show off with all his detailed information, the fool, the jackass. The little red Fiat follows the film critic through the rest of his life, with doors eventually he can't even close. Like another symbol of the idealist's, the art lover's, botched and threadbare reality.

My father loved Rome, because of all the major collections there. He compared the hardships Michelangelo had to suffer while working on the ceiling paintings in the Sistine Chapel to the plight of someone who with his scissors would cut out important art reviews from all the Nordic newspapers over a long period of time, an epoch.

"What is an epoch?" I asked.

"It's the time period from the first time you heard me cut into the newspapers until something else starts to happen," my father answered.

Terrified, I thought how the door to the cellar was shut closed and a simple dead bolt separated me from the collected wisdom of the world.

After World War II Ingrid Bergman was the hottest movie star of her time. Americans have found a new wonderful Swede, a replacement for Greta Garbo. A blonde, beautifully fresh woman who speaks English so innocently correct it's as if she came straight out of the reindeer corrals and early morning visits with contented cows—where no one knows anything about Al Capone or pre-marital sex. The core strength brought to life by Ingrid Bergman represents the dream of the innocent and pure woman of that time. She fits perfectly with a rough and scarred man like Humphrey Bogart in *Casablanca* or against a hardened seducer like Cary Grant in *Notorious*. The Swedish actress reminds America that a woman is always without a past and plants a seed—a dream that always must be fed in the present and not soiled by history or everyday complications. She must be a man's dream.

Ingrid Bergman lives in Beverly Hills with her Swedish husband and a four-year-old daughter. She is the talk of the town in Los Angeles. Samuel Goldwyn thought about making her the movie star of the century. And she even had some success on Broadway in a play by Maxwell Anderson. But in the fall of 1948 she's slouching in a movie salon chair in New York, worn out by the machinations and vanities of Hollywood. She is watching Rossellini's film *Paisà*, about how the Allies and their supporters liberated Italy from Fascism. This is something very different from what Ingrid Bergman is used to. She has seen *Rome, Open City*, but as she said to a friend: "That much drama in a film could be a coincidence once, but not twice..." Ingrid Bergman is speechless. In this case the story isn't turned into propaganda about love and honor—but an adventurous tale of resistance soldiers. And society is changing all the time. There's some kind of nostalgia in the fact that people can betray and tarnish ideals. Honor is not solid but terribly liquid—not at all like the myths that Hollywood often portrays.

Rossellini looks to another subject for a new film —and is contemplating a location on the volcanic island Stromboli—when his secretary reminds him of a letter that had arrived. He has no idea who sent it. Ingrid Bergman, who is that? Rossellini doesn't have time to follow Hollywood productions in his search for truth.

But finally someone is reading the letter to him: "Mr. Rossellini, I have seen your films *Rome, Open City* and *Paisà* and I like them very much. If you need a Swedish actress who can speak English well, hasn't forgotten her German, can make herself understood in French and who can only say 'I love you' in Italian, then I'm prepared to come to Italy to work with you." Signed: Ingrid Bergman. In the year 1948 the film *Rome, Open City* is nominated for the Best Foreign Film Oscar in the USA and Rossellini travels to Hollywood to discuss his next project. The working title of the movie is "Story without a Title Portrayed by Ingrid Bergman in Italy." The main point is that Neorealism is getting a new prominent figure: Ingrid Bergman.

Rossellini in Hollywood is a story in itself. "Casanova in Hollywood" the tabloids read and focus on the really important thing: that Rossellini at age forty-two is about to go bald. Samuel Goldwyn always called Rossellini "Mister Mussolini". After a special screening of *Germany, Year Zero* everybody is quiet. The looks on the producers' faces hint that nobody in Hollywood wants to lose their money on this kind of artistry. When Ingrid Bergman walks over to Rossellini and hugs him, the others look on, perplexed. Howard Hughes becomes Rossellini's saving grace. It is decided that Ingrid Bergman will work with Rossellini in Italy. And Bergman's arrival in Italy becomes one of the high points in her life. "To arrive in Rome was like a dream," she wrote in her memoirs. Hundreds of people waited for her at the Ciampino airport when "The Star of Pennsylvania" arrived.

Rossellini and Bergman became a love-couple for the tabloids. And long before they started working together, the world—and especially with the double standards in Hollywood—claimed their love doomed. A highly esteemed actress left her husband and four-year-old daughter to throw herself into the arms of a Communist spaghetti-gigolo who thinks he's about to reform the art of cinema with his ideas of truth and reality. What a mistake!

Then what is Neorealism? Is it more than Realism, new Realism, or a total absorption into what it is like now out there in real life? And which reality? You can't avoid connecting "the birth of Neorealism" with *Rome, Open City*—the movement grows out of the resistance —the resistance against Fascism, the resistance against lies, against the official historical record and aestheticism. Neorealism is an attempt to elicit the artistic potential within existence, to raise the artistic representation beyond a mere product, to find details, feelings, expressions, and gestures that captivate—art meets reality with devotion—and this creates more than reality.

> Myth and Art are not systems of answers but systems of experiences.

One of the idealists is Pasolini who could walk on to a pastureland in South Italy in his film *Comizi d'amore* and ask a farmer by the plough what his views were on love, tradition, and consumerism, at the same time as he was quoting Sophocles and Petrarch. The answers he received were surprising because he didn't bring anything down to a lower level with some ingratiating question. Respect for humanity was grounded on complications and intents.

In high school, with my season tickets to the concert hall, I was a lone wolf, a Tuesday dreamer high up in the cheap seats. Niels Lyhne, Martin Birck, and Harry Haller were my ideals. During this time I wrote a screenplay based on a reading of *The Magic Mountain* by Thomas Mann—and in the film that was shot but never completed, I played a consumptive youth who escapes from the Malmö General Hospital to a friend: All the way to the end. I was not true to the times. I assigned to myself all the important roles that were strongly linked to the late nineteenth century in this fantasy theater. Literature became a veil thrown over my arrogance, my precocious wisdom. Bearded intellectuals unfolded banners on the street. They knew even more about something else, but I was escaping into the Malmö City Theater's chandelier crowd, hurriedly taking my seat. There I let my mind immerse itself in the sounds of classical music. Another place in time, in history, a moment of deep emotion, and a magical inscription: Only for the deranged! I was enchanted: "Take me along, over there!" There is a freedom to be found in music, not to be confused with anything else. Music wasn't something cut apart, not realistic, not heavy, not stupid. But most importantly: it didn't know anything, but it asked a lot. It opened a whole new world. It shut things off; it gave permission; it let be. My brain tapped into something bigger, my thoughts could catch flight on the wings of dreams, and every little part of what I had seen and was about to see came to me there, in a word-less embrace in pianissimo. For two hours I was released from Malmö's condescending question: "What's it good for?"

The birth of Italian filmmaking can be dated to March 13, 1896, when Vittorio Calcine, (1847 - 1916) presented the Lumières brothers' inventions to startled Roman journalists and businessmen in a photo atelier next to the Trevi Fountain. In the fall of the same year, the first Italian motion picture went beyond recording swinging gondolas and terrified pigeons in an attempt to tell a little story about a young lady in a fashionable bathing suit who sets out to take a bath in a Milanese fountain: *Diana's Bath.* The first real silent feature film with widespread circulation was *The Conquest of Rome* in 1905. A number of historical productions followed that film such as *The Last Days of Pompeii, Quo Vadis?* and *Julius Caesar.* The decade of the 1910s saw the birth of melodrama and crime fiction on the Italian screen as a reaction to the events of the First World War. Documentaries were still rather rare and marginalized. When Mussolini marched into Rome on October 28th, 1922, with the support of the Industrialists and the Vatican, and seized power from the King, he provided the movies with events to project a political rectification, which however turned out to be rather futile. Neither of the masterpieces from 1932, *1860—Garibaldi's Thousand* or *The Blackshirts,* show proof of anything but simplification and glorification. The fictional films during those fascistic times were produced as attachments to the studio system that was growing in Hollywood, a paradox for today's audience. Fascism had the same goals as Hollywood: distraction, populism, and escapism, and a glorification of petty bourgeois values. The motion pictures were distributed like little Middle-class cookies to the general public whose individual thinking was executed or transported to concentration camps. Lack of aesthetic and moral values were the primary "virtues" of these films, and that made them popular. The Neorealistic film was born during the resistance struggle against Fascism and Populism. Originally Roberto Rossellini had planned to make a documentary film about the priest Don Pietro Morosini, who functioned as a messenger for the resistance and was executed on April 8th, 1944. But the film manuscript grew to a whole examination of Rome at the end of the war, with many solid characters, actual war sites, side stories, and quotes (Michelangelo's *Pietà*, for example). Rome was liberated on June 4th, 1944; World War II was over on May 9th, 1945, and Rossellini's film *Rome, Open City* premiered in August 1945. Cinematography and history were united in a blessed work situation. This is the background that De Sica, Visconti, Antonioni, Pasolini, Fellini, and Rosi represent. Francesco Rosi is the final survivor of that select group. The brothers Taviani, Ettore Scola, Bellocchio, Bertolucci, Moretti, and Benigni are their heirs. At the film club in Rome, Francesco Rosi said about the art of Neorealistic cinema: "It deals with social, ethical, and moral categories. We try to portray man in relation to political and economic powers. A film's potential depends on its appeal to feelings rather than the intellect. The viewer is guided by the rhythm of the pictures as they pass on the screen. You can lay down a book while you read it and then pick it up again, but a film absorbs your entire senses. As an invention I think cinema was humanity's first medium through which to understand fellow humans' physicality. Neorealism attempted to create a critical conscience, in contrast to Hollywood—built on the paradox of physiological understanding—by portraying mysteries about people, urges, passions, burdens and virtues without ultimate solutions. We never prioritized the intrigue or the end of the film, but rather the complexity of the plot. We were inspired by life and documentaries. While directing *La Dolce Vita,* Fellini captured the problems of the Italian post-war recovery period by avoiding the action and focusing on the young journalist's perplexity. Our existence can no longer be arranged as before, and that is reflected in art."

I go through about twenty of my father's binders, which I saved from oblivion. His elegant handwriting, the strips of scissor-cut articles, each one glued into several pages in those red binders relatively limited in space. Exhibits, artistry, and debates from long ago. Everything forgotten, most of it buried. The value of his work appears as his way of energizing himself with meaning, sprung from a keen urge to understand, to rise above simple comforts, a constant demand for insights and growth. The scissors move in an attempt to organize his reading into its own system. Understanding as a cultivation of the transitory, unfathomable present.

The cultural birth of a nation occurs when the majority of its population realizes that art injects life into its troublesome and forgetful citizens, into a homogenous society's inhumane spaces while challenging our preconceptions of ourselves. As a child Luchino Visconti had an English-speaking tutor. At six-thirty every morning he practiced his cello. Horseback riding was his first great passion. During the 1920s he was a young aesthete with a taste for opera. During the 1930s Jean Renoir's film *Toni* made such a strong impression on him that he decided to become a film director. Through Coco Chanel, Visconti became acquainted with Renoir and was apprenticed under him, as a director's assistant during the filming of *A Day in the Country*, an adaptation from a novel written by Guy de Maupassant. In 1936 he drives his silver-gray Lancia Spider on the Monza autodrome. The family's chauffeur Mercerati has been persuaded by Luchino to come along. Suddenly Mercerati stands up in the front seat of the roof-less car and is hit by a protruding part of another vehicle. He is killed immediately. This incident makes an indelible impression on Visconti: fate is an evil and threatening

Life is a mosaic of
red and black days.

force. Visconti's father dies during the winter of 1941, and he inherits the grand villa at Via Salaria in Rome. In June of 1942 he makes his first film, *Obsession,* with a screenplay based on James M. Cain's novel *The Postman Always Rings Twice,* transposed to a little Italian country hamlet. All this takes place during the German occupation of Rome. A few months after the film is completed, U.S. troops land in Sicily and begin marching up to Rome. Visconti left Rome in 1943 together with Mario Chiari, who later became his cinematographer. But in February of 1944 he returns under the pseudonym Alfred Guido and continues his work with the resistance movement. Guido was arrested on April 15th, 1944, carrying a gun in his pocket and Luchino Visconti's initials, LV, on his shirt pocket. The brutal chief of police Pietro Koch interrogates him in the Hotel Oltremare. He is starved for twelve days. Italian Fascists and German Gestapo want to execute the prisoner. But this time History is on his side: on June the 3rd the Americans liberate Rome. He escapes death. Visconti's interests at the time have to do with existentialist questions in conflicting situations. Who is a bad person? Do good persons really exist? Which values do we support? Do we have to feel like participants in the story—take some action? In *The Earth Trembles* the Sicilian fishermen's everyday lives are portrayed as an absolute chaos, a beautiful insanity—a condition of total strife and struggle. Visconti portrays either complexities in the lives of the lower classes or threats to members of dynasties and royal families. A returning theme is the demise of the powerful and worlds marked by death. In his late film *Ludwig* from 1973, the King of Bavaria's thirst for beauty is seen as crazy in the eyes of the outside world. His corpse eventually floats up out of the Starnberger Sea, expressing a definite sympathy for the playful and dreamy king. Visconti's focus is on the unconscious, the repression of coherence; human beings, forgetful of the forces of history, become administrators of anonymous forces or evil intentions— mere bouncing balls. At the same time, the longing for beauty is an uncontrollable force. In the 1970 film, *The Damned,* the von Essenbeck's iron dynasty is stripped of all its glittering persiflage in Nazi Germany. The economic administration's link to power is described as "the twilight of the gods." Sympathizers and the guy with the long knives are seen as two sides of the same coin. The downfall of the family is the story of a treacherous loyalty. *Rocco and his Brothers* from 1960 deals with an escape from Southern Italy. The young boxer, Rocco, masterly played by Alain Delon, a Prince Mishkin figure, a good man in an evil world. In Visconti's films the characters portray passions in search of a soul.

As a young boy I felt a deep sympathy for the mood within the works of poet harald forss—*I am a lover of nuances*—and Gullberg's nightingale, lonesome and melancholy: *I had friends in so many lands, but why was I still lonely under the sky...*I let my fantasy play in the silence of Beckett. When I attended the plays at the theater (and stopped squirming in my chair) it was because the sound of the actor Göte Fyhring's enunciation approached a note from Carl Nielsen's *Det Uudslukkelige, (The Inextinguishable).* When words suddenly were let loose into rare harmonies; yes, they were pulled free from their clean and tidy connections and pretentious reproductions of intrigue in the normal world. I was free then, like the music, and sometimes I paid special attention when there was a "rest" in the music, when the language of the music had gone silent. Like Fyhring taking a breath. So quiet, so pure, among those bodies on stage, every movement, every facial expression unusual, a deep, human riddle. Fyhring's glance alone opened a door to the Malmö night, out to the nightingales of the Theater Park. And behind that theater door, another one, and then another, and yet another. I was waiting for that moment. And I would always recognize it. I wanted to open all those doors.

In 1967 I heard the melancholy in John Lennon's brilliant sounds, and I saw Frank Zappa and The Mothers of Invention spit on the floor of the Student Union Castle in Lund. I was only thirteen-years-old then but I realized immediately that Zappa knew everything about my situation: *Plastic people, oh baby now, what's got into you?* When Keith Moon beat his drum-set to pieces at the Malmö Soccer Stadium, I understood that there are rituals other than wandering about on Regement Street wearing a coat of cloth from Cason to muffle out everything: despair and delight. I dragged my feet along the dreadful streets of my hometown with Dylan's raspy voice in my ears: *It's all over now, baby blue...*I was somewhere else, a stranger with secret tones re-echoing in my head, constantly playing different tunes. "Desolation Row" was the name of all my childhood streets. My life was nothing compared to the feeling in *the beauty parlor is filled with sailors, the circus is in town.* I went to the barbershop Eccentric on Regement Street and asked for "The Who-style". Those straight cut whiskers and the fluffed-up hair were my weapons. Those straggly hair tassels were the first signs of rebellion against the norm. I embraced the universe to the sounds of Cream's "I'm so glad". I was living during a prosperous time of acceptance. Malmö City Library was my launching pad.

On December 3rd, 1953, the day before my birth, my father, while cutting out an article about "82 residents of Göteborg," was interrupted in the middle of "among the latter a small bronze by Astrid Noack and a lithograph by Cha-" That sentence was left incomplete. My father had put down the scissors. Did my mother for once call for help? Did he have to come with her to the women's clinic at Malmö General Hospital? Were many newspapers left lying on the table? Not a single cut until the 8th of December, then one with a graphic illustration of *Women on Ibiza dressed in black.*

I belong to a class of people on its way to extinction that does not seem to fit in anywhere, stuck between old and new worlds. And I am completely without illusions, says prince Fabrizio of Salinas in *The Leopard* by Lampedusa and Visconti. His nephew Tancredi gets married to Angelica, a girl of the bourgeoisie. Their money is pumped into the dying aristocracy, a stingy pragmatism in league with the upper levels of society. In the beginning of the film the Garibaldi-followers march for a new Italy; at the end they are lined up and executed. *Il Risorgimento* enters and restores order. Tancredi thinks practically, where does the real power lie? With the king, naturally. But old Don Fabrizio declines the offer from the politically engaged public administrations officer Chevalley to enter the Senate in Rome and work for the new order. He knows that he belongs to the old. He belongs to a lost world. He does not speak, he does not administer, he can only be. His influence is in his example, his conduct.

Visconti's love for European decadence involves a consciousness of death and respect for the past—a kind of resistance. The portrayal by Dirk Bogarde of Gustav von Aschenbach is not as a pathetic aesthete but as a man on the knife-edge of life. In Visconti's world holding on to threatened values is something magnificent, bathed in purple and beautiful bodies—with dripping makeup.

When I was young I looked at art as something like a cloak, a shroud for only a select few. I felt connected to Hjalmar Söderberg, Verner von Heidenstam and Selma Lagerlöf when I was eighteen; perhaps all youth is precocious, endowed with defiant self-confidence—"I already know everything"—and it's only later on in life you discover that the knowledge not encompassed by science is the most important—propelled by art and conviction, like falling down on your knees in the presence of eternity. Currently, for me, art has a lot to do with respect and reverence, like that cool and liberating air in a Roman church on a hot summer day, candles lit for the dead and the power to believe in actions and circumstances without expecting anything in return. To live without too much strategy.

In Ibsen's *Rosmersholm* the sunlight that shines through an open window of the manor house produces a strong contrast against the dark and enclosed interior. "The children never cry and yell, the adults never laugh here", says the housekeeper Mrs. Helseth fatefully. The onlookers follow Johannes Rosmer, a former clergyman who lacks self-knowledge, and Rebekka West, an enigmatic and seductive woman about to take the place of Rosmer's dead wife as they search for their own personalities. A disgraceful and complicated past lurks in the background of Ibsen's "crime-tragedy". Every line is riveted to the stagecraft's iron clad inner logic, every fact expressed as if a witness is under an investigation for a crime. No mercy, no emergency exits. Eleonora Duse and Olga Knipper-Chekhova have played Rebekka West.

Ibsen's words swing between justified consequences, sudden insights, pure terror and major turning points. The audience of a play must feel awe—down to the last drop. We hear cracks in the actors' lines and as onlookers we have gone astray, like players in a false world with a taste of ashes and ruin. What does Rebekka say about Johannes Rosmer's staunch point of view? The Rosmer Glance kills happiness.

In Visconti's film *The Leopard,* the long grand ball scene after the wedding is shot from old Don Fabrizio's point of view. People eat, converse, drink and dance. While he is walking through rooms, he stops next to a painting and sinks down into deep thought. At last he's invited to the dance floor by Tancredi's beloved Angelica, for a last dance. She babbles away the whole time.

"I must thank you, great-uncle, for all you have done for me."

"Don't thank me for anything, my sweet girl, you only have yourself to thank for everything!" it says in Lampedusa's novel.

But Visconti adds:

"Or are you making us responsible for your loveliness?"

In 1943 Vittorio de Sica sets out to make *The Children Are Watching Us,* a film about a boy whose mother leaves her family for her lover. The story is told with a strong focus on the boy's reactions and perspectives. The mother returns to her family and tries to live with her husband for the sake of their child. The family takes a vacation trip, but her lover is following them, and when the husband returns to his work in town the mother is an easy catch for the lover—she forgets her son, the ever present witness to the irresolute world of the adults. The grown-ups become marionettes in a game they can't control, and the mother's desire to get away from husband and child brings disaster to the family. Coldhearted and unemotional neighbors and vacationers make up an implacable mob commenting on the inevitable steps toward catastrophe. It is not, however, the fateful and tragical moments the film is concentrated around, but rather the childlike open consciousness in conflict with a complicated adult world. The expression on little Prico's face is the barometer telling how the world is getting along. And while the adults, based on the mother's inconsistency, approach the unavoidable (and the father's suicide—never shown but only mentioned), it is Prico's eyes and face that become the projection surface for the viewers. It's as if the boy is aging before our eyes. And in the final scene, at the Jesuit boarding school, when the boy receives the message of his father's death and then is ordered to "Go to your mother!" we see a suffering soul, a crying child-man walk away. The little scarred, aged child refuses to understand and accept his mother's love.

I have been able to save my childhood idols from the cold-blooded world: Prince Fabrizio of Salina in *The Leopard* and the old art lover in Rome from Visconti's Gruppo di famiglia in uno interno, called *Gewalt und Leidenschaft* in German and *Conversation Piece* in English. Burt Lancaster played my heroes in both of Visconti's films. Resistance is an obscure defiance, a regard for lost worlds. *Gruppo di Famiglia* is Visconti's next to last film, produced in 1974. They are a family of parasites pushing themselves upon, and taking up house with, a collector in Rome. They are semi-criminal, and sexual disintegration is the theme, another political radicalism, the old man's perfect art-world—characterized by things—is threatened by the exploiters' noise and menace. The paradox to the theme is that the shady existences of the exploiters become important to the old man's life. This is constantly portrayed by the nuances swinging between closeness and distance, devotion and disloyalty. In the final shot of the film the old professor is in bed listening to the sounds of the others. Like the narrator in Proust's *Remembrance of Things Past,* the old man is trying to hold on to everything. The only thing left now is the noises he earlier considered annoying. Did he live or did he only try to avoid life? Did he organize his life to get away from painful things only to find himself in utter loneliness?

What did the movie stars of the 1950s—Lollobrigida, Bergman, Gardner, Kelly, Monroe, Hepburn, Loren, Ekberg, and Bardot—have in common? Dream and illusion, romance and adaptation distinguish these films. The women are sacred icons, representatives of the American Dream. They submit themselves to the myths of individualism, materialism and male dominance. Everything is based on their choice in adapting to their situation. Mae West had— at her time—more substance to offer the female role. She knew that men with sweaty palms didn't need yearning looks, but instead, she gave them a surprising one-liner that would keep them on their toes. Their ideal from the 50s failed because these women opted out of rebellion in order to serve a cultural matrix. The compromise and victimization became an ideological sacrifice. The movie stars were consumed by the radiance they projected on the silver screen. Marilyn Monroe's suicide made logical sense; her attractiveness had dissolved her true personality and become her enemy. Roland Barthes considered the cult of stars a mixture of dissolution and identification. Myth lives in the stars. Perhaps the greatest challenge to that cult was Ingrid Bergman's rejection of Hollywood by accepting to work with Rossellini. The current popularity of transvestitism could be a sign of man's desire for an outsider's role, an extreme longing for the liberation of a sex change. To give up the false superiority of a powerful position is another result. To choose the other side within oneself.

Johann Sebastian Bach put on black gloves to compose a requiem

Gina Lollobrigida reaches for her still-life camera, standing before the gods' temple of truth. This movie star, who always had painted and sculpted, takes photos of the Italian people. She is dressed in a blonde hippie wig, unsuitable glasses, worn-out blue jeans and with a mouth full of plum pits in order to distort her lovely profile. Nobody should recognize her, but sometimes someone calls her name anyway—like the workers at Fiat. She has a personal charisma that can't be concealed. Her entire being is a struggle against clichés: that intellectual ice. Her photography captures the common man's greatness.

Gina started to attend the art academy shortly after the war and the German occupation of Rome while her destitute family, her parents and four children, lived in a one-bedroom apartment. Gina was supporting them by making sketches of American military personnel, GI's on the street. She had always been sculpting and painting and now decided to start photographing her own people.

Alberto Moravia wrote the introduction to the book *Italia Mia* that also consists of photographs, taken by Gina, as bright as her bliss. Here you find children, workers, pedestrians, the over-worked women, the staring men, priests, princes, artists, De Chirico, film directors, Fellini, art students, places of origin, three thousand inhabitants of the city Subiaco—all standing on a soccer field looking open and frank into Gina's photographic lens. Moravia asserts in his introduction that Gina Lollobrigida was not interested in creating beautiful photos or conveying original photographic interpretations of what is considered "Italian". In his eyes Gina creates a picture of her country, which is also a self-portrait. He compares her with Raphael's painting *Portrait of a Young Woman*. Moravia further thinks that Gina has a face reflecting The House of Mysteries in Pompeii or Greek vases from the Mycenaean era. She is part of the collector's world.

One summer evening, sitting by a garden table, someone asked me why I write. Without considering my answer too deeply—the thought that language has its own claims (not to be found anywhere else)—the guests start discussing the writing between the lines. Why is it that a minority can make everything so complicated?

How much longer will they be allowed to go on with that? Who wants to read it? Why not say it as it is and be understood and respected rather than showing off by delving into nuances and mysteries? Our society has reached the point where Populism objects to all writing that does not express established opinions and values already set in stone. This fawning populism—its aesthetics being imposed upon everyone like a dictatorship—has produced this change. Works of art cannot have any secrets, it would be unsettling if the written word has a meaning of its own. The addressee is everything, and increasingly people refuse to become absorbed in what lies beyond their own horizons. If intellectual language demands something beyond what is recognizable, then it appears to be unpleasant, provocative, insensitive, dark—hateful. Our current civilization is permeated with the thought of our troublesome culture's inhumanity. "Trash-television" causes this development to move more quickly by adjusting the soap operas to appeal to the lowest possible levels of literacy. Degradation and treachery by overpowering the weak become a winning strategy. Wisdom is an enemy, clarity is unpleasant. My motivation for writing and reading is generally based on a paradox. People who read and write are filled with energy and improve their ability to concentrate instead of taking part in our rapidly accelerating social scene. My writing is based on my feeling of personal insufficiency because I don't understand. Therefore, I am convinced that I need to piece myself together on paper. I'm in the same condition as the young Brodsky was within the oppressive culture of the Soviet Union. "To the extent we hit upon ethical choices, they were not based so much on the surrounding reality, but rather on moral guidelines taken from literature." Towards the end of *Diary*, Witold Gombrowicz declares that pain is the determining factor in existence. It is this point that Populism and complacency are trying to reject. After a long attack on the structuralists' pedantry and a critique of a new novel for being pretentious, Gombrowicz's point is that he craves a relaxed normal character just as much as a character thoroughly weighted down with pain. Gombrowicz remains centered in himself instead of abandoning the self altogether. That is the empirical approach in his writing. The work has to be characterized by an individual who's living his own life, he writes, thus his mysterious digression from a general sense of time in literature. In *Diary* Gombrowicz's opinion is beautifully focused by his wonderful words to his wife: *"I am the center of the universe, but so are you."* The necessity to come up with one's own authoritative answers is a response elicited by the art of writing.

> The center of my life is the struggle for my own identity, for the Unique in me.
> The right and the obligation to perform the struggle.
> Incessantly.

My father's collection was to me the greatest sign that truth and beauty, in a world in decline, still existed. I was always advised to disregard money and self-interest. At forty-two-years of age, I lived with my wife and son in a coal-heated apartment on a back street of Berlin. When friends came on short visits from Sweden, they experienced my existence as romantic and desirable. It was too late when I realized that I was marked for disaster and attempted to resolve the dilemma through extreme workaholism in order to provide for my family. However, I lacked the ability to throw things away, or to put the brakes on my imagination. My desire for new material and the growing collection of black notebooks spoke in clear words: I am the collector's son.

A few years ago, I rented an extra attic, where I set aside some storage space for my European Trash, which during times of hard work spreads out in all corners. Everywhere in that place I safeguard things that might be of value later on. That's the influence from my childhood. The collector lives as if there are always more parallel and continuous lives. All those things have grown up to my neck, and since my father's death I constantly battle with containers, boxes and paper bags which have to be moved from here to there. I don't know where anything is anymore, but I feel the need to preserve it all not only for emotional reasons, but also as a matter of common sense. The collector's predicament is based on an attempt at keeping himself together with the help of things. When I have become aware of my problem, I have fled into the loneliness of a hotel room, where I have been able to put things in perspective. I can quickly make myself at home with my photos and traveling-library in a hotel room; it transforms itself into a little treasure chest holding my life. The rest of the time I focus my attention on existence. Always the same disciplines, same times, same walks, in cities I've already seen or visited. A dispersed personality tries to hold himself together by observing others.

In Berlin's Schöneberg neighbourhood I can feel closer
to Sweden than anywhere else because I have decided to
live within my native language—a kind of double life.
Germany has remained my outsider; everything I write
is linked to the land of my fathers. It's like the unlucky
lover's dilemma: how to live *with* or *without* the loved one.
I return often to Sweden and my foreign glance helps me
see my country differently because I always seem to be
turning my back and taking my leave. I am not alone. It
feels like life in general is slipping away from us. As long
as I remain in Berlin, I cling to my own language like
a drowning man, one who, in the end, can only feel at
home that way. I feel more at home with the dead than
with the living. In the evening, I go to the theater to see
how things stand with the rest of humanity. When the
actors have put their make-up on and the curtain rises,
I have the feeling that Truth really exists.

A man is the sum of all his failures.

"Spes Desperantium"
Ulf Hallberg, black notebook

3. The Return of Baudelaire

One time my father said that Baudelaire ought to come back because he was one of a few who really cared about the insignificant and the weak. It was Baudelaire's combination of eternity and intimacy that my father appreciated most. His sister, Fasse, however, said that Baudelaire seemed unreliable and never would have been able to stand a single day as a telephone switchboard-operator at the County Government Office in Malmö. Not even on a light Tuesday with few calls and the Governor Gösta Netzén on a business trip to Kristianstad.

"What do you think?" she said.

I answered that Baudelaire was fortunate to be alive during a period when society had no place for the obviously antisocial type he represented, and, thus, he was unable to become an accessory to society's crime of male supremacy.

She stared at me with sincere astonishment.

"Bah to you! It ain't that bad. No one understands what you're saying anyway. You have to think for yourself if you want people to listen to you."

"What am I supposed to say, then?"

"Well, not stuff like 'the obviously antisocial type he represented.' Say an ass, but turn it into a story, then they'll understand. You have to come up with new ways to say it. You don't think I'm being 'a realist,' do you? That would turn me into a pitiful dwarf that everyone would have to feel sorry for."

No one is so poor that he never, at least once, was the owner of a castle in the air.

"Then what are you, Fasse?"

"I am Marianne Hallberg, with a sharp tongue that everyone is afraid of. And everyone at the County Government Office knows that I tell the funniest stories. When I make them laugh, they forget how short I am. I am my own circus."

Baudelaire put away his opium flask, pushed his papers aside and picked up the phone.

"It's not been invented yet," he yelled at Jeanne.

"Don't you have any imagination, you ass?" she shouted from the bed in her dark voice.

"Hello?" said Baudelaire.

In disgust, he glanced at the filthy, messy bed and Jeanne who had thrown off the covers and lay there sweaty and swollen from alcohol, drugs, and rows of insanely demanding lovers with violent tendencies—himself included. Baudelaire was sick and tired of her clingy hands. Now she stood up to her full height. Jeanne's uncontrolled outbursts made it hard for him to hear what the person on the other end of the line was saying. "All you do is sit there and masturbate with your papers!"

"Calm down!"

Her broken-down body was one grand assault on optimism. A solid justification for my poetry, he thought. Jeanne, himself, and the room did not smell good, but in spite of that an insane feeling of love overpowered him. What for? For their fate, for the lonely, real, formless, abnormal, weak, and harassed humanity. A wreck.

Walter Benjamin and Baudelaire converge in their prophetic intuition: they tear down the veil of dreamscapes and illusions that they are barely aware of consciously. The messengers of what is to come are, according to such intuition, not the powerful, the fortunate and the renowned, but the insignificant and the weak (the ones who experience that change directly). As a history writer, Benjamin's focus was—after a study of Baudelaire—on the losers. He put great emphasis on the characters found on the edges of life in huge cities: prostitutes, second-hand dealers, flâneurs, and bohemians.

"Oui" answered the indolent Baudelaire, while he, for some unclear reason, felt a pang of guilt.

At the other end of the telephone line a worried voice talked about a troublesome threat on the other side of the Atlantic. The voice was practically gasping out the information, which, to Baudelaire, sounded more like meddlesome village gossip.

"The devil is pulling on us like puppets... You're an expert on crowds. An imminent event... probably in its dimensions the worst you can..."

"I need to know more," said Baudelaire.

These observations were unclear. A real threat isn't just a conjecture. The knife knows its goal. The bullet hits exactly where it's aimed. The voice on the other end asserted that he was the only one who could possibly solve this unexplained riddle. "Not anyone can write a book that's an asylum for all illnesses," the American voice added urgently. "That is why we don't care about birth—and death—dates. Your particular sensibility is needed here and now. Human empathy is about to vanish from the earth."

There were no witnesses, no leads, no crime, only a suspicious investigator named Hansen, with no trust in the FBI, which caused him to appear rather paralyzed. He was completely obsessed with the idea of getting a French investigator.

"I'm on my way to Honfleur," hissed Baudelaire.

"But you hate nature," objected Hansen.

"That's true, but I don't hate the ocean—and I must see my mother. She's the only person I need to stay connected with in order to survive."

"I see," said Hansen. "But we are in need of expertise, and we rely solely on you. We are offering you the ocean. New York itself has no small resemblance to a ship on a voyage to distant lands."

"So, you have read my writing," Baudelaire replied.

"I beg you; can you come, monsieur?"

Hansen spoke broken French, especially in an emergency. Then it sounded more like the bleating of lost sheep. *"Monsieur"* came out sounding like "mosquaire"— which was a forbidden word—but Hansen knew, as an experienced strategist, that there was an unanticipated charm in his imperfect command of a foreign language. What he didn't know was how close he was to a cave man—in his spoken expressions and his level of culture, including his images of terror. But maybe he had a hunch because he was a sensitive human being.

"Why me?" asked Baudelaire.

"Because of all the unique information I gathered from your work, it is absolutely necessary to call on you, Sir," said Hansen. He spoke more softly and sounded more courteous. "You are needed here. Everywhere on a deeper level, your poems about Paris tell us of the transient and brittle state of any big city."

Baudelaire scratched his forehead and moved his fingers through his disheveled hair. He thought that now was a good time to bring up the question of an appropriate compensation. Maybe this was a chance to pay back on some of his more urgent debts.

"This resembles a modern *sortie,*" said the voice belonging to Hansen (with his absurd American accent, interspersed with incorrect French words), "with all the technicalities of modern times. That's your area of expertise."

"I'm tired of all that prattle about modern times," shouted Baudelaire.

"Forget it!" said Hansen. "We are not looking for innovations, but rather some alleged criminals! And we have learned to keep our mouths shut about anything but concrete leads. The modern mystery stories are exclusively about sex and criminality."

The voice on the other end of the phone line fell silent.

"It's the same thing," said Baudelaire. "People think I sit here and read pornographic proofs."

"Perhaps yet another good reason to consider our request?" added Hansen quickly; he was used to negotiations and long-winded court proceedings.

"$70 per day," said Baudelaire, "$45 in-city allowance, $7 a day for risk charges, and $7 for meals and subway fares. Total sum: $139 per day. And you will telegraph 3000 francs to my mistress here in Paris, 18 rue d'Angoulème-du-Temple."

"Let's make it $140," said Hansen, but changed his mind quickly: "No, $170! And I will telegraph the money to Mademoiselle personally, this morning."

"Banque de Rothschild, monsieur? The Ocean liner is already booked; we'll expect you around 4:00 PM in four weeks. Take the train from Gare du Nord to Le Havre. A man balancing a book on his index finger by the news stand on the Atlantic pier will give you the ticket and further instructions."

"Poetry or prose? *The Wonderful Evening, A Criminal's Best Friend*...Ha! And on his index finger?"

"No time for jokes: *The Lady in the Lake*."

"And at the port for Ocean liners in New York?" asked Baudelaire. "How do we identify each other?"

"East River. I'll be there," said Hansen. "You'll wear an English-cut frock coat and an extremely long vest;

just like a British ambassador's secretary, or whatever.
I'll be white as a corpse,
lurking along the walls of the
buildings in a torn up trench
coat of the worst kind—like
a stale Humphrey Bogart.
But I can handle all the
formalities."

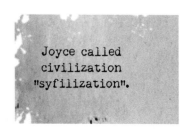

Joyce called
civilization
"syfilization".

"Torn up or torn out?"
asked Baudelaire.

"I'm sorry to say that I wear steel rimmed glasses,"
said Hansen. "I'm ill suited for shoot outs that way. But
the others underestimate me. This city is more nearsighted
than me; it shouts out its *nonchalance* at the pressing
matters of the brain."

"Professor Bogart!" Baudelaire laughed. Deprived
of cognac and opium, he had only read one author,
Raymond Chandler, during his long slumber in the
twentieth century.

"Can I call you Marlowe?" asked Baudelaire.

"Yeah, a newspaper is sticking out of my coat
pocket."

"*New York Times?*" wondered Baudelaire.

"*L.A. Times,*" replied the crime investigator.

"Twenty-six thousand street numbers on one street;
you need Haussmann! Something tells me that Los
Angeles is a victim of the Blue Problem," he continued.

"What the hell do you mean?" asked Hansen
surprised by this foreigner's terminology.

"I'm referring to my own experiences on Mauritius,"
said Baudelaire. "Everyone suffers intellectual impairment

when surrounded by blue and very appealing environments. Furthermore, the problem of America's stupidity can only be resolved with the help of poetry."

"That's why I've called you in," said Hansen.

"Back to basics; the crutch knocks against the stone floor."

"You actually look like a straggler," Baudelaire said concisely, used to giving proper descriptions—after his study of rhetoric with Satan. "But you did learn how to go by foot again?"

Hansen gave a dry laugh. "Yes, I learned it twice. And I only have one eye. But I have very sharp vision in it. I have a patch over the eye that was shot. But that's another story."

"Later I'd like to hear it over a glass of whiskey," Baudelaire said in a businesslike manner. His own tone of voice surprised him a bit. One near sighted eye? Is that enough in our complicated age? Ice cold, thought Hansen.

"I can trust you to come then?" the reconnaissance chief, Jonathan Hansen, from New York's 34th police district probed. "I have a feeling that the incident will unfold soon."

"*Évidemment,*" said Baudelaire. And concluded: "The world and its epochs will always merge, I know that."

He then hung up the phone with a real bang, though he knew that the only thing Realism has been able to produce was police spies.

The young and rebellious discover in Baudelaire a kindred spirit during the insecurities of their young adulthood. The need for the death mask of a Dandy is the greatest at that time. I bought my first copy of *Les Fleurs du Mal,* from one of the Bouquinistes of Paris along the bank of the Seine River. The author's name was printed in gold letters below an oval photograph of the aged poet. A sketch of Baudelaire in his twenties was on the flyleaf. At the time it was like looking into a mirror: dreamy eyes and arrogantly twisted lips—closed and rigid—a recklessly pretentious person. The foreword reads: "Our suspension in eternity." It is possible to identify with Baudelaire from a universal estrangement. The entire cosmos is at play in his prose poetry—for the isolated person. The devaluation of family, motherland, beauty and gold is the plot of the first part in *The Stranger.* That appeals to adolescents suddenly losing all belief in the claims their parents and other adults are making. Society's reality causes its own demise, carried along by a total exasperation stemming from the body's transformations taking place. You leave the domain of the safe and secure, you gravitate toward dangerous influences, develop a taste for the forbidden and the unknown. An unfamiliar, alluring melancholy comes from contact with the inexplicable. That's the immeasurable period of Dandy obsessions (in which no days are actually numbered). The estrangement can serve as an occasional drug and isolated feeling for the sublime: "I love the clouds—the clouds passing by… over there… the wonderful clouds." You lie down on the grass under the burning sun, free and privileged, enjoying the first jolts of death. Protected by his youthfulness, the Dandy can dream about decline and fall. This feeling for art consists of an intuitive understanding of painful longing. It is difficult to move out of the cavern of dreamscapes and Dandy-infatuations, and some stay there for their entire lives (often dying young). Their life style is pretentious and pathetic, both grand and unrealistic and largely contradictory to life itself.

Hansen opened the bottom drawer of his desk and leafed through an old book with more or less undressed female French vaudeville artists in revealing poses. "I really love Europe," he thought. Suddenly

```
Rilke's admiration for
Baudelaire is complete, and
what he appreciates is the
French master's ability to build
strong Greek temple columns, so
to speak, under the dreadful
idea of existence falling down
into a bottomless abyss without
purpose.
```

it struck him that his room may be bugged or even under video surveillance. He knew *they* had some new equipment. "Right now in a remote room of a tall building far away, the essence of my very soul is being sacrificed," he thought. The trademark of our time bears the stamp of the FBI, he wrote in the little black book he always carried in his coat pocket. He didn't want to go home. "I must work," he thought, "that's the only thing that keeps me going. Nobody wants to be a man of the world any more," he sighed to himself. He felt deep respect for Baudelaire's frantic belief in hard work, and he admired the manic, shabby elegance so essential to that French poet. He considered getting a welcoming gift for that crime-investigating poet but quickly stifled that impulse. "Baudelaire probably hates sentimentality," he thought.

"I have traced the connection between language, emotion and power," Baudelaire said at the press conference Hansen organized. "This caused me to glorify estrangement. But it strikes me how all licensed power can hold sway over an empty heart."

That took the journalists by surprise. CNN called in extra specialists in French poetry as interpreters for all up-coming press conferences with this foreigner.

"May I please refer to my *correspondances*," Baudelaire continued triumphantly.

Baudelaire's *correspondances* are glaring evidence of the irreconcilable contradictions of experience—in spite of the massive attacks by time, technology and indifference—and they coincide with what Walter Benjamin called "the category of indifference". "When we say a face is like another face, does that mean certain aspects in the second face are superimposed on the first without a cancellation of what it originally was?" These phenomena are productive alternatives to losses in regards to truth and experience marked by the breath of time. The feelings contained in the *correspondances* expose the Dandy as a contented Philistine. The purpose of the artist, according to Baudelaire, is not to "innovate" or to proliferate the conventional (parlor-establishments), but to perceive and develop the passing moments of struggle. And those *correspondances* are captured in the battle searching for resemblances—the struggle for identity—and (as with Benjamin) lead to respect for the pursuit of truth, though it never can be reached. "Therefore every truth refers to its opposite and, out of these conditions, doubt makes sense." Even self-contradiction, the most radical expression of doubt, is included in those moments of struggle—by dint of that struggle for truth, in its attempt to reach definite, but fleeting, results: "The truth takes on its own life, but only a life in the rhythm in which thesis and antithesis are deferred in order to encompass their own explanation." The precursor of modern times directs us, with his eyes on the future, toward traditional ideals: honesty, righteousness and integrity. But he is killed in battle, at forty-six-years-old. Just like Vilhelm Ekelund, with a keen sense for the mistake of "incurable feather-brained poetry", adds in *The Ancient Ideal*: "Formative enthusiasm for education can no longer be found in the sphere of the home. Beauty is something quite uncomfortable. It has the inconvenient tendency to fade as warmth and comfort take over."

My father once said that Baudelaire seldom took part in pastoral pleasures because he found the green colors of trees to be too tame. "He could imagine," my father said, "that the fields were colored red, the rivers orange, and the trees blue. Nature lacked imagination according to him. The city, however—we're talking here of Paris— is interspersed with all kinds of human energy and fantasy. The trash collector triumphs over the successful businessman. Paris becomes a panorama of messengers."

"Who are they?"

"Those who show us how we should live."

"Who turned them into messengers?"

"No one. They themselves don't realize what they

are."
    "Can I become one, too?"
    "That depends on you."

From the moment of his arrival in his hotel room in New York and during his entire stay, Baudelaire had his "Do not disturb!" sign hung to his door. Night after night he sat in a Windsor chair, half awake, staring out over the city lights.
    Life is a fantasy creation.
    Every once in a while Hansen calls and says: "So far only minor signs of an impending incident."

The poet remains alone among the pressing crowds of people. He rejects a general identification with the masses based on an understanding of himself: the feeling of being destined to eternal loneliness. Baudelaire goes against the flow, and, as an outsider among the masses, he remains faithful to his mission: to always shift his sensibilities and pursue *correspondances*. Since he refrains from contact and communication, relationships are for the most part imaginary, dreamlike, mysterious. They take place in secret—but they actually occur on the sidewalk, a meeting between two people, two inner worlds, and reciprocal spheres of longing. The confrontation between dreams or harmony and the naked heart being ripped asunder leads to the *correspondances* appearing as "a translation of human lamentations."

Baudelaire was gazing out over the Manhattan skyline. The buzzing sounds of answering machines made their way through the thin walls of nearby apartments.

A sort of public principle is created by the gleaming windowpanes with their curtains pulled back, he thought. That great estrangement occurring out there on the streets is a substitute for everyday insight into intimacy. Naked people move behind transparent curtains, from the window seat the night owl peers at unfamiliar embraces. The solitary person moves around in his apartment as if on a stage, the stage props common to all, but here every human being is proven to be unique, daring and unafraid—with walls around itself. Anonymous bodies throw off their clothes, piece by piece, and bathe in each other's flaming eyes.

And beyond the myths
and the masks
there is the soul
which stands alone.

The flâneur has surrendered to the intoxication that the surging and constantly moving masses of people offer him. His experiences underscore the supremacy of the visual, at the same time as they are an expression of modern man's thirst for the "new"—a thirst the Flâneur quenches with the moving crowd's illusions of reality. The intoxication of the flâneur, according to Benjamin, is due to his identification with the exchange value in things, and taking a walk through an arcade is like wandering through a world of decay, the commodity's kingdom of dead things. The flâneur's enchantment, his romantic illusion, could be seen as a counter part to the stuffy businessman's thirst for a conventionalized past, full of velvet interiors: "The dazzling wallpapers of past interiors. To live therein can be likened to residing in a deep cobweb, woven and spun, where our world's events hang, here and there, like dead, impaled insects. One does not want to be apart from that cavern" (*The Arcades Project*). The flâneur's impressions of crowds of people involve both empathy and contempt. He or she can either spin into a soft, butterfly-like chrysalis of passion or go against the current and get recharged by other people's energy. Baudelaire does both. His usual method consists of pushing through his own disillusionments in order to be saturated by others' shabby, degenerate lives and using that as a source of power for his creativity. His sullen contempt, the suggestive beautification of death and poison, is the outsider's protest against comfort and tranquility, the enemies of life and art. Baudelaire's Dandy can be found standing at a crossroads which doesn't only lead to adjustments and consequences. *Les Fleurs du mal* and *Spleen de Paris* also deal with penetrating into transparent illusions—the perforated, shattered and dissolved loneliness of the being himself. Those wanderings can be read as two sides of the same coin: flirting with death and searching for *correspondances*. When the caterpillar passes through the elegant chrysalis state, its existence is revealed as a serious matter.

Baudelaire's *correspondances* appeal—despite the limited duration of happiness and the nauseating insignificance of everyday things—to values beyond one's own being, an existence of a kind of life formulated by observations and poetry. His deep insight into departure is a conversion. Through anticipation of his own and everything's destruction, the poet garners strength and energy in the present to live a life facing death, instead of living an inert life awaiting its end. We can never say goodbye to ourselves just before the moment of death, no matter how deeply insane we are with compulsions or repressions. This predicament looks like a kind of mission.

When Baudelaire listened to Frank Duval, he was surprisingly at ease. The sky over New Jersey was the color of oranges. Darkness was settling over the northern parts of Manhattan. *"Endless nights, endless talks and despair begin. Covering everything, you and me, we know the truth, and we have a time to lose."* He had just bought this music from an Arab down the street, and it would accompany him on his investigations through this foreign century. He would never show anyone his real identification documents. Hansen had provided him with a falsified green card.

That's the way it is here; everything works—as long as one has good connections. But what does Hansen want?

"When we view people from a distance we have a tendency to turn them into insects," Baudelaire said to Hansen.

"You escape into the crowds of people even here in New York," Hansen pointed out. "What do you really think about the *Happy Hunting Ground?*" he continued.

"Such a disastrous taste for pretentious expressions, citations, and allusions," thought Baudelaire. "This crime investigator can't think without running into footnotes barring his way."

"The *Happy Hunting Ground*, I don't know," he replied. "Why not say *The Infinite Emptiness* instead?"

Does Baudelaire have a lack of self-confidence, a judgment he chose himself based on cowardliness? What is there to say about Vilhelm Ekelund's comments from *The Ancient Ideal?* "The feeling that you are a déclassé, that famous illness of the artist which Baudelaire grits his teeth over, and countless others regard as superior, is basically a feeling of self-pity. It has its root in fear, not being able to look oneself in the eye. In other words, not having reached the first level of education, where the insight of life's only joy is to transform, reform, and ennoble one's self." Baudelaire is active on the forefront of education, that point where the lion's share of words and formulations is lived experience. But Ekelund is right about one thing: the bitterness of Baudelaire is impossible to reform. That it always transforms itself into poetic energy is paradoxical. It becomes constructive. The fact that joy is not worth the effort is difficult to face in Baudelaire's compositions. And there is a cruelty lying in his hatred for everyday happiness. In some ways his work is a barrel of gunpowder where the welfare-chiseler and the business man are sent to enjoy a puff on a cigar: "Someone else might light a cigar close to a barrel of gunpowder *to catch a glance, to know, to tempt destiny…"*

Life without art is like breathing stale air—when all you'd have to do is open up a window. You are immersed in commonplace banalities—a sign of your direct and immediate time, where the so-called authentic ones link up, treacherously, with falsehoods and other similar strategies. Why not allow the *correspondances* to come to the rescue? A puff of cloud over *Île de la Cité* can give a sharper image of infinity viewed through a dirty window. That might be what Baudelaire thought, in his bitterness, one night from his limited standpoint behind an Indian curtain covering up a total mess of papers and manuscripts, a bed in disarray, and an empty wine glass. The poet, on his sofa, suddenly heaves himself up and out of his own degradation and with defiant dignity he writes himself out of desperation and agony. Through his writing he could shut himself off from the humiliation of everyday life most humans are exposed to, especially those humans who are inclined to have empathy for the fates of others—which is the predicament of the poet and the comfortable inability of the businessman, he who would much rather have "fried poet" for breakfast. Baudelaire jotted down the following quote from Emerson in his journal: "Great men have not been boasters and buffoons, but perceivers of the terror of life, and have manned themselves to face it."

"Primarily I hate satisfied faces," Baudelaire said to Hansen when they quickly made their way along 9th Avenue. They were discussing crime locations.

"Why do you reject common comforts?" Hansen asked.

"They transform humans into senseless drones," Baudelaire answered. "A human being must continue to grow; life is a puzzle."

"It's the puzzle that is unique. Our crime setting is focused on a terror attack aimed at some kind of symbol representing the Western world's transition from the industrial community to the information age," Hansen said.

"How many moments in a person's life are unique?" Baudelaire asked.

"You really paid attention to the pauvres et petites in Paris," Hansen concluded naively. He dropped his focus on which building could be the target. "But that continuous struggle keeping you in suspense all the time probably demands an amazing amount of self-discipline," he continued.

"I always have to defend my clear-sightedness," Baudelaire added.

"But why do you always wear gloves?" Hansen asked.

"Elegance is a weapon," Baudelaire answered, "at least if you lack other means to justify your mere existence."

Halcyon days are what the Greeks called days of radiant calm and quiet winds in stormy surroundings.

"Your intelligence may bring about your unhappiness," replied Hansen, "or your vanity. Those two things are absolutely deadly."

"In your case gullibility and kindness are the problem," Baudelaire said. "Why are Americans so easily fooled? Haven't they ever heard of *le scepticisme?*"

"That is for you to find out!" Hansen yelled angrily.

Baudelaire walks out onto the fire escape and, in the apartment below, catches a glimpse of the girl he met in the elevator earlier that night. She is stretched out on her bed half naked, writing something on a pad of paper. A love letter or perhaps a to-do list, or a journal entry? His bloodshot eyes, weary of nightly vigils, observe the soft lines of her calf. He lets his eyes wander along the contours of her body, feeling awestruck and a bit shameful. She lies there indolently recumbent with all of youth's confidence in herself, life's possibilities and completeness. I am both lovely, and deadly, like a petrified dream. He is filled with tenderness by this delicate beauty. How quickly this moment passes by, without anyone understanding where that beauty went, thought Baudelaire. He takes a breath of night air and feels a bit dizzy. Far down below cars trundle in and out. The lights remind him of emergency rockets, white and red streaks forever restoring something—he doesn't know what—to memory.

There's a banging on the window near the fire escape.

"Were you the guy standing and staring at me from the stairs on the fire escape, you horny old prick!" The young woman yelled from the stairs.

"I'm not an old prick," Baudelaire mumbled.

"I never said that you were, you bloody old bald owl," hissed the girl.

"Romanticism is dead," declared Baudelaire sadly.

"You damn voyeur!" the girl yelled.

"She must be Belgian," Baudelaire thought with a sigh, "without any reflective powers for poetry."

Baudelaire has hurried back to his room. He meets his own desperate face in the mirror that, in a corner of the room like a black hole, expands his private universe. No softly resting female body, no supple and round cheeks, no clear eyes are reflected on the cold surface following the motion of his pen. Only the death mask. At a certain point in life only an uncertain longing remains that may be awakened by unconsumed beauty. Life's inexplicable waste is impossible to understand or capture. He brings an old, half eaten pumpernickel bread sandwich to his mouth and takes a bite and one of his worm-eaten teeth shatters.

Baudelaire's inhumane, radically negative perspective starts to tremble in the face of an unknown, vulnerable person. His Paris is indifferent when it comes to individual successes or failures. With absolute self-sufficiency the city exists only as a sublime background for the poet's struggle—which is about surviving the "new" and to supply life with dignity. The idea that the city is owned by everyone is disturbed by the poet's imagery from the scene of injustice and suffering that the city really is. This vision of the infinite vibrates continuously through Baudelaire's poetry. The city belongs to history and art; streets and houses create a feeling for everything that's ever taken place there. Walter Benjamin defined Baudelaire's heroic position with a similar insight into the city's *correspondances*. "Out of Baudelaire's perspective nothing within his own century comes closer to the functions of ancient heroes than the portraying of modernity." This means, for Baudelaire, that with the help of the *correspondances* he can create a connection between the living and the dead in that city of the night where flâneurs are startled by sounds of high heels against the asphalt.

Baudelaire goes out to buy another sandwich in spite of his rotten tooth and the unsympathetic woman. Down on Broadway, next to the deli, two African-American children are looking at some shiny and curly haired Barbie dolls.

"I want to be Barbie," the girl says.

"But you can't, you're black" her brother points out. "That's ok," the girl sighs. Baudelaire takes note of this unbiased clarity like something remarkable, and for a moment regrets that he never has been able to generate any real interest in how children think. The child is a boisterous egoist without tolerance or respect, a moment of annoyance. Baudelaire was always occupied with himself. What if children are the messengers! A black hole in his poetry. The child is looking at Baudelaire through binoculars.

> Then you are faced with the enormous fact that, for just a few moments, you feel as if your own life suddenly, unexpectedly, and completely fuses together with the life of the protagonist.

"Looking at you is like facing illness, Dad."

As the elevator is slowly moving up Baudelaire is looking at the woman from the side.

"You don't need to worry; I was in a real bad mood yesterday," she says. "Totally depressed. We're killing the whole world now. The weather is crazy. You can't find a single fish without sickly tumors. And I have no sense of self-respect. I look at myself constantly from the outside. I've lost faith. How long does it take to build up something? Everybody seems so helpless. Just touch some power structure and you see selfishness. Furthermore, everything seems to be falling apart, above all myself. I am an isotope."

The elevator is slowly rising, swaying a bit at the floor landings. It is hanging by peculiar chains and ropes, which are checked every other year by tired and overworked men in dirty overalls.

"What were you doing out there on the fire escape," she asks, "if you weren't just spying?"

"I was dreaming," answers Baudelaire.

"I'll tell you something," she says sadly, "I think that sounds really nice."

Baudelaire feels a kind of freedom in being surrounded by the same movements so many others—walking like them, and being intoxicated by the sense of community. The laugh of a woman who kisses her companion. He loves the rustling fabrics, the voices of lovers, and the sound of footsteps. He exchanges rue de Seine, rue de Medicis, rue de l'Ancienne Comédie, rue des Beaux-Arts, rue Visconti, rue de la Harpe for Avenue of the Americas, Houston Street, 6th Avenue, 42nd Street, Columbus Avenue, and Central Park West. "Poetry must express both the outside world and the artist himself," Baudelaire mumbles to himself as he walks around the Reservoir in his black frock coat drawing attention from the joggers.

"I get the feeling you only care about your work," Baby Jane says, "and with such tenderness!"

"I ruin every single printing house with my variations and corrections," he hisses back in his coarse voice. "My life has always consisted of anger, insults and dissatisfaction with myself. I want to portray a seamless mind, an eye that never shuts."

"What you are confronted with here in America is injustice that's extravagant and ecstatic."

"But Hansen is referring to groups that don't accept any Socratic debates, Platonic ideals or any kind of Aristotelian diplomacies. And according to the interminable principles of the year 1789 we are all equal before the law."

"That does not help here," Baby Jane replies, "authority wrings the law from the hands of those eternal principles."

"Hansen is talking about a darker power that's associated with destruction."

"That's like you and your constant chatter about death," answers Baby Jane.

"Each individual death is a starting point for the values of the European Trash."

"What kind of trash are you talking about?"

Baudelaire looks at her with sad eyes. Will she ever understand?

"All that I put in my sack, as a junk collector."

"It doesn't pay to be kind anymore. Have you ever felt that panic connected with no longer being able to measure up to nature?"

"No matter how much of a poet I am, that easily fooled I'm not," answers Baudelaire. "Nature can only give us incorrect advice. I strive for the ideal."

"Then you'll encounter problems here." She stares with perplexity at the disarray in the room. Her own handbag is definite proof of her spiritual condition, but this goes beyond her own flighty existence. Everything turned upside-down. As if the room has been searched for something that will never show up. Desperation's crime scene. All these damn papers! Baudelaire feels like he needs to explain himself—as if he has to defend the room. "The agony of writing is connected with the writer's attempt at marking out the limits of his own imagination while he's in the process of writing," he says and hates himself for what he lets slip through his lips. "You pretentious rat!" his internal commander hisses.

"I don't think I'd like to be called an artist," Baby Jane says.

"Desolation and despair are my only precepts in writing," says Baudelaire as they sit down and look out over Central Park, surrounded by tall, slender skyscrapers on parade.

"Relax, now it's my turn."

Up on the roof garden of the Metropolitan Museum of Modern Art Baby Jane tells Baudelaire about her love life.

"No one can figure me out, I don't make sense. But I like that."

A desire to never be pigeonholed. She says she'll have her own show, at least for one night, filled with parodies. She wants to summarize all her neuroses and failed love affairs, into one grand performance down at the Cornell Club. That night will be proof that the pain and struggle was worth it, one single life, one single show: *Still Crazy After All These Years.*

"It reminds me a bit of my own euphoria," Baudelaire says.

Naked, they stand facing each other by the window. Baudelaire hopes that someone out there can clearly see them, perhaps through a pair of binoculars. Or through a telescopic sight, he thinks in fear, and the thing down there goes flaccid.

"It's the devil's viper," he exclaims with sadness.

"It's so small," Baby Jane whispers.

"The size is not what matters, it's the energy with which it's used," answers Baudelaire with a crooked smile.

"I apologize. Sometimes I have such a hard time covering up my disappointment."

Baudelaire argues that to Baby Jane it only looks small because she is seeing it from above.

"You have to be at an equal height or look at it in a mirror, from a distance. If you only could imagine everything I feel and hear in your hair," Baudelaire says— with an erection that is now obvious to Baby Jane. She laughs sharply and teasingly.

"Do you really understand what poetry can accomplish?" he continues in a shrill voice.

They share a cigarette and he wants to die while she looks at him. Salty tears run down the tip of his nose.

"Do you have a cold?" she asks. He's sitting quietly on the bedside, strangely shrunken.

"I heard someone say that love is like moving one's naked arm through the cold water of a lake and letting the seaweed sift through one's fingers," Baby Jane whispers and thoughtlessly surfs the TV channels. "Was that you?"

Baudelaire shakes his head.

"Just as I think I'm beginning to figure out who you are, you fly off like soap slipping out of my hands," Baby

Jane yells with annoyance. "Why are you so confused and depressed? Haven't you been lucky to find me? You're just standing there waiting for someone to start crying over you."

"Sometimes I just want to be an ordinary person," Baudelaire says reluctantly with a dark face.

"And more? Tell me more!" Finally a desire within this horrible and helpless but yet so sympathetic stranger, now between her bed sheets, fitting into her own little absentminded world.

"Do you know Balzac's secret?" he asks.

"Did he drink too much coffee?" Baby Jane laughs triumphantly.

"No, it was his love for goodness and humanity," Baudelaire mumbles shyly.

"I love you for your enigmatic brain," Baby Jane whispers.

"The point now is the relentless feeling of rage against the complete dominance of what is false," Baudelaire groans. "It feels a bit like Belgium. I'm re-testing my thoughts about artificiality."

"Why do you hate the commonplace?" Baby Jane asks.

"Speakers for banalities can not, or don't want to discuss what life's about anymore, but life goes on, more and more impenetrable and foggy. That youthful, golden, mythical life filled with clichés is not challenged by art any more, but is lived within a musty, raw and solitary puzzle," answers Baudelaire.

"Stop bickering about the unfortunate day of August

20th, 1857!" Baby Jane yells. "Things of the past shouldn't be underlined in red. Didn't I prove that one has to move on? Don't you believe in my show? And where is that Creator of beauty you say will come and redeem us?"

Baudelaire doesn't quite relax until the evening. She is soft like a bird then, whose wings embrace him with silky affection.

"Why are you so crude?" Baby Jane asks. "You can be open and vulnerable, so beautiful in your bitter decline—like a little neglected child."

"I have, for literary reasons, always avoided happiness and solicitude," Baudelaire replies with a laugh that could be likened to the sound of a saw-blade. It makes it hard for Baby Jane to fall asleep. Staring out over New York's nightscape doesn't help. "If that is what has to be sacrificed for aesthetics, then I hate art," she thinks defiantly. But she passes her hand over his forehead.

Hansen gives Baudelaire a short briefing about the impending threat. The attack will focus on a symbol for the new financial, insurance, and real estate monoculture. The name David Rockefeller is mentioned. The FBI has made a list of buildings, which, in their architecture, are a sign of mankind's insignificance and the power of economic structure.

Baudelaire wants to leave his body, become air, and be like a cloud. His investigations are being done in space.

"Ladies and gentlemen, we are now number one for departure."

The airplane glides like a silver bird over the East

River; all of a sudden Queens is clearly visible. He takes flight up into the clouds to think, to dream, and to fantasize. He dozes off, billowed in pieces of fluff, draped in mist. New York from above reminds him of the Pére Lachaise Cemetery. Baudelaire takes a day trip to Boston and walks in to a library on the Harvard University campus. The library is dedicated to Harry Elkins Widener, graduating class of 1907. He went down with the Titanic into the deep on the 15th of April 1912. His mother founded the library to commemorate her son. Baudelaire writes something down in his black notebook: "Lost in this wretched world, elbowed among masses of people, my eyes belong to a miserable man who, deep within past years, only can see broken illusions and bitterness, and faces a storm containing nothing new…I think I must have come to the wrong place… But I leave behind these pages—because I want to capture the essence of my anger."

Why do we read? Someone has said: Because we are searching for material for comparison, that is, for the characters larger than us when things go well and, above all, when things go wrong.

The leaves of October come floating down around the students. A cool wind blows the tresses on carefree heads into neat hairdos. A black girl standing at a door opening calls: "Come in!" Baudelaire hesitates because he feels old. He feels as if he is aging with the universe, like an old windswept tree with sickly red boughs and a purple trunk.

Three wine-red shields on which are engraved "Veritas". Wood paneling, balconies. Dirty grey statues, one on each side of the stage, red exit signs. A gilded brass lamp fixture with about seventy light bulbs attached to the ceiling. Seven smaller lamps like the ceiling fixture on the balconies.

"The Sacred Seven," Baudelaire thinks.

He sees a man and a woman.

"I have to portray them," he thinks.

He takes out the FBI's list of possible targets of attack.

"They are all too political," he thinks. "The FBI never thinks outside the box."

No one takes political power seriously any more.

The White House, Rockefeller Center, Chrysler Building, Statue of Liberty?

A lot of excess pressure in his head, the images are gasping for air in there, buzzing like airplane engines. What would God have said about present times? Wouldn't he have ordered seven days of destruction!

Baudelaire asks a man on the street why people don't notice each other.

He longs for the nineteenth century, when you could stare at the passers-by as if they were rare and unique objects from the collector's world of things, or shop-windows along the arcades. Back then curiosity was natural. By being blasé he was a sensation in those times. Today such an attitude melts in perfectly with the indifference of the masses.

Hansen has contacted him with a text-message about the harmonies of hell, and how the routines of everyday life have such a crushing power over us, dripping glue into every seam of our existence.

"Which building do you think it'll be?" ends the message from Hansen.

"A building that gives the impression of providing space for dead matter, rather than space for people," answers Baudelaire.

"Excuse me, but is it possible for you to drive me somewhere?" Baudelaire asks a young woman in Williamsburg who climbs in to a monstrosity made of shiny lacquer.

"Somewhere where?" the woman says.

"Away from here," answers Baudelaire.

"What's the matter with you?" the woman asks.

"I think it's my naked terror of the weariness of life," Baudelaire says, "or a stomachache."

"Jump in here, and tell me about your problems," says the woman while she laughs and opens the door to her car. "I'm not doing anything in particular."

Baudelaire looks at the elegance of the leather seats, the pulled-out ashtray and the woman's cigarette holder made of silver.

"Why do you trouble yourself during your leisure time?" she asks.

Baudelaire feels unsure about a suitable answer.

He leans back and feels more relaxed as they drive across the Brooklyn Bridge.

"Look at the stars up there," says the woman, "aren't they the best evidence of eternal principles. How many countless multitudes have suffered the pangs of love under them? In the end everything is forgotten."

"Would you mind dropping me off at the Lower East Side," Baudelaire says, "I don't want to bother you with my spleen and my hatred for progress."

"Get out, then!" the woman says, "I didn't realize you were an Arab."

"All of my writing deals with the life I do not live," Baudelaire says. "To keep myself together I evoke a female character in an existential situation. If I do my work at a feverish pace, then my existence is a hard won victory."

On the 101st floor of the north tower in the World Trade Center Judith L. sits by her desk at Cantor Fitzgerald. She is reading a newspaper, then she looks through her day planner, jots down yet another meeting she forgot to add earlier and thinks about calling her mother to find out if everything is ok with her four-year-old son.

Letters appear on a screen. *Flight ready for departure. Captain running crosscheck. Thank you.*

Number 1 takes a seat next to a corpulent priest who's looking through some papers.

"We're going to take the extra runway. Just waiting for the signals," says the flight captain with confidence in his voice.

Number 1 feels a thigh of one of the stewardesses against his upper arm as she shimmies down the aisle holding drinks, smiling like a doll with red lips. The priest is falling asleep in the middle of an "Ave." To fill his emptiness, Number 1 reads the priest's papers. The latter is fingering his rosary.

"Is everything ok, sir?" the stewardess chirps in a

bright voice. "Anything to drink?"

I will have as many women like her as I want—later.

He clears his throat.

"Anything else, sir?"

The airplane is jolted by an air pocket and the stewardess grabs at his shoulder, by reflex, to keep her balance. Their eyes meet at the moment of contact. Her fingers are warm and a bit moist; in one place the long nails make microscopic scratches in his flesh.

He sinks, as if drowning, down into his dark fantasies with the memory of her perfume clinging to his nostrils.

He sees bridges and freeways that remind him of ticker tape streamers.

The roofs of the buildings shimmer like giant cooking pot lids. The sun reflecting off of the car roofs looks like gray-blue fish scales. Giant letters announce: Alexandria Satellite Parking.

Hansen uses the name "terrorists" in reference to the attackers. He's been clearly stating, the whole time, that the attack will have something to do with an extravagant exterior. Suddenly it strikes Baudelaire that the creators of the skyscraper as well as the terrorists are not interested in matters of everyday concern. They build their sense of reality based on an abstraction. There is no universe outside their own dream world. The illusion of reality and the shiny exterior of the building have mutual origins. Physical force is plotted against an abstract target.

Paul M. is a window cleaner who's in an elevator on the way up. Red digital numbers indicate the floors. Two sevens flicker by.

"Seventy-seven is my lucky number," Paul says and laughs.

Baudelaire grabs the list out of his pocket again. A very famous building is missing from the schema. He walks along the lower parts of Broadway and looks up at the skyscrapers. Always those clouds toward the end, here in Manhattan, barred by the facades shining like silver.

The fighters are pushing their way in to the cockpit, the crew is overpowered, and some of the others are keeping guard.

Judith L. types up an e-mail regarding some transactions that later on in the day will be delayed.

Number 1 holds the controls with steady hands. On the horizon he can see the Verrazano Bridge like a giant padlock against the ocean. The New York skyline appears like a towering shiny mirror against the bright morning sky.

Without civil morals societies cannot exist; without personal morals their existence has no value.

Baudelaire turns on his walkie-talkie: "Baudelaire to Hansen. Twin Towers! Twin Towers! Can you hear me? The threat! Oil, the hatred of progress, the Arab world, world trading, World Trade Center." Only crackling noises, technology proves itself to be the weakest link in that crucial moment. He is alone with his instincts.

Between the East River meander belt and the grey-brown squares of New Jersey, the skyscrapers protrude like glimmering spears, thrown against Earth by Satan in a reckless assault. Like barbs shaking in the last fragments of light.

Paul M. looks at the woman next to him in the elevator. A rare beauty, he thinks. Life is full of possibilities. To simply look at someone with joy.

Baudelaire rounds the street corner rapidly and turns on to Liberty Street. His coattail is flapping behind him. Sweat beads form on his forehead, he looks worried. He is facing the entrance to the north tower now.

With restrained breathing, and small, shiny beads of sweat forming on his upper lip, Number 1 drives the airplane straight into the building façade.

At the Concourse Level, connecting the two towers, shop- and elevator doors shatter, windows burst out of their frames and violent wind gusts move through the ground level.

Baudelaire hears the crash and observes firestorms where the plane hit the skyscraper.

"*My God!*" somebody screams.

"Some people think I lack human warmth," Baudelaire thinks. "I've had to pay a ghastly price for my insights. That's the point people who slander me hone in on. Those well-dressed people in their bright meeting places with exuberant buffets speak of humanistic promises. None of them can imagine my relationship with death. Or my frantic belief in fate's triumph over man.

"Lezz go!" Baudelaire calls with a strong French accent.

Baudelaire hears Hansen call out orders outside the south tower.

"Hansen to Baudelaire, Hansen to Baudelaire!"

"I hear you!"

"South tower hit by unidentified airplane at 9:03 AM. What do we do now?"

"The same things art demands."

"What does that require?" Hansen, who never made it through *Moby Dick,* asks.

"Art is a duel where the artist screams out of complete terror before he is defeated."

"Understood! How do I convey this to the firemen?"

"We're on the same mission."

Baudelaire, in a terrible accent, shrill and croaking, talks into the walkie-talkie:

"Go, go, go!"

Group divisions, equipment control, and adjusting hoses while the towers are burning and objects fall and hit the streets. People jump out from the uppermost floors. A thousand degrees up there.

Baudelaire's walkie-talkie only rattles. Hansen's voice distorted by noise and screams:

"The tower is collapsing!"

Only noise.

"Which tower?" one of the firemen yells.

"Which tower? Which tower?"

Loud noises. Then Hansen's voice drowning in screams and clamor.

"The entire south tower."

Baudelaire is running for his life down Liberty Street, to escape giant whirls of dust and heaps of ruins, black clouds of iron filings, steel particles and glass. Together with a group of firemen he escapes into the north tower, just as a black cloud covers the street in sharp particles and gravel. Baudelaire is handed tools—an ax, extinguisher and a pick—then he and the firemen rush up the stairs of the north tower.

Respect for Duty.

The last thing they think of are themselves.

They are the messengers at the moment of devastation.

Hansen remembers with gratefulness, year after year, his French colleague's unselfish contribution.

"Baudelaire knew a lot about the hopeless infirmity of a big city," he says during his speech at the Police Department's New Year's ball.

Baby Jane says at a less successful party many years later, with a melancholy sigh:

"Baudelaire and the firemen are the only ones I believe in. He had something very special. He was a hero of the old school. Wasn't he? In spite of everything?"

The world is not immoral to the extent that
those who are better off are the better ones.

"SAID ABOUT ART"
Ulf Hallberg, black notebook

4. The Machine Man

The idea of the world as a laboratory has left its stamp on the development of technology. Items on the collector's desk, our living room pictures and works of art have shaped my own development. In this laboratory, curiosity of the world was the starting point, challenged through art, which was considered the highest form of existence. Technology works at creating new "necessities" which generate money, whereas art satisfies a deeper need beyond money and machines.

When we took over Fammi's apartment after her death, my father hung up Endre Nemes' *Machine Man,* in the hallway between the living and the dining room. That colorful *Machine Man,* a line drawing with the water colors painted in, was reminiscent of a puppet or a robot, a being that could be controlled by stimuli and hands-on manipulation, a spirit bereaved of executive function—and nonetheless, like a sympathetic circus clown painted with an unusual understanding of how cosmetics and frozen movements are evocative. On second thought, you get the insight that the Machine Man's existence is everyone's fate, but that sometimes the robot overcomes that mechanized condition; for example, in his protest against rapid and unreasonable overconsumption. Through Art, mechanization allies itself with humanity.

Karl Marx explains that, from the sixteenth century until the middle of the eighteenth century, during the period of development from handicraft work to the Industrial Revolution, there are two building blocks of manufacturing: the clock and the mill. The entire theory of "perpetual motion" was unleashed from the mechanisms of the clock. During the eighteenth-century the clock inspired the first idea of using machines with moving parts in production, more specifically those which are driven by springs. Friction, wheels, and cogs—all of these already existed in the mill. From these principles the first machine was constructed. And this was the raw material that stretched forth as an extension of the human hand. In 1748, the French doctor, Julien Offray de La Mettrie describes in his book, *L'homme machine,* a human as a mechanism made up of moving parts. He proclaims that the body is simply a clock. During this period "automatons", as well as human-like machines, based on clockwork principles—some of the most famous were Vaucanson's flautist, Jacquet-Droz' pianist and Kempelen's trumpeter—were built in various parts of Europe. In 1815 the German Romantic writer E.T.A. Hoffman writes the novel, *The Sandman,* about how

Nathanael falls in love with a mechanical doll named Olimpia, which becomes the inspiration later on for Offenbach's opera *The Tales of Hoffmann*. The American science fiction writer Philip K. Dick produces a novel in 1968, *Do Androids Dream of Electric Sheep?* which was the basis for the film, *Blade Runner,* in which an android named Luba Luft returns to Earth in order to perform in Mozart's *The Magic Flute*. In the genre of Science Fiction, Dick gradually introduces a new element of human-likeness developing within the machine. In the same manner that ordinary people can become cold-blooded destroyers of our environment and culture, the androids are beginning to show feelings and understanding.

In Ridley Scott's film *Blade Runner* the factory production of replicants have artificial memories that don't comprehend living experiences of life, but rather depend on certain photographs they carry with them which have been developed by the manufacturers of the *Nexus 6-series*. As in *Blade Runner,* street level things are just like an underworld. Society is completely vertical. Hierarchies and life in the fast lane are the "in thing". Efficiency and adaptation. No still-life pictures anymore, no originality in everyday life. *"All those moments will be lost in time. Like tears in the rain. Time to die."* Running around on meaningless missions constructed in order to increase the need for artificial stimuli, always a step behind those public-relations media identities, we lose our way. In *Blade Runner* the point of burn out occurs at the moment when the dialogue forces its way into our consciousness like words as true as the ancient Sibyl's: "She's a replicant, right? She is starting to suspect that.

How can it not know what it is?"

The world is a second-rate hotel crawling with lice and a whore house, where people with the help of ironic wit, quotations from the movies, and snappy repartee attempt to tranquilize themselves from a growing panic— mainly by submitting to economic powers and breaking free from feelings, carrying sticky emotional connections between beliefs and morals. "I want to pay from home! This collateral damage I now refer to as 'Love,' might perhaps exist in a tightly monetary household." The hookers' dedication to their work illustrates the oversimplification of feelings resulting from the method of payment used in a consumer society. To describe that experience as relaxation and release in relation to genuine feelings is a paradox about something not less unpleasant, but definitely more provocative. Insight always arrives too late. We drag our words behind us like tin cans tied to a dog's tail. We shout out because we don't understand. Today feelings are both genuine and paid in full. That's what makes it feel so inhumanly real.

The slackers suffer no defeats.

Trash, in this case, refers to useless things such as advertising letters or chewing gum wrappers, or yesterday's newspaper. All the discards we can't find room for. All the waste we accumulate, our own mess. That trash starts to multiply if you don't keep a close eye on it. For example, if you have some junk scattered around in your apartment and you go to bed, there will be twice as much when you wake up the next morning. You can be sure of that. This very morning, for example, when my alarm clock rang, the whole apartment was full of junk. My wife was lying next to me touching her mood stimulator.

"Get your dirty paws off me!" she said when I reached for the tuning knobs.

On her schedule for the day she had programmed six hours of self-accusatory depression.

That's the way it is. Things fall apart. Everyone's burned out and the junk just keeps on growing.

Mary Shelley's novel *Frankenstein* from 1818 prefigured the entire nineteenth century's eagerness to deconstruct the various parts of a human being and put them together again into a new construction. The god-like act of creation in Shelley's novel is especially appropriate because Frankenstein's monster is assembled with body parts and an ordinary mortal's abnormal brain. From Jewish Golem clay figures to Frankenstein and on to androids and robots, it's all about men being able to create a being that doesn't have to gestate in a woman's womb, but is constructed by someone who is playing God. But it is precisely this *hubris* that causes such a reactionary uproar against the machine. The inventor Rotwang's creation of Maria in

> Imagine studying human history with the help of x-ray pictures. Much of what is now so magnificent and obvious and admired would then be thin shadows, while what is hidden from view perhaps would be exposed as life's backbone.

Fritz Lang's film *Metropolis* exemplifies the fusion of science and magic. The mechanized Maria has a hypnotic glance, but she also sparks a reaction against the machines. When self-interest is the only motivating factor in human relations, the androids must come to their rescue, or a scenario such as the one in *Blade Runner* might eventuate, where the residents of New York are moved to a new New York on Mars, where the true humans are supplied with servants and don't have to work so hard. Left behind on a contaminated Earth are all the chicken brains and losers stuck in their own junk—just like me.

> Hegel dreamt of an absolute consciousness that could melt down everything.

Consequences do not matter for the androids. They can change personalities in a split second from compliant test subject to cold-blooded murderers. The replicants don't give a shit about history. They have no responsibility. They have no idea of concepts such as honor and respect. It doesn't exist in their program. Their memory chips are constructed to see their struggle for their own advantages and their own winning are preferable—even humane. *The Matrix,* the reverse side of *The Interface,* is the connecting point: a dream world with the purpose of changing humanity so that it can be programmed like a machine.

In the 1930s, Moscow became a society where Stalin was unapproachable by day (when he slept). During the night, with a smile on his face, he signed death-sentences for family, friends, and co-operatives. As a consequence, he made himself indispensable, at a frantic speed removing all potential competition. The turbulence and fury of Stalin's Soviet Union is similar to today's *marketing* and *life style* strategies: "If you have everything under control, you aren't moving fast enough." Everything is in constant motion, nothing is certain.

> It is impossible to be truly terrified of anything but one's self.

"A glass of mineral water if you please!"

"We don't have mineral water."

"Do you have beer, then?"

"We should have beer by evening."

"What do you have, then?"

"Apricot juice, but it is lukewarm . . ."

"*The Machine Man* on our wall is a messenger from Prague," my father said, and I didn't get what he meant.

"What about Prague?"

"It's Kafka's city and the City of the Jews'"

"Eastern Europe," my mother said.

"Yes, with all that music."

"*The Moldau.*"

"Have you ever been there?"

"No."

"Oh yes we have. We are always there. *The Machine Man* transports us there."

"We play that music."

I looked up at Nemes' watercolor painting.

It was as if I saw the *Machine Man* nod at me.

"When I get a chance, I'll travel to Prague, become

Jewish and pay Kafka a visit," I said.

"Sure, sure, but first you need to lie down and get some sleep," my mother answered with a smile.

"Why do you always have to keep me from seeing the stuff I really want to see."

Without the Voigt-Kampff test, you can't distinguish between an android and a real human being. The differences are hair thin. My job is dedicated to a search for what, or who, is real, and to separate out the androids. So I return to history. The first true-to-nature machine men where constructed of clockwork, with pendulums, and various cogs and wheels. But much earlier, at the dawn of history, it is said that Prometheus created humans out of mud and water and, against the will of Zeus, he gave fire to them so that they could assert their independence over the whims of the gods. As a punishment Zeus allowed the skillful Hephaestus to build an artificial woman, the beautiful Pandora, who in her box carried all kinds of evils to the Earth. Ever since then there are many kinds of fake people, no construction material is considered too base—dirt, leather, compressed air, wood, roots, or corpse fragments—in order to create an artificial human.

Thinking must liberate itself from the absolute power of technology.

Strictly speaking, androids should remain as slaves on other planets, but some of them have returned to Earth in order to get ahead here. They have murdered people on a certain spaceship, and made their way here illegally—

because they don't like other solar systems, but actually want to belong to this totally trash-laden reality here.

Memories have been created like soft pillows inside the androids' consciousnesses in an attempt to keep them under control. But when I hear Rachael's voice I understand Deckard. Rachael's radiance is more human than any of the others'. The android, during its short life span, understands something that Deckard and all of us repress. It is death that imposes our values. The android wants to live longer. Just as we need more than four years to come to grips with things, so does it.

For Deckard, the android hunter, in confrontation with the Machine Man—whom he will kill—there remains only one feeling beyond fatigue: a foolish love. He can't get rid of Rachael's image inside his retina. Not even the recently purchased goat can divert his thoughts about her. And animals in the world of science fiction are as priceless as a Picasso painting might be. Can a human being love an android? Has he gone insane? In a world full of trash and chicken brains, Rick Deckard has nothing but his feeling of what in his inmost innards he believes can be right, and his love for an android—a Machine Man. And perhaps Deckard realizes that the android, Roy Baty, really says the most important thing about life: *"All those moments will be lost in time, like tears in the rain."*

Philip K. Dick got a chance to see certain early scenes from Ridley Scott's film, *Blade Runner* before he died. He was overwhelmed. When the completed film was shown to a confused public, expecting another *Star Wars,* the producers decided to change the ending. Instead of having an elevator door close on Rachel and Rick Deckard, in order to convey their uncertain fate, a narration voice-over tells how Rachel was an experimental model without any limit to her lifetime—and then she and Deckard sailed off together into the setting sun. But then in 1991 Ridley Scott produced his "director's cut," where the distinction between androids and humans is blurred. Rachel and Deckard head for the elevator, and Deckard catches sight of a piece of paper, folded as a unicorn, on the floor. You hear a man screaming: *"It's too bad she won't live, but then again, who does?"*

When my father sold Endre Nemes' *Machine Man,* it was as if a member of our family had been auctioned away at a bargain-basement price. I called my father a slave merchant. It was impossible for me to understand his rationale. We weren't that much in debt. And if you were to sell, why not to the highest bidder, instead of a colleague of my mother's who would get such a fine deal? My father thought it would be best to sell to a friend or an acquaintance, personalizing an otherwise uncomfortable transaction. What hypocrisy, my sister and I whispered. As children we realized that there were higher powers that would disprove of us if we brought up questions of payment, money, or proper compensation. We had been brought up to believe that we were only to be dedicated to culture and that art work must be treated in the same way, with a resistance to seeing them in terms of a financial transaction. The important thing for my father was not to sink to the level of filthy lucre.

So this was the reasoning that appeared to lead my father to sell *Machine Man* at a loss, and, in turn, it led immediately to regret and the cursing of the buyer's ignorance of true Art. The buyer was the subversive; he had broken the contract between the collector, the *objet d'art*, and the infinite. Endre Nemes' *Machine Man* had become a refugee from its rightful place on the wall, its links to Danish nineteenth century painting and the most select examples of European Trash that had been such a natural home for him. "I wonder how's he doing now?" I thought in my deepest soul. Of course, he was hanging on the wall of the colleague's family apartment, but how would he handle the separation from our family? His absence from the place where he had observed us and made us contemplate games of life in a technological age, the unlit wallpaper gaped with an unbleached emptiness, a rectangle where something of value had been lost. The sale was an embezzlement, and that it had not provided us with a legitimate sum of money was a sign of how everything becomes sordid when it comes in contact with the awful measuring stick and inhumane whirlwind we call finances. It took me half a century to get to the bottom of an argument for which I still have some sympathy. Opposition, greed, and calculations have so many self-confident representatives and so little pure energy. The practical and pragmatic

I think other people have incorrect impressions of me, just as the face of the Earth is transformed in the false light of the Moon.

allies itself with money, worshipping it, always to need more of it, to gain financial security. The problem is that it doesn't lead to that result and sometimes, quite the contrary, to an abyss. In a way, money is more strongly linked to Death than Baudelaire himself, as my father used to say. His point of view was foreign to everyday reality and naïve in the extreme, but in spite of all that, he was on to something. Emotions, origins, the essential. The many paths of Art and the collector's fostering measures are a mystery, but I can see Rachael's form being painted somewhere on a wall in Prague, where Kafka is being arrested at the very same moment. And I know I will always be searching for Rachael and freeing Kafka because, just like Deckard, I am on a mission. It's left to me to incorporate the *Machine Man* and place him in the collection again. And that Kafka needed help was clear to me the moment I heard his name.

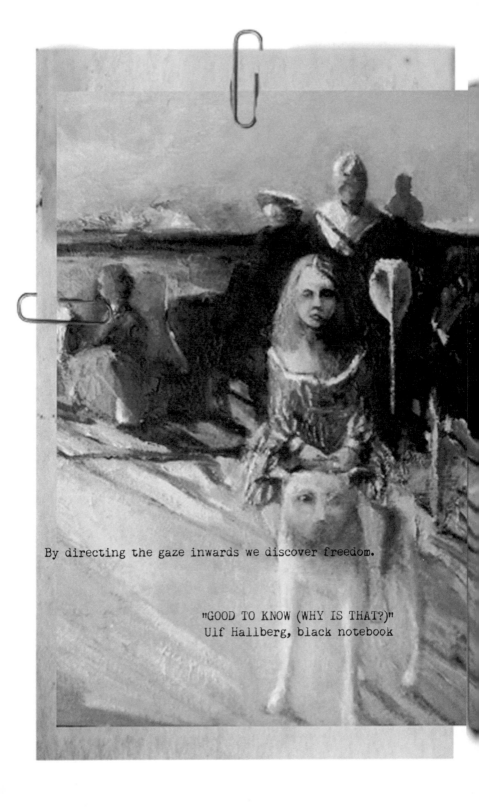

By directing the gaze inwards we discover freedom.

"GOOD TO KNOW (WHY IS THAT?)"
Ulf Hallberg, black notebook

5. The Messengers

Their questioning faces express dumb astonishment, as if their errands have already been abandoned and only dread remains. Two of them are totally turned around, one holding up a child, perhaps an heir; it's as if the expectations of the nineteenth century are being blown away from the deserted beach that constitutes the future. The atmosphere of the Crusades or of the age of knights-errant can't be maintained any longer intact. Sand blows up into their faces and makes these messengers impatient and irritated. Yet their manner of unwavering dedication appeals to us if we don't mind facing suffering and understanding their melancholy mission.

It's all about sacred idiocy.

Someone in armor says, "Truth can't fly. It lies right there on the ground beneath your feet. Donkeys and human beings trample on it and slime it over, but all that doesn't matter. It still lies there on the earth. It is in a certain sense the earth itself, stretched out under us like a safety net, deeper than we can ever fall. Therefore, there is no reason to fear. There is no defeat."

The trust of animals expresses the same hope

as one had in childhood. The strange dog barking out of fear and the young elephant loping forward, a coal-black bandaged Babar, which a little girl proudly points to, express an aspect of time in art—like sticking a hand in your pocket and pulling out something you thought you forgot—the possibility that, in a complete synchronicity of time, you could triumph through a combination of paradoxical stories and complete confidence. First and foremost with a grandiosity that is otherwise fading. The bygone messengers are standing in wait, almost politely, because someone else is always in power and, above all, abuses that authority mercilessly. In the future they will look out from their beach—under a violent orange and blue-grey sky—somewhere near the horizon in back of us, appearing nonetheless completely willing to pull out one last cigarette or offer us the last glass of water.

It is as if art is that last glass of water, some cool gulps before the watchman slams shut the doors again to sleeping or restaurant wagons and then forces us out onto a painted ramp that looks like a train station from the window. From the station's painted mural over the entire wall we suddenly detect that there are faux windows and doors painted in happy, eye-pleasing colors. Over the ticket window a diagonal strip is placed with the word, "CLOSED." It's a little masterpiece with its foreshortened sill in false perspective and panels painted with such exact strokes.

Departure times to Warsaw, Bialystok, and Wojkowice have a similar blackish pigment painted as if they are also related to eternity. To the left of the barracks there is a sign that says "HOSPITAL," on top of it sits

a nailed-down pile of wood saying "WOJKOWICE."
Over the other gate are the words: "TO BIALYSTOK."
They lead to the undressing area. The messengers on
the beaches between Binz and Neu Mukran see it all:
first the painted stage scenery of life, then the secret
room behind. How the nineteenth century's dreams and
expectations will sink into an indifference never seen
before by previous generations. And he who paints those
messengers belongs to the Pinocchio cavalry and was once
a student under a strange ceiling lamp, with an inverted
umbrella hanging down pointing out instructions to
the aspiring students at Snickarbacken in Stockholm.
There a bearded young man was standing sucking on
a corncob pipe in contemplation, excited by Velázques
or Piero della Francesca, and he slept in the art school's
studio by night on the models' platform—mad for art's
pretentions and claims, a true *massier*—as in Paris.

Åke W. Pernby, Snickarbacken 7, Stockholm.
1.9. 66.

Herr Henrik Bager, Malmö.
Registration into the Art School begins on the 15th of
September in the morning. You are welcome there and I
hope you will get the intended profit from your studies.
Yours, Åke W. Pernby

Art school is a time machine where you work to earn
a relationship with eternity. So it is good to begin as a
massier: to maintain order, keep clean, have everything
in the right place, so that nothing wild or irregular might
take over and corrupt the student into a lazy dandy or
self-satisfied prima donna, dressed in the mantel of a

phony artist. In the studio's smell of oils, turpentine and dirt, he finds Baudelaire's words: "In every moment we are crushed by the thoughts and feelings of Time. And there are only two ways to overcome that nightmare and to forget about it: amusement and work. Amusement undermines us. Work will strengthen us. Let us choose."

As a *massier* he has the keys to the school in his pocket, his few belongings lie in a box, he lights his fires in the iron stove and dreams at

> Life is not a matter of achievement but of what we learn.

night about all the women art will send to him—faces of light that he paints in unreal blue tones, lusty ladies behind thin curtains. "Like at the Jeu de Paume in the Tuileries Garden," his master, Åke Pernby mentions, "the same shy longings, the same celebration."

"Now we shall go out and have lunch, Bager!" Pernby chats about Toulouse-Lautrec and Van Gogh, about Pissarro and Degas, Picasso and Cézanne, about history and humanism. With the coffee and brandy, the instructor raises his voice suddenly, looks intensely at his massier and gathers together his thoughts on the incision wound. "Art is a mission, young man, our forebears are messengers. Now let's walk up to the school. I have something important to tell you all."

"The incision wound, *par exemple!* The paintbrush isn't just a piece of wood with tough or pliable bristles. It can be an extension of the lifeline, the timing of the paintbrush and the color with the movement of waves or birds in flight, a question of survival. You can paint the possibility of being seen by the dead. Identity is perhaps a certain blue tone that suggests absence. The true time is found in the incision wound. The color touches the beholder like when you cut yourself with a sharp knife and don't know if the incision is superficial or cut deeply down to the hard, naked bone. The surface wound widens to red, and you see the bandage's colorless, grey-white tone. Airy light hints at the leap between dream and waking. Faces remind us of those questions we tried to pose as a child and then forgot all about."

And the teacher who knows what he is saying and teaches his gifted ones to impose boundless claims on themselves, so that they shall serve art, this otherwise tongue-tied man in an impeccable suit, pink tie or dark blue bow tie, then walks into his office in order to ponder the critic's words about his art. Even though vulnerable, punctured and cut, he never shows it to anyone (trusting that art is stronger than the fear of getting hurt). I speak of the paintbrush's wound but forgot to talk about the stinging pain from the knives of the critics. He worries about his hands trembling as he approaches the easel and doesn't seem to be able to hold up the paintbrush in the right way. Can students see that? *Massier* Bager, the remarkable one, with his ardent talent and intuition?

"Then he was fully conscious of the inadequacy of his work and couldn't boast about his past, but he believed that, in life as in art, he always found himself at an apprentice stage, and deep inside he felt like a powerful and ingenious machine in waiting, though yet not in motion. He always lived in wait . . ." Italo Svevo says. Isn't that always the artist's condition? Pernby walks over to his young student, who then increases his stride as the other heads home and takes him by the arm: "You have the gift," he says. "The rest is hard work. You perhaps don't know what cold and warm colors are. But that's exactly what makes your paintings appear different from the others'. Always think how André Breton stresses the free-association method as a way to make unforeseen connections! You yourself will set the conditions for the truth." Like grandfather did, the young man thinks.

And thus he hears the teacher's voice rise, as if it has been injured by something unknown and disgusting. "A clever marksman hits the target after he has practiced aiming a lot, but a true artist hits the target without even having seen it!" Like grandfather did, he thinks again, but without those strict limitations. When grandfather went to art school in Paris from 1910-11 he didn't see Picasso, rather he only saw the Impressionists' nineteenth century. Grandfather was too clever; preconceived notions shut his Paris in. His personal rebellion was to become an artist instead of a jurist. He allowed his art to become formulated. But the artist must always formulate his own mission himself. Grandfather's genius was that he created the city of Malmö instead. He drew the Malmö of the sixteenth century just like James Joyce wrote about the Dublin of 1905.

> Each and every word carries the whole universe.

Out of the archives of the City Hall cellar Einar Bager

134

creates the Malmö of the sixteenth century from stories and legends, rumors and statistics. His drawings, sketches, cardboard models are products of the imagination. He creates his own stage scenery of sixteenth century Malmö. Then when archaeologists excavate the basements of the real houses, Bager's model matches reality. Intuition and contemplation, constant cataloguing, more research, and artistry—a messenger from the sixteenth century with his so-called "pipe organ" over his huge working table with so many files and envelopes for directorial material à la Carl Theodore Dreyer—right there in Mölle. Grandfather as an artist was a brilliant craftsman, but as a research worker he was an ingenious discoverer. For what we know about Malmö's sixteenth century, we have a fallen angel to thank. He was a man who suddenly understood how Flaubert must have felt when he began to doubt the value of art and drew the dreadful—and, thank God, the false—perception that art is nothing more than a stupid, childish game. "History is taken seriously, my son!" grandfather might say. "I remember when I met the dying artist P.S. Krøyer in Copenhagen in 1908. Krøyer was blind, confused, in the last throes of his syphilis. He knew that his most renowned painting, the one with his wife Marie and the dog on the beach, was his worst. His last wish was to see his beloved Marie one more time, from whom he so long had been separated—because the composer Hugo Alfven had used his influence to keep her away. It wasn't true that Krøyer in that moment couldn't reconcile himself with death, because Marie

Seraph = an angel of the highest dignity, especially glowing in its love, the colour of Seraph is red.

arrived sure enough just at the end and stood there in front of him, but he grumbled so about everything he hadn't managed to get the time to paint."

Then I said: "Now Herr Krøyer must calm down. Who can say he has had time to..."

And then the ninety-five-year-old Einar Bager turned to the young artist and said: "But you are just lazing around and lapping up old stories. As a twentieth century man and artist you are responsible for your share of monstrosities."

He stood on the train platform and remembered the summers of his childhood on the beach in the former East Prussia between white summer cottages with carpenter Gothic facades, the smell of flowers, of skin and of freshly baked bread. He was sick to his stomach when Lalka marched by with his subalterns. The trains with Jews were sixty cars long and stopped just a hundred meters from Treblinka. Of course, it would have been much simpler just to let the train roll right into the camp. But the unloading area wasn't long enough, and if the six thousand deported Jews were to step out at the same time it would cause an undesirable uproar, chaotic confusion—maybe even worse. The first problem was how to give a minimum of hope back to the deportees. So the idea of the phony train station occurred to Lalka as head of the concentration camp.

Now it was time to inspect the last paintings. The painters were still working on the finishing touches on the intended ticket box office, the window and its curtains when Lalka arrived. He let some gardeners do some planting during the afternoon, all of which looked quite cozy and tidy. But, despite all that was done, the head of the concentration camp wasn't pleased.

The artist felt the irritation written all over Lalka's face and feared immediate punishment, which for several of his predecessors had been an instant death sentence.

"This won't do!" Lalka screamed. "You have painted an awful station that doesn't stick to the purpose. You're not a true artist! Any kind of Jew would notice that it's a fake."

He snapped his fingers at the guards.

They had already got a grip on the unfortunate artist.

"Maybe what is missing is the station clock," the artist said as an afterthought.

The carpenter looked around and put a clock together. The artist was allowed to paint a clock over a cylindrical piece of wood with a diameter of seventy and a thickness of twenty centimeters.

"What time should it be in Treblinka?" the artist asked from his perch with paintbrush in hand.

Lalka looked at his own watch. "It shall be three o'clock in Treblinka," he answered.

While he was painting that clock with arms that would always be pointing to three o'clock, he dreamed of the ocean's overwhelming freedom and power. He saw his sister standing on the windy beach, the nurse maid holding his little brother in her arms, mother and father had just come down to the beach to call them home for dinner. Someone is being patted down with a big white bathing towel, they are lifting up the food basket, and even though they had died in the gas chambers behind him, his family kept him from falling down now. He remembered the sounds of bare feet in the sand, childlike laughter and the parents' urgent pleas. It was in that moment that he knew that he would survive Lalka, the SS-storm trooper Commander Kurt Franz nicknamed "The Puppet," because there exists another eternity of justice. No one shall try to make time stand still and go unpunished. Everyone is still alive, he thought: Sara, Olga, Emil, mother and father. There are no dead ones, so long as we keep working on rescuing them. And it was his paintbrush and his dexterity that gave him that skill.

On the face of the clock, Hans Bevernis paints his initials, H.B., as a sign to be noticed in the future—as a sign that he would be inquired about as a witness in that future.

Åke Pernby's favorite story dealt with one of the old masters at the famous Grand Chaumier art school who once insisted on taking him through the Louvre, where he pointed to one of the paintings and said:

"Don't you see it?"

I nodded confidently; then Pernby said:

"You don't see it! Look again!"

And I saw a garden with trees, bushes, light and greenery that I accurately described; the teacher went on:

"But you didn't notice the bird!" the old man cried so loud that the people in the gallery turned themselves around.

And then I saw the symmetry: everything that damn little bird among the leaves up to the left, conveyed.

And then Åke Pernby always smiled, though he had told the story for the hundredth time, with the same understated bravado.

In the color blue there is a trail that leads to the roll-down window shades of childhood; the dread of chartered trains; all the wide, questioning eyes the adults had seen and been terrified of but so seldom discussed. The maid's room where the boy Henrik Bager slept had been divided in the middle by a thin partition and on the other side there was a bathroom. Frightful sounds came out of that place of terror, words like enemas and stomach pains, constipation and intestinal blockage were mentioned, amplified in the boy's dreams. Those hours in lonely contemplation—outside his normal sense of security—the dead idylls of linen and lavender came alive. It was just like the big production at the end-of-the-year program for Miss Nordenstjärna's Kindergarten class near Fridhemstorget in Malmö in 1953, where he played the role of Prince Charming in a pageant of *Sleeping Beauty,* which didn't include a successful theatrical triumph but rather seemed a testimony of future disasters. The roll-down window shades' fantastic tales symbolized everything that adults didn't talk about. In the shifting lights in the darkness the boy perceived all the mysteries he had to be shielded from. When grandmother called him to the breakfast table, he was rigid with that fear. There was something else, something indescribable outside that he would always be afraid of.

> I am in the middle of Plato, in wonder of the dialectical method that sharpens my brain like a blue-shimmering knife.

On the beach between Binz and Neu Mukran on the island of Rügen in the Baltic from 1936 until

1939 the Nazis built the Prora summer camp, which was never completed because the war broke out first. The German labor front would be sent there for their summer vacations—hard-working laborers with at least three children. There were huge sports arenas there and auditoriums—the great hall had room for 20,000 people—and everyone participated in collective recreation. It was considered to be a worker's duty to keep himself in shape, everything sickly was excluded. The body should be strengthened in Prora, the soul hardened, the family welded together—everything forged to the mission to become one with the nation. The state would be one welded body: fit, hard, sun-tanned and ready. That summer camp was exhibited at the World's Fair in Paris in 1937. But as Walter Benjamin wrote: "All efforts to aestheticize politics culminate in war."

In 1945 the camp was partially demolished. During the four-decade-long existence of the GDR, the German Democratic Republic, Russian soldiers were quartered in the old Prora constructions. In 1992 these constructions were opened to the public as a kind of historic chamber of horrors which sailors from Scandinavia found as they sailed along the coast. A painter among those sailors perceives figures on the beach

Conatus (one of Spinoza's concepts) = the essence of all living things.

that no one else sees, blind or blinded children, knights of the crusades or Good Samaritans, mute messengers from another era. In that blue light, sand swirls up into the eyes of the beholder in his boat on the sea beyond Prora.

The artist turns himself around on the platform in 1942—
and on the beach between Binz and Neu Mukran in 1993—
in order to attach himself to Cocteau's formula: "Save the
messengers' blue mystery!" That blue comes from a long
way off. Along the way it hardens and turns into a mountain.
The Culture Industry has changed the conception of the afterlife.
Today's triumphs cannot be revised. But the grasshopper is
working there. Birds are working there. The artist is working.
In the word alone we know nothing. That's why he paints.
One speaks of Prussian blue. In Naples a fresco of the Holy
Virgin still exists in the cracks of more recently painted walls
while the sky withdraws. Now he paints the arrival terminal,
the clock and its hands of wood pointing to three o'clock.
That's his mystery. The blue roll-down window shades'
mystery, the sapphire's mystery, the Holy Virgin's mystery,
the soda fountain's mystery, the white gowns' mystery, the
clock hands' and the blue beams' mystery. And a long time
later his follower paints what he sees behind Prora, on the
beach between Binz and Neu Mukran. All tales, all words,
all resolutions and explanations disappear into color; the
bright nuances carry along tones and feelings with them that
are only grasped by the eye and the heart at the same time.
That's the way life is illuminated. Even her blue eyes piercing
his heart. The messengers have given him the mission to
save everything. They are standing there on the beach and
looking out to sea. Thus his brain directs his hand—just
as on the platform to the train—to the muffled barking
of the dogs, the rhythmic clatter of the oncoming train,
everything that is heard beyond the railway ties, along the
coast of childhood—to lift his brush and create illusions
of truth on canvass.

Through the studio's skylight the stars of the pact shine clear. The artist breaks away from normal life and walks into his own time. Sometimes he thinks he is constructing a Gothic cathedral, but he realizes suddenly that he is standing in a baker's kitchen and is squirting syrup on a rococo layer cake. In the cloud over the beach between Binz and Neu Mukran on the island of Rügen he paints very bright parts and a bluish contour looking like the shadow of someone. He sees in front of himself the corridor between the hall and the large studio at the art school in Snickarbacken. In the bright light the door opens into the teacher's room and Åke Pernby peeps out. The darkness in the middle of the painting is only the raw material, the necessary antithesis.

"Tunnels" in the universe connect various locations that are light years apart. The tunnel becomes both a fast short cut to other worlds and a time machine, where we can travel either back in time or into the future.

It is a darkness that simultaneously describes and is rendered harmless by the messengers—human figures who live outside of time.

"Don't forget to turn off the light in case you go out, massier Bager!" Pernby says in a fatherly way, a little proudly. "But I assume your head is full of art tonight. Good evening!"

In solitude memory begins to move, the present time
and the past are mingled and flow together. The dead
return to the poor little room of our imagination.

"WORDS & AID"
Ulf Hallberg, black notebook

6. Those Beyond Repayment

My father hated his own father. When the subject of my grandfather (who died two years before I was born) came up in conversation, my father said bluntly: "There was nothing good about that man." I had many questions about my grandfather Victor. My father told me how Victor made his four children share one room while the other six rooms were allocated to his wife, Fammi, and himself. My grandparents had separate bedrooms, and Victor also had a separate workroom. He was a pediatrician and the dowry from the marriage had been used to start up a practice on Söder Street. Victor's mother ran a tobacco store, so he married into a substantial rise in social status. Fammi was one of the four daughters of Rudolf Asp, founder of *Skånska Daily News*.

When I was in my twenties I pestered my father about Victor. It led to an odd conversation. I was not given any definite answers, only a feeling that Victor had released an unreasonable hatred in his son. I can remember details about my father arriving home to witness his father fondling the hired maid. Or about Victor hitting my father's older brother, Stig, for drinking out of the whiskey bottle or the punch. Stig was something of a street urchin and a charmer, a kind of elegant double of my father—without notebooks —but with exceptional manners and captivating eyes. I only met my cousins once before my father's sister, Fasse, died. It was a Christmas Eve in my childhood. I remember how they attended Fasse's funeral, with my other aunt Britt, dressed up nicely, then quickly departed with the most valuable things from her apartment. I had not seen them for over twenty years. They barely had anything to do with Fasse before that. My father was defenseless against such people. As my parents prepared dinner, the guests made up lists of what they would take home with them: the chandelier, the parlor cabinet, and so on. My father never spoke with his sister Britt again after that.

Fasse was part of our family; she was frank and wonderful. My father was the only one who couldn't quite handle her toward the end. Throughout my father's youth, he was probably saddled with the fact that he was the only one who cared for "The Little One," the dwarf who cried and yelled at her father to find some medicine that could make her grow. We children loved Fasse because she always understood our needs, always made our games the center of interest. Fasse and I were inseparable. I've always measured myself against her; first height-wise, and later as a storyteller.

My grandfather, who according to my father was a morphine addict, tried to sign over all his assets to his nurse when he was on his deathbed. It's a story I heard many times. I can visualize that blonde nurse sitting on a swivel chair waiting for her share, Victor crying in the agony of death, and my father running around the office in a frantic hunt for the false will. I always pictured Victor, foggy eyed and spitting up blood, just at the moment of death making one more demand on his son: "Can you promise me to finish your law studies after I die?"

Against his will, my father had studied law for four years and in another half year would have taken the exam as a Candidate for a Law degree.

"I said yes," my father told me, "but as soon as he died I began my studies in Art History and didn't give a damn about the law. And I managed to secure the money for Fammi."

I knew this to be true since during all my childhood my father went to the bank with Fammi every Wednesday. He always said that without his help Fammi would have been dirt poor, and later on he pointed to his study of the Law, which gave him insight into the economics of stocks and bonds.

"Going back and forth to the bank is a full-time job," my father would say, "but I do it for Fammi's sake."

They always dressed up when they went to the bank. That always made me wonder what kind of transactions were taking place with my father wearing his best suit and Fammi in her fur boa. In hindsight I think it was a symbolic act, purely for the sake of Fammi and my father. When I became a writer there were still people who welcomed me at the Bank of Skåne, in spite of my economic circumstances.

Perhaps my father financed some parts of the art purchases on Thursdays in Copenhagen with Fammi's retirement funds.

In addition to being a pediatrician, my grandfather was the company doctor for Yllefabriken. He also took ice cold showers every morning, my father said in disgust. "And when I worked as a mail man on Söder Street during Christmas break in order to earn some extra money, he didn't even greet me when we met on the street."

As a pediatrician Victor was apparently appreciated, and it has always been hard for me to get a clear insight into his personality. When I look at photographs of him I see a decision maker and a man interested in personal gain. A pragmatic, razor-sharp man of power with a mostly-ignored, melancholy wife. At the edge of the photo I see my father with dreamy eyes searching for a way out.

"I don't understand why he became a doctor. He cared as much about people as any circus horse or drum major!"

I never understood the image of Victor as a circus horse or a drum major until I experienced the market scenes in Büchner's *Woyzeck*.

"A doctor who can't respect vulnerable people should choose a different profession!" my father said.

During the 1970s when my father and I had intense conversations about Stanley Kubrick's film *A Clockwork Orange,* one of my father's favorite films, in regards to the staging of violence, my father said "Alex is a bit like Victor, totally amoral."

My father's aversion to power and authority seems to stem from this paternal hatred. Sometimes I also had a feeling that the significance he assigned to objects early on, had to do with a loss he suffered in relation to his father, an injustice regarding his identity and everything he was truly fascinated by and believed in. It's as if he was ruled by an unsatisfied need to be seen and noticed for his true beliefs and desires.

My father didn't move away from home until, in August of 1949, he married my mother. He was thirty years old. When Eva met my father, on Walpurgis Night in 1949, he lived in an attic room above grandfather's and Fammi's apartment on Fersen's Road in Malmö. The attic room was filled with books and objects— among others, Büchner's collected works—that he used as weapons of defense against my grandfather.

"Büchner had faith in the poor bastards," he said. "He saw the human body as sacred and the desire for power as worthless. In Victor's world it was the other way around."

My mother, whose father Oscar was a farmer in Bårarp just outside of Jönköping, thought that my father's family was something new and amazingly fine.

When she entered the attic room she asked astonishingly: "What's all this?"

"I've collected everything that those beyond repayment have created," my father said.

"There's no room for us in here," my mother answered.

She had studied at a teacher's college and worked in a small village school in Småland; now she had her first employment at Rörsjö School in Malmö.

Eva saw things with a view to practicality, but remained respectful of that European Trash.

"I think we can work things out eventually," she said.

It was the only time she thoroughly misjudged a situation.

In 1831 the University of Strasbourg had four faculties: medicine, natural sciences, political science and theology. There was an anatomical museum and a chemistry laboratory. George Büchner studied pathology and surgery. Lectures and instruction were often conducted at the hospital as well as the morgue. Psychiatry was in its developmental stages and medicine explained psychosis based on weather or moonlight and was often in conflict with physiology. Cold showers and bloodletting were acceptable forms of treatment. Human anatomy as a science had a key role in the nineteenth century. Anatomy formulated criteria for a "normal body" and indicated what was normal and abnormal, healthy or sick. Instruction in medicine was developing around an anatomical understanding of the body. Dissection was the initiation into the understanding of medicine. Students penetrated, surveyed, and assimilated the inner workings of the human body at the anatomical theater. While Büchner was living in Strasbourg, the fifty-four-year-old Doctor Lobstein, of European renown, authored the first textbook in pathological anatomy. His enthusiasm for science culminated in his will, in which he specified the donation of his own corpse for a complete post-mortem examination. Until the end of the nineteenth century his internal organs, preserved in chemical liquids, could still be viewed at the anatomical museum he himself founded.

My strongest memory of the Wall is of a white line located

at the border crossing on Invalidenstrasse; that's where we West Berliners crossed over. At night I traveled out of East Germany, walked up to that same white line, made an about-face, and traveled back again. I was living in two worlds during the 1980s; inside me these black-and-white worlds remain etched like a personal problem.

If the fall of the Berlin wall in 1989 is viewed as a moment of truth, then it's not entirely about a collapse of political systems and fundamental oppositions. It wasn't only the simple friend-foe, East-West, mainstream-underground antagonisms that disappeared, but their entire foundations were shaken up. Since then the prevalent ideas about nationality and national individuality have dissolved—both through nationalistic border issues (the Balkan Wars) and through encroaching border disintegration (the EU's influence on member countries' border control and economic, political globalization). "Social movements" and the "working class" have been substituted by the arrival of the "elites" and "management"; culture has lost its dialectical character and has become a mass-media phenomenon. Personal identity remains, nonetheless, alone and abandoned.

> To limit oneself is a mechanism of escape in order to save one's life.

Collective confusion and high anxiety are the results of personal breakdowns and a civilization's dissolution. Everything has become bitter. Reality and hard-nosed politics produce shock, outrage and falsification. The individual is torn apart. But language continues to protest, it gets amplified, halts and explodes—and cries are heard—in the real world and on stage. The fawning proletarian worker is turned into a virus laden e-mail message. The head officials and those responsible have become obscure. It is an airy, impalpable world where individuals are supposed to realize their feelings through the purchasing of merchandise. More and more often, uncontrollable shrieks are heard.

My father and I had a shared interest in the Austrian writer Robert Musil. My father said the portrayal of the main character Ulrich in the unfinished novel, *The Man Without Qualities,* came so close to his own shattered self-perceptions that he could thoroughly picture Musil's internal conflicts as he sat at his writing desk.

"He writes day and night and can't ever stop. It's just like me with the scissors and the European Trash. By summoning up his extremely developed ability to understand human psychology, he attempts to organize everything in a novel that shatters all borders. It becomes a whirling essay about humanity's modern conditions," my father said. "He is a collector, you see that! He's understood that, it's very important! He has read that; it must be written down! I can really picture him at his writing desk!"

And my father grasped the scissors, raised his arm and cut out the article about Robert Musil in *Hufvudstadsbladet,* and carefully glued it onto a page in his notebook.

The German cultural theorist Aby Warburg is, together with Walter Benjamin and Sigmund Freud, one of the representatives of Cultural Studies that analyze history's "affects," its strong mental agitations and critical conditions, by looking at traces of these affects in pictures, texts, and events. One of Warburg's special contributions has to do with analyzing antiquity's influence on Art History as a kind of archive for "agitated forms of expression." In his doctoral thesis on Sandro Botticelli's famous Renaissance painting *The Birth of Venus* he coined the idea *das bewegte Beiwerk:* "the moving irrelevance", and simultaneously "the irrelevance that moves us." For example, he analyzes Venus' hair or the expression in her face rather than proceeding from Art History terms or classical symbology. According to Warburg a scarf or a shell is not part of the whole, but rather an interesting detail in which the whole can possibly be deciphered.

During the 1920s the photographer August Sander documented "The Twentieth Century Man" in facial portraits. "I've been asked many times how I came up with the idea to create this work of art," wrote Sander. "Through observation, study, and thought," he stated laconically. Sander divided his portraits into seven categories (farmers, craftsmen, women, professionals, artists, big cities, and just everyday people) with many sub-categories (23 a: the National Socialist). It was the type, or the role he was after: the teacher, the mason, the gypsy, and so on. He collected the people of his time in portfolios to take a stand against decadence.

It's twelve noon on Wednesday, January 5th, 2005 at the S-Bahn Hohenzollerndamm station in Berlin. A group of 4th graders have just been ice-skating on a sports' day in strong winter sun and are boarding the train. The sensation of skating is still in their bodies, their legs feel light. When the skates have come off, each step is like floating on air. Life is full of possibilities, lap after lap of machine-polished ice, with someone close by to pull off the skates and help with the backpack. Everything is perfectly clear: the train and the winter day, walking next to one's best friend, the teacher holding the universe together, the protective care from the parents. A girl stroking her hand softly down her friend's braided hair, a boy putting his arm around his best friend's shoulder.

Suddenly a voice from the loudspeaker announces that all of Europe will unite in silence for three minutes to honor the victims of the tsunami-catastrophe. From Kiev to Copenhagen all trains stop. The adults in the train cars are immediately quiet.

All power, no matter what form it takes, is ruled by an instinctive need to consume, an impulse to deplete and totally exterminate other people or Nature.

The children look at each other and try to suppress the giggles that burst out inadvertently in this unfamiliar and formal situation. Then their faces change again and become solemn. It's as if they have grown old for a moment and can take part in some experience beyond their own innocence. What kind of pictures do they look at within themselves? What do they have for images in their minds? People grabbing cement pillars or trees and suddenly torn loose from their fellow humans by an uncontrolled, senseless natural power? People being hurled toward a nearby embankment or down into the deadly waters? Glimpses of despair among lonely children or bloated bodies turning blue while lying on the beach? They recall images they haven't been protected against. Images that witness fate's power to crush every certainty and truth, to tear apart all bonds and trigger immense and lifelong grief. I look into these children's serious faces, one of those children is my own, and can feel Europe's immense grief—incurable, yet shared and full of insights.

After March of 1933 Walter Benjamin was in exile. Throughout the 1930s, Paris—especially the Bibliothêque Nationale—was his place of refuge. In the reading room of the library he tried to take a stand against the *Zeitgeist* of the times, the breakdown of popular movements and his own destitute situation with more and more focus on material studies. The master test of fragmentary forms, the history-philosophy of the *The Arcades Project,* Paris, capital of the nineteenth century Metropolis grows incessantly, quotes upon quotes enveloped within labels such as "Fashion," "the Flâneur," "the Interior," "the Collector," and so on, broadening and getting thicker; quotations and collections of comments—all nourish different aspects of the former century viewed from the present-day's "bloodstained fog."

The interesting part of twentieth century family epics is the struggle between intimacy and distance, community and freedom. The family is not so much a cradle of civilization, rather more of a communal fact, a battlefield, a mirror. Although none of us, not even the childless lone wolf, can be cloned yet, we are all affected by its continued existence, and can learn a lot from an epic family saga. How the art collector Soames Forsyte struggles to put out the fire in his travelling art gallery, how Thomas Buddenbrook tries to uphold his own family's merchant traditions in Lübeck, and how colonel Aureliano Buendía fights injustices on the South American continent, how the persistent Melquíades, writing on his parchment papers, gives an account of the Buendía's family history one hundred years in advance, anticipating the infinite solitude that always hangs over and always has been hanging over the family, not some false intimacy but a protest against loneliness. García Márquez' clever title *One Hundred Years of Solitude* offers a surprising freedom to the description of the Buendía family in Macondo, because its framework is always cosmic loneliness. And therefore the family is not only a sanctuary but also a location for dedicated unity, constructive contradictions, stubborn defiance, and vigorous opposition.

People's heads are being hollowed out by aesthetical decay.

If an historical truth exists it is in continuous motion between the past and the current historical situation's present—it is the moment of writing or reading. The salvaged manuscript of Walter Benjamin's *The Arcades Project* mirrors the struggle between ideas and the historical world: the world of experience breaking down, the fate of art, the mechanics of traditional processes.

The texts live through our fascination in the not-so-small parts of this historic reality. The arcade windows, the cafe mirror-image worlds, the changing slants of light, the sidewalk reconstructions, the development of the light fixtures, the death principle's supremacy, Utopia's collapse. Everything is absorbed into language and transformed into an endless commentary on the developments of the nineteenth century—foreign to us today, yet establishing laws forward to a new world. Those descriptions live in an "intimate pathos," an attempt to pull those artifacts closer together, to let them step into our lives.

"Are you going to die, too?" My youngest son asks, and I understand that even his small world of experience is changed by the tsunami. "Yes, I answer, we all are." "Doesn't anything stay behind?" "Yes, memories, experiences, and emotions." "What about me? Am I going to die, too?" "Yes." "And the lamps, will they die?" "No, the lamps won't die." He has to think about this: "Will Santa Claus die?" "No," I say, "Santa Claus will not die." His smile reflects his insight into the incredible joy of eternal values—a quick glance behind the curtains that screen the scenes of life.

In one of his final letters, of May 7th, 1940, Walter Benjamin writes to his friend Theodor W. Adorno, "A child's charm primarily provides society with a remedy, a hint we receive about some 'spontaneous happiness.'" At another place in the letter, Benjamin points out that the origin of his "theory of experience" can be found in childhood memories. In a first draft of the *Berlin Chronicle* Benjamin portrays an afternoon in Paris, where he sketched a graphic timeline of his life. The sketch looked like a genealogical chart—or rather like a labyrinth—and was lost. But at that moment when he sketched out his "bio-graphy" it seemed obvious to Benjamin that the city of Paris, with its many brick walls and wharves, its passageways and kiosks had a special potential for letting the connections to the past appear as dream pictures and reveal their true faces. Before the failed attempt at fleeing across the Pyrenees in 1940 ended in suicide, Benjamin left a typewritten copy of *Berliner Kindheit um 1900* for Georges Bataille, the Head Librarian of Bibliothéque Nationale at the time. That's where Benjamin, throughout the entire 1930s, wrote down his thoughts on Progress, the Interior, and the Flâneur, his philosophical comments on childhood memories and starting points for a new way at seeing old traditions. The present day creates or abolishes history; experience can be found in the remembrances of or the interpretation thereof. Benjamin recalls to mind an object or an incident that he gives a new meaning to. A name or a taste is the only thing needed, just as in Proust. It is possible to interpret reality, but only at certain moments: "The writer can hold living hours in his hand just as the collector holds up his art pieces. He does not have to speak of them, but they are visible; because he is so devoutly searching, questioning, evaluating and, full of knowledge, turning them around in his hand, looking at them from every angle, but without giving them the life of false insight but instead that of true tradition." That's what Benjamin writes about Max Kommerell, but it's more like a self-portrait. The lightning-like pictures in *Berlin Childhood around 1900* could be viewed as

Benjamin's final Utopia: "children as representatives of Paradise," with the intuitive ability to elucidate and criticize the glorification of the status quo. "Each childhood accomplishes something great and beyond repayment for humanity," as it is written in *The Arcades Project*. The child, disguised in his "alphabet-turmoil," on the threshold between two centuries and gazing at the ray of light under the bedroom door constructs likenesses. The collection in the dresser drawer is a renewal of dead objects; words are holes with innumerable connections. Time contains an urge to interpret the past that remains incomplete; that is the fundamental thought in Benjamin's concept of tradition. He states that the majority of humanity does not want to, or cannot create, any new experiences; and additionally are blocked by their convictions, but he adds that a connection between experience and observation remains to be demonstrated. "Like a mollusk I dozed through aspects of the nineteenth century that now are spread before me like an empty clam shell. I hold it against my ear. What do I hear?"

Some voices are intolerable, thin and self-sufficient without any contact with the rest of the world. We can hear them everywhere nowadays. Then there are voices with a ring of depth, voices in contact with both beauty and sadness. Marianne Faithfull's voice portrays the rise and fall of pop-culture, how myths turn into experience, how dreams of a different life turn from grief to drugs and disillusionment. But in spite of rock n' roll and rebellion evolving more toward mainstream and commercialism, her experiences are deeply personal. Both a singer and an actress, she always mixed the two art forms. In 1966 she acted with Anna Karina and Jean-Pierre Léaud in Jean-Luc Godard's *Made in USA*. She's sitting at a café table turning toward a man next to her: "Say something!" "I'm tired of this," he answers from the depth of every barstool's loneliness, and Marianne Faithfull hums to herself *As Tears Go By*. As if Godard, with that melancholy song, wishes to capture the sounds of time. In her autobiography *Faithfull*, published in 1994, Marianne Faithfull relates the golden years of the 1960s: "to drop down on Indian pillows to the music of Ravi Shankar over at George Harrison's and Patti Boyd's, have a joint or an acid trip fixed by Spanish Tony, and think you're on a quest for the Holy Grail like an innocent child." In *Memories, Dreams and Reflections* she describes *Swinging London* with Mick Jagger and Keith Richards posed in front of the painting of *Vesuvius* on the outside wall of Spanish Tony's club in London: "We all lived under a volcano, lit up, dressed up, were together, went around to clubs with clever names, while forces we couldn't even imagine were lurking around corners."

> Nobody survives alone. A conversation with someone who has passed away embodies that someone's life in one's own self; one can step into his or her footsteps, start walking, and in that way visit the many nooks and crannies in the house of history.

My father thought I ought to bring Walter Benjamin back. He felt a strong link to Benjamin, both as a collector and a thinker. In a way I had done that when I translated his works, but my father demanded more. He said that

Benjamin must have felt deep disappointment when he was refused Spanish asylum at Port Bou on the 25th of September in 1940 as a Jew fleeing the Nazis, possibly also a despair over not being able to finish editing his great work about Paris. My father knew how it felt to be surrounded by stuffed envelopes, folders about to burst, binders, quotes, and loose-leaf notes. He stated that Benjamin at that moment had the full weight of all the European Trash on his shoulders and that despair over the amount and complexity of the Trash—still not entirely organized in proper clusters and categories—was the determining factor in Walter Benjamin's suicide.

The envious fly in Purgatory with eyelids sown together.

"If nothing else, I think Benjamin, when he lost his belief in his own ability to organize that Trash, must have felt an obsession to communicate with someone other than that dry Adorno about what he really thought as he was facing death. That person must have been his darling Asja Lacis, his grand and unfortunate love. And it would be a great loss to the European Trash if nobody found those letters soon and added them to the collection. They are probably stacked away in a desk drawer somewhere in Hostal Francia in Port Bou. I think he wrote more than one letter that day, before he took those morphine capsules. He could have put the letters on the reception desk, one by one, and then the idiot of a receptionist might have placed them in a compartment somewhere where they were abandoned. It's tragic how the European Trash has been so mistreated over the ages."

Port Bou, 25th of September 1940

Dear Asja my angel!

If only you were here so I could say all this and look into your eyes. It would be like returning to Capri, forgetful of the stomping boots out there, and breathing in the scent of bougainvillea and your skin. My memory of you is like a folded fan, which doesn't provide any breath of air until unfolded, and that in its new embrace contains your lovely features within—that is, in my ailing heart. When you were standing there in the store trying to buy some almonds without knowing the right Italian word, my education, for once, had some practical relevance. I was able to help you and get acquainted. But I was lost from the beginning—a bouncing ball in the confusion you always brought upon me. Yet I always knew that even a one-way feeling has absolute value. My life is fulfilled at the borderline of two nations and two languages. My race from the war has ended; I wasn't able to complete my Baudelaire or my *Arcades Project*. Once I described myself to Adorno as someone shipwrecked. He had safely climbed up to the top of the mast, but its wood was rotten. Nevertheless, I argued that he could always send out an emergency signal and be rescued. But that is not the case anymore. Being Jews, we wait and wait and wait. Then we meet up in the camps.

We have been walking across the Pyrenées since seven o'clock this morning. When I glanced down over La Côte de Vermeille and saw the vermilion-red autumnal earth and the ocean I thought for a moment that I was rescued. But new regulations had taken effect that delayed our departure, and I didn't have the strength to confront that stooping dwarf any longer. The hunchback had, with customary precision, emerged again. I told the truth about myself in the Proust-essay: "He died because of his alienation from the world, and because he was not able to change the conditions of life which started to have dire consequences on him. He died because he didn't know how to start a fire in the furnace, or how to open a window." All this can be observed here and now, with this addition: Life wasn't his medium; perhaps he belonged to the sphere of the angels, or to the back yard of the useless ones.

My briefcase, which I have carried around with me all day, contains my *Theses on the Philosophy of History* and the most recent notes and envelops belonging to the *Arcades Project*. The material that is already edited I deposited with Bataille at the Bibliothéque Nationale in Paris. In those theses you will find the total sum of my historical intuitions. I completed them in February with a feeling of clarity and conclusion. A text I call "The Angel of History" I'm most proud of. But in general the aversion I have for completing my projects and texts has always been my weakness to the point of self-destruction—this urge to always keep the wording open for yet another thought or investigation.

Dear Asja, I have the feeling, here in this dark room, while my heart beats irregularly and my breathing is strenuous and painful—the morphine capsules lined up neatly in a row on the table—that it was my greatest failure and yet my most powerful revolt this lack of realism, this attempt to embrace a whole epoch and to safely deliver the nineteenth century into our times, to mirror the threshold of a new insight, like an awakening that probably never will take place. As you know, Baudelaire and Blanqui were my lodestars. The former because of his outmoded anger and his exemplary fabrication of alienation, the latter for his crushing criticism of Progress and the unreasonable urge to put right everything unjust in spite of who is in power and what is to come next. This ought to be my attitude now, but my energy is at end, my unfinished work is about to defeat me.

I am a paradox, even as a refugee, since I always flee from every possibility to build up what might constitute a personal life – at least outside the focal point of writing. You probably laugh heartily at these scholarly subtleties and my aristocratic fear of the middle-class. You have always been able to see the pristine origins in me. My grandmother's twelve-room flat on Blumeshof, the encased existence, the protective coverings, yes, all of my terribly proper complaisance. You never saw what I call "my courage," the philosophical aspects of enduring, and fulfilling, my insights. You only saw me as the fallen bourgeois, never as the revolutionary professional writer. You, who lay claim to the revolution! You never imagined the state of mind necessary to adjust to that cozy and homely life between the jaws of the crocodile, with a fountain pen in one hand.

Your Walter

Port Bou, the 25th of September 1940

Hegel's definition of philosophy is "time summarized in thoughts."

Dear Asja, my angel!

As we, the Jews of Paris, stood in rows at Stade de Colombes in the oppressive heat, holding our small suitcases waiting to be transported somewhere, to a camp in the south or to another country, I saw Fascism as a force of nature, turned loose by the unharnessed and destructive powers born out of people's inability to tolerate conflicts and paradoxes. The absence of ambiguity postulated by Fascism has the character of death. There is no life in something absolute, just as art that is too plain, isn't art, but a lifeless, censured artifact. Truth is not a disclosure that destroys a secret, but a revelation that does justice to it. Positivism has, in the development of technology, only moved forward in the natural sciences, but not in human society. In all politics I only understand one thing: revolt. During the ten days we were locked up at Stade de Colombes we had to climb up onto big vats to take care of our bodily needs, and eventually those disgusting sewer tanks, reaching the height of a man, obviously overflowed. The stench was deplorable, just like our uncertainty and the inhumane way we were spoken to, the constant intimidations. Perhaps you remember that I wanted to develop concepts of aesthetic theory that would be impervious to Fascism. What was important for me was the fighting power of my theses. What I called "aura" was an account of an experience, the loss of something inexpressible. As if no longer able to grasp tone qualities in music, or its purely sublime and freedom-intoxicated sounds, its youthful and bright life with all its expectations. But how do you take a stand against physical threats with their absolute commands? You know that I always felt drawn to Adorno's words about Alban Berg, "He undercut the negativity in the world with the despair of his own imagination." At the work camp in Clos St. Joseph Nevers I did, however, teach a class "A Continuation Course in Philosophy," and charged three cigarettes (of the brand Gauloises) for admission! At the same time I read, with great profit, Rousseau's *Confessions*. Not until I was in Marseilles did a wretched melancholy return from the past, the fateful feeling of my fortieth birthday and the dark hotel room (which reminds me of this one), where I wrote farewell letters, which I never sent. The designers of those World Fairs reached out, for the first time, to abolish all the borders of the world. The brutal self-enterprises of Capitalism show that modernity really is the first stage of Hell. Hell, as an absence of anything new, the place where everything is void and becomes the same as everything else because the fundamental understanding of history is false and untruthful. Baudelaire was the first to see the angels' tormented features, "to sell one's soul to the devil, what's that? Is there anything more absurd than Progress, where man always acts the same, like a barbarian, which is something that is witnessed daily. What are the dangers in the forests and open meadows compared to civilization's daily shocks and conflicts? Whether man embraces his unsuspecting victim on the street or stabs his prey in the unknown woods, he is still not the eternal man, that is, the perfect beast of prey." Modern barbarism has a joyful but falsely positive foundation, reminiscent of hiking songs and the first steam engine's triumphant whistling. No one seems to notice anymore that the purpose behind, and consequences of this euphoria is to shatter everything: personality, traditions, memories, the efforts of the past, and, last but not least, "modernity" elevated to absurdity.

Your Walter

Port Bou, 25th of September 1940

Dear Asja,

Here in this village on the border, under these huge magnificent mountain ridges (which proved to be insurmountable), I am completely without the protection and the shadow given by the presence of a loved one. I am nothing but a broken down torso of an ill-treated thought. I put my empty briefcase behind some garbage cans before I was moved up here. I set my notes on fire in the little furnace and I'm studying that fire through its open door while I'm writing this. At the sight of those flames I am reminded, with a certain sadness, of the words of *The Storyteller,* how the wick of life burns up in the pure flames of the story, and how in *On the Image of Proust* I attempted to pursue the blind, unreasonable urge for happiness within this child of an old man, and his immense stream of *soit qué's* revealing an account, in a tired and depressed mode, of the countless illuminating motifs it was based on. "He is completely possessed with the fact that we all lack time to experience the real dramas of the existence granted us. This is why we age. Nothing else. The wrinkles and folds in our faces are traces of sufferings, burdens, insights, that came by to visit us, but we, Ladies and Gentlemen all, were not at home." I'm burning the papers because it is true, all too true, especially about myself.

You must know that I always loved you. Even as I face my own death, I can't think of any greater gift to offer from my life's story than the suffering I felt when

166

I glanced at you. Therefore I want to communicate everything to you; the final movement from now to back then, and the leap through that small gate where the Messiah can never be seen, or if he is put in motion due to humanity's insistent demands, always a day too late. That instant I dreamt of, filled to the brim with the past and the future—which I called present-time—appears, at the last moment, to give shelter even to the memory of my expected death. In other words, memory can transform the unfinished (happiness) to something finished, and the finished (suffering) to something unfinished. It can even reach ahead and anticipate its own end, voilá! I meet the eyes of the angel in the darkness and I am sure it is your glance. Happiness always leads to ruin, but that doesn't make it any less powerful.

With love, your Walter

I pass by the customs house where Walter Benjamin and the other German refugees were sent after the Spanish border police had arrested them on September 25th, 1940. They had exit visas from France, but no entry visas into Spain. That had not been necessary before. World War II and the concentration camps initiated rampant escalations of unrestrained decision-making, the inhumane categorization into the useful and the unuseful. Everything around here has the air of an abandoned region today. "In about a year the high-speed rail will be here, the TGV between Perpignan and Barcelona; it'll make this place into the world's 'arsehole'," the female cab driver says. Then she tells about when Robert Duvall and Charles Bronson were here and filmed during the 1970s. "We're already living in the past! We are passé. But Duvall was a gentleman." With that last comment she touches upon the experience of Portbou, the border—a matter of dignity. The Israeli sculptor and visual artist Dani Karavan created in 1994 his *Arcades* in Portbou, a location dedicated to Walter Benjamin and all those who were forced into exile from 1933 to 1945. In a small iron tunnel, a passage down the rock ledge, eighty-seven steps lead down to the ocean. At the lowest step a huge piece of glass, and beyond that, the whirling ocean, the cold and unfathomable, the unreachable depth, the whirlpool downward. Etched into the glass, only one of Benjamin's quotes: "It is more difficult to honor the nameless than the famous. The true construction of history is done so as to consecrate the memories of the nameless."

Now the wind blows so sadly through the branches as if it were crying.

An invisible crowd of people beyond repayment.

What is a journey other than a life summarized?

"QUOTATIONS & REFLECTIONS"
Ulf Hallberg, black notebook

7. Hotel de Dream

My father really enjoyed Icelandic sagas for the spareness
of those stories, and for the associations that terse writing
creates. He often spoke of traveling to Iceland in hopes
of experiencing barren and unreachable environments
beyond our material world. Imagine a person thrown
onto a moon landscape, he said, where a new way of
life suddenly appears more threatening than a potential
eruption of a volcano. The story about the residents of one
of the Westman Islands, Heimaey, (who returned home
from the mainland only to find their entire community
covered in lava, and they had to dig out their houses)
had a strange effect on my father's fantasy. As if their
circumstances symbolized his own. How at the end
of his life he tried to hold out against his increasingly
technological surroundings by going to flea markets,
antique stores, and thrift shops. As if a small statuette
could save the day, a lithograph resolve an epoch.

Sometimes it feels as if I travel in order to lose myself,
but in spite of that attempt to escape I constantly long
for the feeling I had as a child when I looked out over
the ocean and knew that here in Southern Sweden—
near the Archaean Rock and the Kattegat—here I am at

home. Nevertheless, I am—in the anonymous loneliness of a hotel room—unsure of where that place is that others keep calling "home." The hotel is a sanctuary, and its anonymous rooms give me the strongest license of freedom possible. Everything is contained within this room, where the present is crystallized into memories and reflections. I feel liberated when I put my little travel library on the bedside table and sort out my papers. What if home is a condition or a memory, an atmosphere or an illusion? Sometimes I encounter that "feeling of home" while I'm on the run, as if from an unknown angle; it overwhelms me and my agony disappears. As fast as it appears, it disappears. It is like getting a glimpse of some unknown people at a small-town train station under faint station lights, just as the train is about to depart, and I know I will never see them again.

My life appears to have been a flight away from something I have been afraid of, so now I travel in order to find out what it is I fear, at least if someone were to ask me what I think about my own condition. I have been a bouncing ball in my employers' eyes; they have all used my work for their own purposes. Where does this ingratiating and servile attitude come from? My betrayal of my inner self is rising to the surface, eating a hole through my repressed past and tearing me apart. I now lack a substance that was lost in perpetual motion, in the attempt to understand everything else —in the belief in an infatuation beyond the doors and borders of my "home." The images of memory I earlier thought so important disgust me now. I write in my black notebooks in order to keep myself together. These notebooks are the only things I have left;

the urge to hold on tight to my thoughts and the events of my life. A persistent wish to find a few pieces of the puzzle, or I must take off again, disappear, be snuffed out for good. How far back do I have to go?

In a kind of scientific obsession, I embarked upon a concentrated study of death; I called it my "indoctrination." I read what philosophers had postulated and what novel writers had described. I made tables and diagrams. Everything was included: different forms of death, statistics about accidents, the permanency of death, various progressions toward death of different diseases, suicidal catalogs, as well as fantasies about Hell and Paradise. I followed the tracks of Death in history. And I began writing notes and excerpts on the subject that I collected in black folders.

Do humans have fragments of their past that can save them—if they take them seriously? And does a true descriptive art exist, pure words in the confusion everything is tainted with? Do I develop a tendency toward clarity when I write, or is it just a therapy for panic? Language is a lifeline that should not be drawn too taut. Hold on to the words, pull the lifeline through them and secure yourself to some tree with big and strong roots. At least I'm trying to avoid the trap of continual decline. I can't stand that. I have been alive for a long time yet I don't know anything. I am empty. Perhaps I need to fight for *my* position. Actually, I tried to organize what I saw. What did the psychiatrist say? "Your empathy is injurious, in fact, pointless. You must get away from all that." Modern times have given me that prescription over and over again. I didn't believe it. But she was right about one thing: we always try to put the blame on someone. I have visited many locations of importance to the stages of history over the last decade, but the images—that I took myself and could remember for a while—have faded, become overripe. They were too manifold, too notorious, and too malicious; my camera ejected them into living rooms others call home. Was I a tool of destruction? Or did it all have some meaning? I seem to flounder within my own fate. "You are not Isadora Duncan," said Christiane Schramm, the psychiatrist. But I answered, "How do you know that?" And then I told her how Isadora Duncan dances for her dead children in my dreams. Schramm interrupted the analysis with some harsh words. "Sort out your impressions!" she shouted. There were voices that tried to get at me by their incessant mumbling; I could not control my reactions. I hear cries of despair from within myself. Cities are unfamiliar, the world is obscure. I have lost the belief in myself. Isn't it possible that I—during days when I feel good at least – can understand that I can't compare myself to Baudelaire? I'm not clever enough. Only obsessed with him.

The airplane, a double engine Cessna, swayed a bit as we approached Heimaey airport. It passed Ystiklettur, where I finally could see the harbor and the city. The harbor inlet had almost clogged up completely after the eruption, but firemen were pumping seawater onto the burning lava and were able to cool it down. I thought about Baudelaire. His mind was overworked; he'd prematurely worn out, the doctors said about him. Violent wind squalls hit against the body and wings of the airplane as we rounded Eldfell and Helgafell and came in for a landing. The old lady in front of me straightened out her black kerchief. There were no other passengers. For the first time I caught a glance of the pilot who announced that it would be impossible to reach the mainland until the winds died down. "We need a miracle in order to leave the island today," he declared—now standing in the cabin—with jolly contentment, as if he was relaying the message from a higher power.

In art it is less about what is being said and more about how it is being said.

"You have to practice patience out here. Nature makes itself heard."

I'll be stuck here for a day or two, and Trailer will have to wait for me in Reykjavik. It's really what I need, a time and place to catch my breath. Perhaps I can round the island in a boat, if the winds die down a bit tomorrow. But at the same time I'm feeling my fear of voices. I was forced to check into a hotel, an old unearthed house. I get the room that's facing the strongest winds, where a dark messenger—the only other person around—tiptoes around outside my door and listens to my troubled pacing back and forth.

I observed the black lava fields around Eldfell through the window of a taxi that drove through the middle of the island, barely a kilometer across. I asked the cab driver if he had witnessed the evacuation, and he nodded but didn't seem to be very talkative beyond that. I thought of a follow-up question, but couldn't bring myself to ask where he'd been at the time of the volcano's eruption. The weariness of what I call "the dumbstruck world" lowered its paralyzing hand over me again. I was so afraid of his obvious answer that I avoided the question. I would have liked to ask the cab driver to keep driving around and around, but all these island people would, within a few hours, have noticed such a strange activity, and that would reduce the possibilities of gaining information that could be useful material for the film. That would have been a waste, I reasoned, while I also knew that my own self-consciousness in

Tropism = what our consciousness is not able to reach and that determines our feelings and actions.

those kinds of arrivals makes any spectacular entrance impossible, which, in a way, is a means for gaining some respect. I simply suspect that my tiptoeing tactics reveal how decadent I am as a person, but there's nothing I can do about that. I'm afraid I move in slow motion. I'm too pensive; everything is up for more questioning inside me. Many, including myself, dislike that attitude, though I don't share the idea that it is tantamount to suspicion and lack of trust. The volcanic eruption may have already been filtered into the cab driver's memory as something natural. He belongs here, so if volcanoes begin to spew lava all over him, he can just call the coast guard and with their help get to safety, and later hurriedly return to his house to start digging it out of the meter-high lava flows, as if it were the most natural thing in the world. Why can't I ever think that way? With clear self-assurance about what is close at hand. Why is my world always in a state of eruption, and why do I seem to look for catastrophes, like a refugee driven out of his own private world by an anxiety that is always itching to gamble on everything. Simply put, this is the cab driver's home, and once, twenty-three years ago he had to re-capture it from nature. He is settled and gloomily drives around living with his sense of "home," but little feelers on the back of his neck are stiffening and registering that the man sitting in the back seat doesn't belong anywhere. The cold that surrounds me is of a particular kind, because—like old-fashioned tourists—I take everything in with unendurable surprise, which makes the self-evident suddenly turn to ashes when faced with my bewildered and questioning gaze.

During my first days on Iceland I thought about Adam again. Something contained in this hopelessness—this too barren and gray earth; only ashes and mud—made me think of him and his photographs. Trailer, whom I worked with in Germany when the Wall fell, gave me this assignment. He remembered a few things that I had said about the Icelanders. Sometimes I can tell stories and people will remember them. But the problem is that our reports are becoming pointless. Our own abstractions destroy us, everything we read and listen to, every detail we summarize and present. We move along some ingratiating line of comprehension, which has become our measuring unit. All the different nuances are about to disappear. We cross them out with our oversimplifications. I have to break away from this choking grip.

The first time I visited Iceland I discovered a strange connection between my visual sensations and my irrational fear of existence. There was no room for revision here, as if all of life is put to the test on this brown-black moonscape. Against a background of severe wind gusts—without any hiding places—people are forced out of their disguises in order to test their own strength, their beliefs and disbeliefs. My failures are two-fold, both input and output. From the viewpoint of a compass, I'm off course. I can't restrain myself from consequences and from obstinately holding on to my views, even in areas where I am not an expert. But I cannot find an antidote to my weakened faith in the substance of things. It's as if my head is a fuel tank always ready to blow up. I try to tie together a bundle of contradictions that is bigger than myself; it is torn apart and everything flies out over a desolate harbor where I stand, God knows why I'm there. My thoughts are slippery and impenetrable; I don't even have a net to catch my poisoned fish. The Atlantic puffins jump down on the rock ledges looking for protection, loafing, hovering under the clouds, and make nosedives down into our past. Intuitively I perceive that someone is following me with his or her eyes. Someone is staring at me here, among these pastel colored harbor warehouses. I turn my ear towards the ocean and hear whispers in the wind. Hark!

During the spring of 1995, Adam had lived a couple of months in Tuzla, a gloomy suburban area surrounded by chemical plants. He had rented out his little apartment in Williamsburg that was more like a photo lab since his life was so focused on the process of documentation. He wanted to portray the human conditions in Tuzla, that dreary and shameful city. For many years he had photographed Muslim women who had been raped by Serbian soldiers, and in Tuzla he photographed children who looked like aging adults lost in the world. But he had also photographed what he called "hard earned dignity."

"It's the face of sorrow I want to capture," he

> I'm not enough of an extremist. I live as if eternal life, and not complete extinction, is waiting for me. That means I live in my own slavery of the future and not in the eternal freedom of death.

said. "As if I need to penetrate darkness in order to find myself and my right to be happy. To search for the look of love, pride, and self-worth. Sometimes a little bit of make-up or a freshly ironed shirt is enough to offer war some resistance."

Adam and I had many discussions on the meaning of journalism. We were both doubtful as to the effects we produced, beyond ourselves. Adam often said:

"If I wouldn't stay here, where should I hide? I don't want to sell these pictures anymore, but I have to keep taking them."

Adam was the first to witness the survivors from Srebrenica arrive by foot, in wrecked cars shot full of holes, or on some bus that managed to get through. How many were they? How many had they been? He couldn't sleep any more, he was out on the streets all the time asking people if he could photograph them, listening to their stories, he even helped to care for the injured and the homeless. Eventually eight people lived in his little apartment, and he took care of a fourteen-year old boy who had lost his family. Adam treated him as a brother. Djilan, the boy's name, had seen men become separated from their women, his sister and mother were shoved into a bus, and some soldiers had beaten his father and brother up because they were protesting. Djilan managed to avoid that kind of treatment because he could speak several languages and was useful, but he had to witness how his own father and brother were shot and thrown into a mass grave. Eventually he was able to escape across a field and through forests and mountains with a small group of survivors. When he reached Tuzla it took three weeks until he regained the ability to speak, and in the beginning he could only speak in fragments of words and confused sentences, as if his ability to speak had been shattered into a thousand pieces. He stuttered a lot and could only repeat their names and cry in traumatic convulsions. "He screamed out in his sleep," Adam said. "When he regained his ability to put together comprehensible sentences his questions were only about why he had survived. I had no answer, but I asked him if he would like to be my assistant." Djilan developed and copied photographs for Adam. He was not on the plane when it was shot down. He was preparing Adam's photos for an exhibit in the entrance hall of B92 in Belgrade. Somebody said that Adam's surviving family gave him Adam's equipment after the funeral, and Djilan is supposed to have documented the trails of the massacres in Srebrenica. There are no people in his pictures. Only car tracks, broken down doors and windows, burned down houses, wooden bunks, torn up blankets, burned clothes, pieces of shoes, melted down gold rings and gold teeth. Enormous machinery must have been needed in order to murder and haul off eight thousand men.

I met a few children who laughingly gathered around me. Eager to find something to give them, I rummaged through my bag while they were asking questions I could not understand. At last I found a collection of postcards with Degas prints, and gave it to them. I explained to them, in my own language, how much I admire the graceful necklines, the movements in the portraits, the slender hands. The children nodded and laughed, until a woman appeared in a window and called them into the house. They waved to me continually, with the postcards in their outstretched hands. I spoke to a fisherman who didn't answer me verbally but pointed towards a small tavern in a street corner. I went there and sat down by a table next to a window, waiting for something to happen.

A man walked in and introduced himself as Jóhánn o' the Hill. He offered to help me.

In my youth I had the most flabbergastng memory. I could remember both what happened and what didn't happen.

"Is it possible to find someone who can take me out there?"

"I dunna ken. Ought to ask."

Then he disappeared and a few minutes later returned with a sailor dressed in a woolen cap, an old-fashioned character, who remained silent while the scheduling of the boat trip was discussed. It is impossible to circle the island because of the current weather. He could go past Eldfell and Helgafell, but not as far out as Stórhöfdi. At a certain point they would have to face straight into the wind.

"This is the windiest place in the world," Jóhánn

181

declared.

I had heard about that before; that was the challenge. I thanked him for his help and followed the sailor down to the quay. It would be a wordless journey, as far as I could tell. The better for me.

Don't forget the storm when the calm is presiding.

I sat outside on the deck with a thick scarf around my head. The waves washed onto the little wheelhouse, where I sat crouched down the whole time. I saw some sheep grazing high up on the distant hillsides, and I saw how the Atlantic puffins had a special liking for the Bjarnarey cliffs. There was a house up there, probably a bird observatory. Ropes hung from the cliffs here and there, but there were no people around, either in boats or on land.

The hull of the boat slapped hard against the wave crests while we passed the eastern side of Heimaey; my body had become one with the to-and-fro swaying and tossing. The black lava fields that surrounded Eldfell reached all the way down to the sea. Everything here was barren, no growth of any kind, but further away I could see Helgafell's green slopes.

I don't know for how long I had been at sea. A hand was placed on my shoulder, and I cried out in surprise. The boy apologized; he just wanted to point out a reef that had been the site of many accidents where ships and people's lives had been lost. I couldn't figure out how he had been able to stay so invisible earlier; perhaps he had been asleep in his cabin. His cheerful eyes ought to have put me in a better mood, but I was far too deep into myself, where time was ticking away faster and faster and shrill cries drowned the roars of the ocean and the closeness of the skipper boy. With surprise he looked at my notebooks and gave a sudden jerk when I started counting out loud. I had to literally count the seconds in order to hold onto them, just so they didn't run amuck again.

"What's your problem with time?" the boy said in a clear Icelandic that I could understand perfectly.

"Do you understand Swedish?"

He nodded, yes.

"My mother is Swedish. She's father's fifth wife, not counting Miss Johnson in New York City, then she'd be the sixth. Wenches are flighty and fickle, my father says."

I pointed out to him that my knowledge of Miss Johnson, out of necessity, was limited, but that I do worry about time.

"Oh, I don't really know myself either. She might have been one of those harbor-women; and there he was, my little half-brother. But time will not worry. Only we do that."

His nauseating breath disgusted me. His teeth were oddly yellow and neglected.

"Don't be too sure," I said, and kept on counting. "If I don't control my time, I lose track of things."

"It's the other way around," said the boy. "The more you think of it, the stranger it gets."

I don't know what I was looking for out there on the ocean. Was it fear? It's as if I wanted to penetrate the very ways of the sea itself. I came to a conclusion about keeping myself mobile that seemed to be logical. But is it so? Did I really want to venture out on the ocean to subdue the horror?

Or was it a voyage of exploration that had to do with the volcanic eruption? From another point of view, I always want to see what I pass by from a different perspective. But I pass it by. I am the motion, and it actually lacks memory. It's a lack of focus, an escape. Every soul on this island knows that, and I envy their circumstances, but at the same time I am unable to renounce my doubts in exchange for their equanimity. I simply don't understand them; they belong to another world. But I am here. Why? They can stand under the stars with that endless ticking strapped to their wrists without any sense of anxiety. When I stop here in the harbor to look up at the heavens, the first thing I notice is the ticking of my watch reverberating throughout my whole body. The sound of the watch is transferred through my pulse into my brain, and a dreadful voice yells out immediately: "You must begin to count, hurry up! Seventeen, fifty-three, ten, seventeen, fifty-three, fifteen, seventeen, fifty-three, twenty . . . " I enter time intervals to calm myself down. After a little while I can breathe more regularly. When I concentrate on this one specific thing the yelling stops. But at the same time it's stressful to keep up the count. I wish that time could take care of itself, but that's the danger. That is when it hits you, without mercy.

I open my journal and place it in front of me so I can study my notes. They are not written for anyone, it is a work of fear. When I jot them down it's as if I serve some great purpose that I stopped believing in a long time ago. Is this my story? I swear by my journals because I don't want to be destroyed. This room is just as cold and gloomy as I expected. And rightly so, the continual tiptoeing in the hall outside my room reveals that the hostess is taking care of her duties, that is, she is acting out a kind of guest house-comedy for me—in spite of the fact that we are alone here. Her body is wrinkled and her posture bent from the pains of rheumatism, a sign that she is walking the border between life and death. Perhaps her entire life has been in this middle ground, a continuous submissive waiting to disappear. But where does the radiance in her eyes come from? A seldom-seen pristine light, streaks of hope, no dead irises or stiff pupils. How can tenderness be nourished? She has a natural cosmic relationship to life that

It's a wonder how a person's body harbors a number of different personalities that at the same time is only the person.

I completely lack. Even though alive, I am dead! My arrogance raises its head, making sure I always remain an outsider; I haven't learned a thing. This woman is at peace within herself. She's moving with assurance within the cycle of time, while I stagger along, or nod over my notes. A spider crawls across the thick oak desk, reaches my notes, climbs over some books—*The Iliad* and *The Odyssey* lay open in front of me—and just as it approaches my hand I squash it with a perfect slap. It was a hairy creature from Hell. Unfortunately I hit it with the palm of my hand, which now is all sticky. I shove the spider-corpse into a dusty corner with a piece of paper, and wipe my hand on one of the curtains. That was not necessary but I can't show respect for everything. 23:20:40, 23:20:50, 23:21:00… They are approaching, they are noted on the speakers' list. The hostess finished making the bed and is moving things around in the room next door. Maybe her work was unnecessary; I'm not sure that Trailer is coming. He let me use one of his Betacams, so I can film anything myself. I turn the pages of my journal, but they are pressing on me now. They are inside of me. Some whisper, others yell.

Spes Desperantium = the hopes of the desperate ones.

I went over to the airport to make a phone call. On the way I passed a landscaped area in the middle of that inaccessible terrain. Someone had planted shrubs and flowers, made trails and collected fine rocks and something like a small English garden emerged next to the lava fields. I sat on a bench and surveyed the picturesque scene.

There was a strange peacefulness in that ill-cared for creation. "Perhaps they are dead," I thought, and imagined an old couple visiting this garden every day to water, weed, and every now and then, plant something new. I sat there for a long time looking out over Heimaey, as if I was in some kind of middle kingdom near Styx, the entranceway to the Underworld. If they were dead, they probably stood on the other side of the locked gates and beheld with sorrow the creature that seemed to enjoy their work. He brought neither water nor shovel. "That is not a person, only a shadow, approaching us."

A long time passed before someone answered the phone at the hospital, and the only information I could get was that my father's condition was stable. Stable, what a word! I don't want to lie in my death throes while the hospital personnel chatters, "He is in stable condition." Someone must cry out "He's dying!"

The little snack shop was open; I went over there to buy a pack of cigarettes. An airplane was coming in for a landing. The wind must have calmed down. But I've said that I'll wait here. I stood there in the waiting lounge hoping to see some tourists, or anyone. Most importantly, they had to be noisy and unfocused, a similar mindset to my own. Tranquility exhausts me and it makes my nerve channels creak, my blood simmer.

A woman walked down the stairs and hur-ried across the landing strip as if she was running away from someone. But no other passengers were there. I began to feel uncomfortable and turned around, taking a few steps toward the door. But she had seen me.

"How can I get over to Heimaey?"

To dare is to lose one's foothold a little bit, not to dare is to lose one's self.

Her English accent had streaks of both Russian and Italian, like an opera singer. She had a thin, hardened, worrisome face, dominated by eyes that wandered all over the place, as if a number of cameras were mounted in there, and were rolled back and forth by quick-footed assistants. Why didn't she hide her feverish activities and vigilance behind a pair of sunglasses?

She had tiny freckles around her nose and on her forehead; her hair was reddish brown. The most remarkable thing was the twinkle in her green eyes. I could not stop myself from secretly looking her way to get a glimpse at the color of her eyes. They had an iridescent depth, and I was pulled into them.

"Take a taxi, if there's one available. Otherwise you have to walk," I said.

I distanced myself. She followed. A certain discord in the sound of our footsteps forced me to start counting seconds. I calmed down a bit, but I realized that she would soon catch up to me.

"There's not a lot of people here," she said, and looked around at the landscape that had been distorted by the wind.

Beware of being sad. Once it starts, it never stops.

"The dark side of the moon is like Paradise compared to this," I commented hollowly.

I walked faster, but she was able to keep up. The wind gusts were whirling around our heads; her light red hair was standing on end, her eyes tearing. She couldn't be more than twenty, maybe twenty-two years old.

She looked at me timidly and let out a nervous little laugh.

"My name is Laura."

She let out a little whistle when we walked past the garden.

"What is this?"

"Central Park."

"Where are the saxophonists? I have seen them in pictures."

"They are out catching sharks."

"What about the whales?"

"What do you mean whales?"

"Don't they sing?"

Her voice rang out into the stillness of Heimaey.

The quality of her voice rang clear, and she held that tone as long as she had enough air. Such a clear-ringing voice struck my senses; those vibrations reached the darkest parts of my soul. It tickled something within me I thought was dead.

The roof is caving in on me, the wind tearing the window frames apart. She's lying there on the other side of this wall, and doesn't dare to breathe. I really don't understand how she ended up here; to me she seems entirely out of place. When we passed the mirror in the hallway she winced, as if she hadn't seen her own reflection for a long time. She talks about things, but what she says does not seem to be what really absorbs her, but rather expressions of calculated maneuvers—some kind of panic-stricken padding for an annoying silence. Now she's humming. Her singing voice is so light, totally different from her speech. The sprinkling from the handheld shower stopped. Now she must be standing—perhaps naked—a few meters away from me, drying herself with one of the hostess' big yellow towels. I can hear the terry cloth rubbing against her skin, and how she balances first on one, then on the other leg. If I could only see the lines of her body, her neckline and the arching of her back! She takes a couple of steps, then wraps herself in something… The bedspread! No, she keeps rummaging around. It's the duvet. It's completely

Psychoanalysis is the madness it tells you it cures.

quiet. I don't dare move. Sneaky steps. A gentle knock on my door. I sit there, motionless, with a pen in hand, not a word comes through my lips. Messy, unshaven, in a red flannel shirt I lean against the tabletop and keep writing. In the star-shaped mirror on the wall underneath the crucifix I see the reflection of a terrified notary who quickly sweeps a couple of things into a desk drawer. Self-portrait with a pen, Westman Islands, December 1999. Am I really going to invite her in?

I couldn't explain it, or it was something I didn't recognize, but when she stepped into my room wrapped in that flowery green duvet cover, I knew she was looking for protection. It was an outward motion, taking notice of the wind, and those eyes. They were never still, but constantly moving and turning towards different details, as if she was taking a reading of the room and myself. I think my piles of books calmed her down.

"Are you afraid?" I asked.

"That's none of your business."

"Who are you afraid of?"

She didn't answer.

"You shouldn't be afraid. No one wants to come here."

"Well, you are here."

"Only because I have to."

"Can I sleep here, in your room? Only for tonight."

I gulp quickly. I feel like I'm sitting in an armored tank aiming the main gun against a hostile world outside, but all the words I fire off just ricochet back at me. I suspect that all my notes are completely worthless. I nodded, but I didn't move from my chair. And I couldn't find anything to say. I just kept on writing. The pillow covers half of her head. That is her nighttime face, for sure, not just smoothed out and unprotected, but catching her breath all the time and undergoing transformations. At times terror-struck, other times affectionate and faithful. Now and then she wakes up with a start and looks at me without knowing who I am. She calms down when she notices that I'm still writing.

"What are you writing?"

"Just my notebook," I said.

"May I see?"

She held the black notebook in her hand and gazed at the little white piece of paper on the front page.

"Hotel de Dream, what's that?"

"There's a hotel in Florida with that name."

"That's a strange name."

"The first time I came across that name was in a novel I read by Stephen Crane called *Maggie: A Girl of the Streets,* which he published under the pseudonym Johnston Smith. It takes place on a little back street of lower Manhattan called Rum Alley, named after the liquor. It was sold in two versions. Crane also wrote a novel about the U.S. Civil War called *The Red Badge of Courage.* I found a well-thumbed copy in Belgrade. Crane married a woman who managed a brothel in Jacksonville, Florida. The name of the nightclub was Hotel de Dream. I have never been able to let go of that name."

"But why have you written it on your notebook?"

> Her passport was in order, but her luggage arose suspicion.

"When two languages are mixed, the words that are used can open up. Since the meaning is not entirely grasped, the feeling is strengthened by music, by pure tones."

"Is that what you're hoping for, pure music?"

"Hotel de Dream is like a formula. If I could explain it, it would lose its meaning. I just love the words we use when we ask ourselves why we exist."

In silence you find yourself

"So, your notes stem from a hotel of dreams? And you feel like a hotel guest in life? Then I have a few things I would like to deposit in the receptionist's safe. If there happens to be a porter around."

She pulled a cloth bag out of her cheap black handbag, made of imitation canvas leather, and looked at me plaintively.

"Can you keep this for room number two until tomorrow?" she said.

"What is it?"

"Don't ask."

"Does someone want to hurt you here? You are so far away."

"Far away from what? In the end they'll always find me."

"Who are they?"

"Those who resent my right to live because they're trying so hard to destroy me."

I put my black notebook and the cloth bag into my big leather case, where I keep all notebooks and valuables. She studied the photograph of the volcanic eruption on the wall, the view of the harbor, the cold light on the harbor buildings and the reflections on the water—and the flames in the background. A threatening and hair-raising normality.

"Why do you look so sad?" she asked.

I shrugged my shoulders. The truth is not for everyone.

"And what were you doing at the airport?"

"I was making a call to the hospital."

"Which hospital?"

"Malmö General Hospital."

"Who do you know there?"

"My father."

"Are you still a little boy?"

"You are protected by a certain glance. Then everything becomes completely different."

"At night the dead seem so close. Just like in Peredelkino."

I had no idea of what she meant. She turned to her side and buried her head in the pillow.

"Are you from Russia?"

She nodded.

"I was a common girl with completely normal dreams when they got hold of me. No one can really imagine what men are capable of."

"But at least you made your way to Italy."

"I haven't been anywhere; I've come straight from Hell. Please just let me sleep here."

I carefully tucked her in. She looked at me in surprise.

One ten twenty, one ten twenty-five, one ten thirty… They tell me, with their sharp voices, to write down the numbers now—as if the numbers make a pattern that will eventually form the sum of my efforts.

She is speaking in her sleep, making disturbing exclamations, waving her arms. "Irina," she calls out. "Stop!" The duvet is on the floor. Funny how she's dressed in old-fashioned flannel pajamas, blue-striped. However, they magnify her fragility, the softness of her shoulders and slender arch of her feet resting on the bed sheet. With all these things present comes a greeting from a repressed world; and I suddenly remember how I once existed not merely as an observer but as a person. The pajama shirt has slipped up to the waist. I can see some skin; she takes a sudden breath. Careless stitches of a scar run across her abdomen. I can hear my pulse tick like a clock. Her breathing has calmed down. Nobody has been in the rooms where I was present in a long time; those rooms were repayable, empty, and inhuman. I have left sexuality behind. I have killed the animal within myself. It was my punishment. There is a moment of forgiveness in her undemanding presence. She is resting as if she has exerted some enormous effort. The gales beat outside, the windowpanes rattle,

Free birds fly, tame birds dream.

and a body of a stranger moves between the sheets as if it belongs there. I walked up to the bed and carefully touched her hair—without waking her—only her eyes flinched a bit. I'm not completely destitute. It was my tears. At her age you are not aware of how you use up your life, slowly but surely, with every action. What do I have left but to adore her peaceful rest?

I didn't sleep at all that night, but sat petrified at the desk watching her wake up early, just as the first rays of light came up. She did not sit up quickly, but she was groping towards wakefulness—as if her insides begged to remain under the protection of the land of dreams. After a while she quickly jumped out of bed, again blinking at me and throwing her head back so that her tussled hair whirled behind her shoulders in a self-conscious motion.

Where danger grows there is the power of salvation.

"If something happens to me, keep away. Anything that may happen to me can be very uncomfortable for you. Thanks!" she said and walked toward the door.

"What about the cloth bag?"

"Can you keep it until I come back?"

Suddenly a feeling of fatigue came over me. I lay down on the bed without straightening out the bedding. Her scent was still there, the smell of another human being. I fell asleep at once.

In my dream she came walking towards me down a long corridor. There was no way to avoid an encounter in that narrow space. When we passed each other I felt our bodies touch for a brief moment, hip against hip. The warmth of her body connected to mine with an electric spark – it was like it was before. I turned around to embrace her but the corridor was completely dark, except for a forbidding hallway mirror. "Halt there!" someone yelled suddenly, and I bowed courteously, with a feeling of wonder, since the reflection in the mirror at the end of the corridor, after all, would have to be my own.

In order to grow,
one has to tremble.

8. Homer in the Moonlight

Everything is very uncertain, and
that calms me down.

"THOUGHTS BY MYSELF AND OTHERS"
Ulf Hallberg, black notebook

Based on the feeling the city of Lisbon invokes, every single European ought to be a Homer in the Moonlight. Perhaps a melancholy and blind one but still brimming with so many stories that the night always includes the possibilities of a happy ending.

"Where is Largo da Olaria?"

"Yes, yes, Largo da Olaria. Of course! It is complicated. The city is a real labyrinth. And time just flies by, right? And all those people who talk so much."

Those who want to avoid heavy suitcases and only travel with well-ironed shirts forget about entropy. That's why I'm thankful my father made me understand this. That was his gift to me—a struggle against the impossible—against becoming an agreeable "runner with the herd." Traveling as a child, the grown-ups at my destination would open my suitcase, and when they saw all the books I had stuffed in there sorted into separate stacks following my own system, they said:

I am my own professor.

"What good will these do?"

"Where are your clothes?"

"Where is the real luggage?"

They wanted to see the socks and the underwear, not the poetry and the dreams.

That was my first encounter with the "Managers."

"They are working on the elimination of Homer," my father said.

When he produced his famous dome in the Basilica of St.

Peter's Cathedral lying on his back, painting the ceiling frescoes *The Creation* and *The Final Judgment* in the Sistine Chapel, Michelangelo created something sacred that rose out of the wreckage and remains of the desolate Roman Empire. The paintings were done al fresco: the paint from his brush dripped down onto Michelangelo's face and formed a motley pattern of colors. He was bitter and disappointed with his life, but he was able to include Pope Paul III's Master of Ceremonies, Biagio da Cesena, among the damned in Hell.

My father and I spoke of Shakespeare's characters as if they were old friends, loathsome enemies, or simply our doppelgangers. My father also marked down in his notebooks the dates when he read the plays (a note made for each book with the date, along with stars, on a scale from one to ten). *Hamlet* was marked with ten stars and so were *Macbeth* and *King Lear*.

Does one turn a better, wiser, happier person by reading books?

"It's not that Shakespeare has a hold on us," my father said, "he certainly applies many theatrical tricks, but his greatness lies in his ability to encompass all human problems with a certain wisdom. His genius comes to light in his approach: nothing shall be oversimplified. Insignificant characters and low actions become large, and our souls grow in awe and empathy. Shakespeare is the greatest of all collectors. He denied himself material things and went straight into adventures. When I started to read Shakespeare seriously I realized that I had to curb my passion for classification."

"Is that why you carried the binders downstairs?"

200

He looked at me as if he had been reminded of a distant defeat, and our conversation broke off for a while.

We had touched upon a painful point, and neither one of us had an answer to my question.

My father's notebooks were full of underlines and side notes. By those expansions the black notebooks multiplied, the European Trash

> Art is the willingness to turn outward via certain chosen mediums.

grew and was crossbred with his reflections on life. There's a Homer in every human being who defies time with his or her art.

"We are perhaps the last members of the lower middle-class who are carried forward by soul and growth, empathy and development. There are, in spite of everything, quite a few of us left. But we are growing scarce. Strong forces are set in motion to make our activities more difficult. It is no longer honorable to serve the European Trash. "You are reactionaries," it is said, when you seek something other than money and comfort. Others buy houses and look out for themselves. We live in the nooks and crannies of the European Trash; we sign the rental agreement, give our thanks and make a bow, then we read Homer in those strange rooms as the sun sets, anticipating the next day's odyssey."

"We live like the Borrowers, on the pages of a book," I said.

"Yes, we are miniature beings on a book shelf," my father added and laughed.

> It was a savage time when rain was kept away by outcries for "Sun", and clouds were driven away for the purpose of reading more clearly.

In George Büchner's *Woyzeck* a grandmother tells a radical anti-saga, forever breaking the good fairies' magic wands. "Once upon a time there was a poor child without a mother and father…" the story begins. It's about a small child's search for someone to turn to for protection on a desolate Earth. However, everybody is dead, and the child continues his wanderings across more and more desolate spaces, where the moon is a rotten piece of wood, the sun a wilted sunflower, and the stars are tiny golden insects stuck onto the prickles of a blackthorn bush. Facing this universal abandonment the child wants to return to Earth, but Earth is an overturned chamber pot. The child sits down and cries — "and there he still sits even to this day, all by himself." The vision Büchner shows is of a society that produces filth and crap, which the poor are forced to clean up. The rich and powerful support themselves with a kind of veneer of language, an extreme untruthfulness, and irascible arrogance in their expressions serve to oppress everyone lower than themselves on the social ladder. Language is tarnished and shot full of the holes of communal lies. Woyzeck's discussions with the Captain and the Doctor are not leading to any new insights or clarifications. He's subjected to an evil fairy tale. The doctor diagnoses Woyzeck, the captain browbeats him, neither of them care about Woyzeck as a human being. Marie cheats on him; that is the filth of passion. He perceives others' lies,

> Poetry never draws any conclusions. It experiences and expresses.

and is relentlessly forced toward his own dirty deed: "It must be lovely to live with morals, Captain. But I'm a poor fellow." Woyzeck wanders feverishly around in this cold universe. Fate empties the entire contents of the chamber pot over him.

"The chamber pot represents Victor's position," my father said, "something that forbids you to visit the circus, to read or listen to music, and forces you to eat fish once a week." My father hated fish. For a long time I put sugar on my eggs because I was convinced that everything my father did was an expression of a higher order of life. In actuality, many of my father's actions were results of protests against Victor's autocracy. Putting sugar on things was the response to a father who viewed art as something parasitic and superfluous, but customs and conventions as sacrosanct.

Once Liberty has exploded inside a human's soul, no gods can exert their power over that person.

Our father took us to museums in order to grade the best Trash with devotion. He was inexhaustible, even inside the largest museums. Sometimes the experience became too much for my sister and me, but he always caught our attention with a story about Gauguin's travels to Tahiti or how Cézanne could represent the entire universe in a pear.

"The whole universe?" my sister asked.

"Sure," I said, "Ryttmästaregatan, Fammi's apartment, and all of Copenhagen."

"But where does the universe end?"

I thought about that for a long time. She could see that I didn't really know.

"In the basement, I think."

My father said that Bertolt Brecht, as a collector, had a unique ability to consider all aspects of life from a materialistic standpoint.

"It is most important to not become a thief, but to give something back. Brecht was good at that. He created a new continuity."

Sadly enough: You suddenly realize that
your claims on the world are in no way
in accordance with what it can actually
fulfill for you.

"KNOWLEDGE APRIORI"
Ulf Hallberg, black notebook

9. The Lonely One

My father and I both admired Greta Garbo. Her enigmatic essence, her nonchalant personality and character, her need for solitude and independence—all that appealed to our own self-understanding. The collector and his son recognized themselves in a woman who spoke with a dark, veiled voice and questioned male dominance. Her sensibility was a matter of avoiding current structures and creating an individual identity. We considered her intuitive separation from public view equivalent to our own belief in the benefits of anonymity and the liberating solitude of a big city. We did, however, talk a lot about her solitude, as if we knew that Greta Garbo had missed out on something we couldn't put our fingers on.

"There's productive and non-productive loneliness,"

said my father.

In hindsight I don't think my father ever was alone.

"What's that?" Ninotchka asked.

"It's a hat, comrade! A woman's hat."

"How can such a civilization survive which permits their women to put things like that on their heads?"

Lubitsch and I were a great mix, Greta thinks. Perhaps I was a *comedienne*. It is said that truth is right beneath the surface of humor. Maybe I've been going in the wrong direction—all my life. Laughter was so hard to reach. I should have had someone like Lubitsch next to me all the time. I have lived my whole life without saying "I love you."

The joke is a declaration of dignity, as assurance that the human being is superior to whatever happens to him.

I think Greta Garbo liked Simon & Garfunkel. She knew that Paul Simon lived on the other side of Central Park. He composed that wonderful song, *I am a Rock*, in such sentimental tones, which reminded her of her estrangement, of the labyrinthine trails in the park, and to live out one's life in a foreign land among people who can be held at a distance, in an anonymity that would give her enough time to think, to protect herself and to rest. She still felt as dull and feverish as in *Camille*. "Life can be very difficult," Greta thinks, "take laundry for example, so many things can go wrong, if you mix up the colors—or if you come home with someone else's clothes." Today at the cleaners the young man looked at the paper she had filled in.

"Garbo, oh yes. But what about the first name? Is

it a C or a G?"

"G."

"Oh, ok."

Another customer calls out:

"Don't you know who she is?"

And the boy answers:

"Oh, yes, it says right here, someone with the name G. Garbo."

Director Mauritz Stiller discovered Greta Garbo in 1923. He cast her, at 18 years of age, in the role of Elisabeth Dohna in *The Saga of Gösta Berling*. Stiller was an innovative director whose reputation spread throughout Europe. He was a wasteful adventurer and *bon vivant* who, in Stockholm, once stopped his racecar *The Yellow Peril*, so abruptly that his dog Charlie was thrown out through the windshield and landed on the hard asphalt of Drottninggatan. Stiller took Garbo to Berlin, where she played opposite Asta Nielsen in G.W. Pabsts *Die Freudlose Gasse*. After that the couple continued on to Constantinople where they were supposed to film a melodramatic story, written by the Russian fugitive-refugee Vladimir Semitjov for the Stockholm newspaper. Stiller had added some zest to the articles and given them the title *The Odalisque of Smolna*. The director, along with his film team, checked into Hotel Pera Palace in Constantinople. Ever the artist, Stiller

To laugh = is good. Releases endorphins. Be around people who laugh. Middle-aged people and retirees laugh the least.

had convinced the German film company Trianon to shoot the film in Turkey because of its everlasting sunshine, the amazing backgrounds, and the large masses of people. Furnished with a financial advance on a large scale, as well as travel budgets, the Swedish director organized an outstanding Christmas party in Constantinople for his film team and some Swedes and Germans in exile. He bought two sports cars, two trailers, and a fur coat for Greta Garbo. After that, Trianon went bankrupt.

Life is full of confusions. One day you're a poor young girl living in Stockholm, the next you stand on a quay in New York being photographed by the famous Arnold Genthe, your pictures to be published in *Vanity Fair*. The magazines were spread out on every desk of every Hollywood studio boss. And everybody asked: Who is she? *Our new star.* In the blink of an eye you are standing on a tennis court in Bel Air, with slick and handsome Jack Gilbert, "the great lover," beating him 6-2, 6-1. He is very good looking and charming, but he doesn't keep his eyes on the ball, and what a lousy backhand—completely without strength. He's just relying on his fame. Soon he became a tired, burned-out alcoholic, a shadow of his former self. And then suddenly he's gone, dead of a heart attack, thirty-eight years old. His greatest sorrow was when I refused his proposal. In an attempt to punish me he married Ina Claire.

She wanted to be both man and woman, not just comfortable in her female role, cast by men like Irving

Thalberg or Louis B. Mayer with their wives, children, mistresses, and souls like bundles of money, filth and greed. She dreamed of another role-assignment. That is why she so often moved around like a man, with her big feet, dressed in a suit or sailor's trousers, a woman in long pants and sneakers right there in Hollywood, on her way to the beach without any entourage—or already leaving the party when everybody else is just beginning to arrive. She is alone in her bed, afraid to be touched, afraid to be undressed, deserted.

Men are so tiresome, so amorous, so aroused: Stiller, Gilbert, admirers. They want to get in under her shell. She has learned to keep her emotions at a distance. The worst part is when they want to marry her. She has to make herself unreachable. Fame has a way of strengthening the feeling of universal loneliness; stardom becomes confinement. Take Murnau, she thinks, the German film director who wanted to move to Tahiti—live like Gauguin, in pure sexuality without responsibility but with all his emotions burning at forty-two years of age. He was a publicly declared homosexual with his head in the lap of his fourteen-year-old Polynesian chauffeur, while driving fast between Los Angeles and Monterey, in order to heighten his presence within the vortex of ideas, projects, marketing campaigns, celebrities, and photography flashes—Hollywood—the car swerves and is hurled down a cliff, *no more Murnau, just mourning,* the grief that Greta knows so well, Murnau's film *Tabu* premiered six days later in New York.

211

Greta Garbo listened rather than talked, her friends said. That is how she played her roles—open, vulnerable, shy. Truman Capote, who took Garbo's poses and ironic distancing and stylized it, wrote: "Of course it is enough that a face like hers has existed, but Garbo herself must have complained about the painful responsibility derived from the fact that it was her face that was in question."

She never really had the strength to be interested in other people. She felt that the sufferings of her own life were enough. Besides, so many others had been watching her. To be famous is to be beyond reach. This condition—sought-after by so many unknown people —she wanted to avoid, from early on.

Sometimes I think I'm like one of those clowns that stomp into the circus arena in their huge shoes and make the children laugh, because at the same time as they say with proud looks, "But I am very very clever," a red light bulb attached to their behinds turns on. They are grotesque because they don't know what's going on behind their backs.

But there is no way back. *You can't go home again.* We are spectators of our own lives, she thinks. That's what I've been, ever since I was very young. Greta Garbo changes her pose and turns on the TV in the Hampshire House on the Upper East Side of New York, among so many paintings and heavy oak furniture, but only a few books. They are so thick, really troublesome, she's only on page 34 of *The Great Gatsby.* But it was Cécile who so strongly recommended the book.

But now suddenly that clever singer with straight bangs is on TV, he ran off with a female Japanese artist, and once they lied down naked in bed to propagate peace. He is so different, a terribly intimate person. It's John Lennon, and a reporter asks him if he is longing for his home back in England. Home? Yeah, where's that? How would Greta answer that? Wachtmeisters, Tistad, Cécile de Rothschild, Hotel Crillon in Paris, Mercedes de Acosta, Silver Lake, the Riviera, Aristoteles Onassis, and that comfortable, extraordinary luxury, to be so focused on avoiding everything that is common. "Of course I'm homesick," Lennon says. "Do you want to say hello to them at home?" the reporter asks. "Yes, of course," says Lennon. Ok, the cameras are rolling... John Lennon smiles: "Well, I just want to say hello to you folks back in England. How' you doing folks?"

> Even though all great values of life are emotional, the weak light of reason is our only instrument for orientation.

"Men, oh how I hate men, don't you?" Greta Garbo says with a low, raspy voice—like a distant foghorn—in her role as a scarred prostitute in *Anna Christie,* the film adaptation of Eugene O'Neill's theater play. Her very first line is *"Gimme a whiskey."* With the advent of the talkies the roughness and anticipated masculinity in her acting are strengthened, the androgyny, a restraint which perhaps is emotionless or just a great actress' absorption in the primary rule of any art form: *Less is more.*

Greta Garbo gives every viewer what he or she needs, a mirror in which they can see themselves. The only intrusion between her and the audience is the viewer's own neurosis. Garbo's face and movements become flycatchers for men and women's insecurities, confusions, and worries. The irony in her shyness is that she chose to hide in front of a film camera, in the public loneliness of acting. Her face provokes the audience into ecstasy. It is heavenly, perfect, its contours are so soft. You want to reach out with your hand and touch it. But nobody is allowed. In 1933 she's the highest paid actress in Hollywood.

> To dream is a way to continue thinking in the dark.

She wakes up in Manhattan, but she feels uncomfortable. It's nice that it is raining. Don't want to go out today. I'm too tired to even hide my face. They are going to show my films again at the Museum of Modern Art. Without me of course. The only one I would like to see again is Ernst Lubitsch's *Ninotchka*. Lubitsch was fun. *Such good fun.* So surprisingly brave and outspoken. Billy Wilder's repartees always had biting truths as undertones—which real humor always has. For example, when Ninotchka arrives from Russia during the years after the October revolution to spy on her comrades and is met by them at the train station, a porter attempts to take her suitcase and carry it for her:

"What do you want?"
"May I have your bags, Madame?"
"Why?"
"He's a porter, and he wants to carry them."
"Why? Why should you carry other people's bags?"
"Well, that's my business, Madam."
"That's no business, that's social injustice."

"That depends on the tip."

There is a pause. Then the comrades ask Ninotchka how things are in Russia.

"How are things in Moscow?"

"Very good. The last mass trials were a great success. There are going to be *fewer* but *better* Russians."

I remember a conversation I had with the English playwright Kenneth Jupp. Suddenly it escaped me:

"I am an unborn child."

We sat in silence for a while. Finally I said:

"I am a lonesome person circulating around Earth."

"What do you mean by that?" he asked.

"One day I'll tell you," I answered.

Her skin feels rough now and uncomfortable, the bed frame rubbing against her back, in spite of all those silk pillows on 52nd Street in New York City. Greta Garbo remembers how she once upon a time was running around on Blekingegatan in Stockholm. The fresh air that dreams are made of, the hat shop in Bergström's department store, the joys of being a poster girl, to be photographed and seen, all that attraction—*with a lady's hat*—so long ago and so far away, with an alcoholic father and an overworked mother. She helped out at Widebeck's barbershop around the corner, foam on the old men's rough cheeks, a coarse hand giving her a pat. "I ought to take a walk," Greta thinks, Miss G. G. G. Greta Gustafsson at one time. A girl full of dreams, now Mademoiselle Hamlet. Why is she wandering around aimlessly in Manhattan in a brown trench coat, slouch hat, and dark sunglasses? She has always enjoyed observing—*a looker on, precisely,* just following the unknown people with her eyes. She calls it drifting, just walking around, dreaming. Imagine being one of the others, unknown! Happiness is always anonymous, temporary and hard to catch—like the really tired girl this morning, who ran for her life, her hair fluttering, down into the subway station, running late, but yet in the moment, anything to fulfill the obligation of reaching the office on time. She herself has all the time in the world and works full time to get away. From what? Public attention, endeavors, other people, life. A movie star ends up on another planet, a planet that looks like death.

The novel is fiction. Fiction is based on
real life, it breaks free, creates a world
of lies and eventually returns to reality,
and attaches itself to life in a way we can
neither control nor measure.

"OBSERVATIONS, MY OWN"
Ulf Hallberg, black notebook

10. The Enormous Emptiness of Things

It was dark outside when I woke up, and I was cold. I didn't have a clear picture in my mind of what had taken place that night, it was as if it had all been a dream that I was trying to understand without success. Some branches, lit by a flood lamp outside, threw shadows on my window shade. Strange figures ran along the weave, changed shapes, looked as if they were fighting or mixing with each other and then dissolving into silhouettes of the branches and autumn leaves thrown from side to side. It hit me that another day had gone by without any real answers. I threw on my clothes and rushed out. No people around. The winds had kicked up again.

Outside on the road it felt as if the gusts of wind could hurl me down the lava hills, down towards the ocean. As an incantation, I started counting while I walked.

219

That's how I arrived at the airport.

When you're upset you forget the simplest things; for example, to coordinate your movements. Just as I jerked open the glass door into the Arrival area a strong air current swept my notebook out of my hands. I saw a man moving towards the exit door. The wind had calmed down enough for me to leave the island. Our eyes met briefly. He had no luggage. Only one of those small handbags dangling in his hand. He had light, medium length hair; he looked like a well-educated hippie, but was dressed in a gray-black suit. I ran outside to catch my notebook that was being swept away through the parking lot. Two loose pages had been torn out and were drifting away over the lava fields. When I turned around to go back into the Arrival area, I saw the man climb into a taxi. Our eyes met again. He looked at me as if I were an object; there was no sign of human interest. Just a black iris, and pupils like the flowers of death. He was fiddling with something in his little bag.

> Every impartial person is a monster.

I went into the little airport waiting lounge, put some coins into the pay phone, and dialed the number to the hospital in Malmö. The nurse answered right away. There was something in her voice that made me realize that my father's condition had worsened. I also noticed that the nurse lacked confidence in her own explanations.

"Things are spinning slightly," the nurse said.

"The mind is a merry-go-round," I said.

Our lives are connected by a few thin nerve threads,

which the blood can flush away at any moment.

Our conversation broke up several times and I kept calling back only to get the same answer: the condition of your father is basically unchanged. Aren't we basically unchanged throughout our life, I thought with irritation, because the word on the other end of the line wasn't enough, even though that was all they could say? The phone conversations dragged on and didn't lead anywhere. When I finally decided to go back to the hotel, it was icy cold and dark.

When I only had fifty meters left to go, and I could see the light in Laura's window, the man from the airport came storming out of the front door of the hotel, running straight toward me. He couldn't have known that I was there in the dark, so I instinctively threw myself down into the ditch. Something told me that a confrontation could have serious consequences. There was something cruel and inhuman about his posture, and when he approached me I heard him breathe hard and swear to himself. At the same time, Laura's window was pushed open and the hotel hostess stuck her head out and yelled something that I couldn't understand. When the man was right next to me I made a pathetic attempt at blocking his way. He looked completely surprised, but just for a second, then I felt a heavy object hit me in the face and I was thrown aside. When I touched my chin, blood was running down from my wound. The man was already gone, and I staggered towards the hotel entrance.

The hostess came towards me and said, in a troubled tone of voice, that she had come home, heard some strange noises from Laura's room, ran over there and found Laura bleeding excessively.

"You take care of her while I go and call the ambulance!" she exclaimed and disappeared behind the drapes around the telephone booth.

In three strides I bounded up the stairs. The open door to Laura's room was foreboding, and I couldn't imagine what awaited me inside. She was slumped on the floor. Her body reminded me of some kind of bundle that had been thrown away. A puddle of blood had formed under her hips, but she was breathing, faintly. In the room around her everything was shattered: the lamp, a chair, the crucifix, and various paintings. Her few belongings were strewn all over. I grabbed a towel from the hanger by the washbasin, and then I placed Laura in a sideways prostrate position. Her breathing increased. Suddenly she lost consciousness for a few seconds. I held her by her wrist while at the same time I desperately tried to turn her over in order to give her artificial respiration. I felt her cold mouth, full of mucus, against my own. Her pulse quickened with several rapid palpitations and then it vanished to my touch. I pressed the hand towel into the deep knife wound on her stomach. I remember the key words: circulation, breathing, shock; then tried her neck, and both her wrists, then the neck again, pulled her toward me, hopelessly blew more breath into her lungs, which, nevertheless, left her still and lifeless. The old hotel hostess rushed into the room. She had called for the ambulance. Her movements were quick and firm. She applied a compression bandage that helped, as opposed to my efforts.

She yelled something at me to the effect of getting

out of the way, and I hurried into my room. I heard them carry her away. My brain shut off, I was pounded into a stupor, as if I had consumed too many drinks and the alcohol had finally knocked out my consciousness —a white night, mental images flickering incessantly.

I woke up, after falling out of my bed, drenched in sweat. My dreams left me without any definite patterns. I could only recall pictures of blue-black scraps of flesh, and the sound of a saw blade approaching my face. Without really feeling my body, other than as something insanely annoying, I got up and peeked through a slit in the blinds. How long had I been sleeping?

I went over to the closet and started to feel about for the leather case containing my notebooks and her cloth bag. I found it, opened the cloth bag and in great surprise pulled out a ten-centimeter thick pack of hundred dollar bills, tightly secured by several rubber bands, and a worn out notebook with a picture of a horse on its cover. The notebook was cluttered with childish-looking Cyrillic handwriting, impossible for me to read. A wrinkled, cutout magazine article fell out of the notebook. It was half a page long, and not much of the text remained. I recognized Laura, though the photo had been taken in 1997, two years ago. She looked as if she was eighteen or nineteen-years-old. A shabby looking, unshaven man with the fly of his pants open was having intercourse with

We have no compassion for who we are.

her behind something that looked like a urinal. Her white thighs were spread out by the man's heavy and aggressive action, her skirt hanging by her waist, and her eyes staring, empty, up against a gray-blue sky. The man looked like a bow-legged black angel of death, wearing some kind of green uniform jacket. It looked as if he had bored himself firmly in between her legs; his face was contorted with an expression of triumphant contempt. Laura's sprawling body looked as if it had been crucified. Two men stood a few meters away, as if they were guards or cronies. They were grinning.

Above the man's head someone had painted a skull with a black ink pen. On the backside of the magazine article something more was written in Russian that I couldn't read. When I inspected the margin carefully I noticed an imprint of numbers.

The Icelandic police force had no definite traces leading to any information about the man's identity; they only had a photocopy of the falsified passport he had shown upon check-in when leaving Reykjavik. Nobody had taken any notice since it was an Icelandic passport. Laura stayed in the hospital for a week, and when she was released she had to undergo interrogations for two days by the Icelandic superintendent detective. His principal strategy was to table the matter. This proved to be easily achieved since Laura's unwillingness to cooperate led to fruitless interviews that always ended in her saying "I don't know." "I don't think so." Or "I can't answer that." Her confidence in the police force was nonexistent. Laura and I met every day and I noticed that she did have a certain need to talk with me: "If I say anything to the

Police, they'll just send another man, haste post haste. There's more than enough of that type around."

When the interrogations were over Laura was asked about her future plans. She replied that she would most likely be leaving the island as soon as possible. This answer was received with great approval by the Icelandic officials. She signed the protocols and was then released out into the damp winds.

Everything was open to question now, and she asked to meet with me in the hotel foyer.

"Do you have my things?" she asked.

I nodded.

"Where are they?"

"In the gray bag on the floor," I answered and tapped it with my foot.

"Have you looked at the cloth bag?"

I nodded.

"That's not good."

"I'm sorry. Where did you get all that money?"

"That's my problem and my redemption. That's why they hate me; the money gives me freedom to move. For a while I thought I had escaped them here on the dark side of the moon."

"Who are 'they'?"

"You must have seen the magazine article if you have looked through the stuff in my bag."

"Yes."

She looked down at the table. When she looked up again her eyes were clear and alert.

"They are men capable of putting something into

your drink, and when you wake up you're in hell without any way to escape. Before, you were reading Balzac with your first boyfriend; now you're trapped in a room like an animal being sold to filthy men without souls. They are men whose minds are set on only one thing. They have let ferocious monsters loose within their beings, which have killed all empathy for others. Don't you know what happened to Lulu? If you have been trapped like that, you're not human anymore. You are abused and you really should die, but something within yourself tells you to survive. It's like some traces of honor and defiance still remain. They will never forgive me for how I managed to escape. I shouldn't have taken the money. That was the weakness of my own presumption and foolishness. Money is always a symbol of power, and they will never forgive me."

"So they want their money back?"

"Money is nothing to them. But since I took it, I must die. They sent a hit man to kill me."

Laura had no idea what to do next. She asked me about my plans.

"I have to go to Trieste."

"What are you going to do there?"

"I'm going to cover a film festival, a meeting of filmmakers from the East and West."

"You are a person who can do whatever you want."

"Come with me to Trieste!"

"That can cost you a lot."

"I can handle it."

"You don't know what you're talking about. You saw what happened here."

"You would've been dead if I hadn't stumbled into that hotel."

She gave me a furtive look.

"Do you really mean that I can come with you?"

We were sitting down by Porto Vecchio—the old harbor in Trieste—looking at a huge movie screen that had been erected along the pier. Besides the captivating films by Jean Vigo, Victor Erice, Alexis Damianos, Alain Tanner, Myriam Méziéres, István Szábo, Werner Herzog, and other great Europeans, we were treated to an unparalleled backdrop. The freight ships and tugboats were slowly gliding in towards the pier in the evening dusk, between the silver screen and the dome of the night sky.

> The story of a man who's looking under a street lamp for something he lost, not because he knows that he lost it there, but because it, is light there.

The Mediterranean Sea lapped, the giant projector rattled; the big film rolls were switched as the audience eagerly waited. In the shambles of an old harbor warehouse projection screens were flapping in the wind. Jean Vigo and his beautiful wife "Lydou" appeared in the colored light from a projector. He was the young French film genius who died at twenty-nine years of age in 1934. The daughter, three years old at her father's death, stood on the pier and talked about her father's films. Then we saw the old masterpieces. The Italian film festival director spoke with great inspiration about every film, interpreted, and validated. Didn't he look a bit like the threadbare film critic in *We All Loved Each Other So Much*?

Laura was constantly worried.

"They'll find us."

"How would they know where we are?"

"You have no idea about their ability to find us."

"Culture is the realization that the dead are in a way more real than the living. Their presence is still alive, the enthusiasm in their eyes, their special ability to merge with life," I say with my philosophical insights, trying to impress Laura, who's keeping me on a tight leash. I guess that's what's making me break free, against all odds. Tighten the leash more and more; what follows is an attempt to be more myself. Without opposition everything is lost.

"You just keep on talking. It's incomprehensible and boring. Think first, speak afterwards."

The airplane bounced a bit as it came in for a landing at the Lisbon airport. The light from the city was so strangely white, as if the whole city was bathed in light.

"Fernando Pessoa was a poor office clerk," Laura said solemnly, the look in her eyes telling me to listen up and pay attention, "on Rua dos Douradores in Lisbon. He died in 1935, forty-seven-years-old. In 1927, from the little office with a view out towards the harbor, he saw the storm approaching that we no longer can avoid: a concern for having been exiled among spiders."

"How do you know all this?" I asked.

"I was a student of literature when I walked into the wrong night club."

She closed her notebook and put it in her jacket pocket.

"Could you take down my carry-on luggage?"

I thought about Pessoa while slyly looking at Laura. Everything Fernando Pessoa jotted down, on thousands of notes he hid in a large laundry basket, touched on the imagery of Neorealism: an irrepressible and enormous affection for the common man. Each and every one of us has many parts, many selves, and multiple selves.

I became anxious and poked Laura on her side.

"Ouch!"

"Pessoa used a lot of different names. We can change names too! I'll be Adriano Lucca. You know how much I love Italy. Your name can be Luciana de la Mar, and you can be Portuguese."

"I have already lived so many different lives that a new name would feel just natural."

"Why should we have to keep our names as if carrying a cross, when we can be whoever we want to be?"

The Four Cardinal Virtues: the feeling of fairness (or justice), prudence, courage, and temperance.

"The fascinating thing about you is that you're able to keep your fantasy world intact all the time, completely uncorrupted by reality," Laura said and with a sudden movement patted my cheek. I touched my cheek with my own hand. What had just happened?

"What's the matter with you? Why do you look so stupid?"

How come I connected Pessoa with Visconti? Was it just an accidental confrontation, or an obvious meeting between two related types of artistry? Visconti's films are full of conflicting characters, enthusiasts looking for their souls. It is enough for Pessoa and Visconti to ride the trolley—or to film from it—in order to experience life to its fullest. Pessoa was the only co-worker who could write a business letter in English; his humanistic views had neither purpose nor conclusions. His message is simple: the enormous emptiness of things lay claim to humanity. Visconti's characters often betray themselves and **Assert your right** their surroundings, but then **to your own self.** all of a sudden they can also, in moments of apprehension, break out in lyrical monologues. It's that feeling of being alone in a big city, for example, Venice at night. Visconti always portrays a situation with a lyrical greatness, like a Chekhovian possibility: if we could only reach out our hands a little bit farther—we could then touch upon the reality of life.

Laura read out loud from *The Book of Disquiet* while we were standing in the aisle, which annoyed many fellow passengers.

"'The monotony, the dull sameness of the same days, the difference between today and yesterday—I hope things stay like that forever.'"

"Some people are always going to bother us with politics!"

"'That I have my soul alert to enjoy the fly that amuses me by flying by chance before my eyes, the peal of laughter that floats up from the street, the vast sense of liberation that it's time to shut up the office, the infinite repose of a day off.'"

"Could you wait until you are alone among like-minded people?"

Laura did not let it get to her; her self-restraint comes

from a recalcitrant indifference to others' opinions about her. When she's furious she's furious. If reading aloud, according to her, is recommended at the moment, then it shall be done.

I have come to know her over the last four months together, on the run from city to city.

I'm about to be saved from the distrust I have in myself by taking on another person's problems.

"'I can imagine everything for myself because I am nothing. If I were something, I would not be able to imagine. The assistant bookkeeper can dream he's the Emperor of Rome, but the King of England is deprived of being, in dreams, any other king but the one he is. His reality doesn't let him . . .' Hey, can you be more careful with the bag!"

"Pessoa is a Visconti character," I said.

"Tell your wife to shut up!" hissed a fellow passenger in a black suit.

"Tell that man to show some respect for me!" Laura yelled back.

She was in the mood for confrontation, stiff arms and legs, heavy headed, absorbed in the discomfort of her body.

"Pessoa's empathy and destitute condition gave him experience," she answered.

That last sentence is so revealing and so crucial to Laura's view of existence. To liberate one's self from permanent clichés or the death masks of frozen identities—in order to experience.

"Have you seen *Death in Venice?*"

"No," she answered glumly and added: "But did you see it during the Bronze Age?"

I nodded and remembered how serious I was back then, the high-strung and cerebral self-sufficiency of youth, the lack of clear-sightedness and distance.

"Where did you see it?"

"At the Camera on Stortorget in Malmö, 1971," I answered. "To me it was a complete work of art, every camera angle a revelation. The lonely composer Gustav von Aschenbach at the Grand Hôtel des Bains in Venice. Thomas Mann's novel transposed into Velázquez paintings, a plague-ridden Venice where an older man falls in love with a young boy, Tadzio. I was the composer Aschenbach. As a seventeen-year- old one can be so 'forte allegro,' artificial and open to manifestos about art."

"Why go on jabbering about that now?" she said. "Just so you can blow your own horn here on the airplane and show that you are so much more mature than me— artificial and open to manifestos, is that supposed to be me? As if I'm just a mouth with lip gloss."

"No, you are genuine! Nobody can change you. You have that independence so seldom seen today. The things that happen in Visconti's films are the exact opposite to today's times and everybody's worn out clichés. Visconti's characters are believable. They are filled with conflicting emotions. They fight superior powers within themselves. We have to follow the entire battle."

She gave me a scrutinizing look. Her mouth moved but I couldn't quite follow what she said.

"I think your words are too ingratiating," she said. "And you never hear what I say."

Had she said something about *La Terra Trema?* Is that what she was talking about? I kept on thinking about the past, as if the person I had been in Malmö in

1971 had managed to drag itself into the present. It was a shocking image: a dismissed actor who suddenly appears on the stage in spite of the stage workers' warnings from behind the curtains, an impatient passenger who insists upon attention in the airplane aisle.

"Did you say anything about *The Earth Trembles?*"

"Yes, I said that even though it was ordered by the Italian Communist Party, in a way it is an idealization of everyday life. It has many wonderful details from the chaos of everyday life portrayed as the beautiful insanity that it is."

"It's the 'work day' we are always surrounded by—everything that both protects and hems us in. There's this buzz going on around us all the time."

"Don't start talking about your being tossed out of history. I don't want to listen to that. That's just too pretentious. As if your own true self is a crate of ideas that's unloaded at different airports and then always reloaded into the wrong planes. You are forced to continue your search because you're flung out of your own private history. And new ideas are streaming by all the time. You don't have time to close the bag before they're gone. Empty in your head, eh? Travel with less luggage. Don't bother with the lost suitcases. You are who you are—or whatever? We're in Lisbon now. Be happy that you still have the weekday! What else could you cast the blame on?"

> I am trying to catch life as it passes, rather than staring blindly at the scheduled plan.

I stuck to the Aschenbach character and mostly spoke to myself. Laura walked ahead of me into the merciless glaring lights of the Lisbon airport landing strip.

"Like seeing yourself in an unknown future now," I mumbled.

She turned around, an angel against the light.

"It is called the white city," Laura said and laughed. "Fresh air! It has come across the Atlantic, all the way from Copacabana. What's the matter now? You're ghostly pale, Aschenbach!"

"I'm adjusting."

"Just try to be yourself."

"Who am I?"

"All the dreams of the world."

We sat by a table at the Café A Brasileira, and Laura kept asking me questions about my father's life, as if she wanted to learn how to see things through his eyes. It all started with her frequently talking about "the enormous emptiness of things," and how humanity is so often exiled and alone in an ice cold universe. I tried to approach her by describing my father's method.

"Every Thursday morning my father used to take the Centrumline to Copenhagen. And before I started school I was often allowed to come with him. He always bought a can of Nescafé to take with him home because there were two free ferry tickets in the can.

"That's how we travel for free," he said.

"If you keep drinking the same amount of coffee."

"Balzac drank 16 cups of coffee every day," my father commented.

"Did that work out okay?" I asked him.

"That's how he wrote *La Comédie Humaine.*"

"What's that?"

"Well, that's a sequence of thirty novels, at least!"

I swore to myself that I would start drinking coffee as soon as possible, despite its awful taste, and I imagined all the Nescafé cans that Balzac must have acquired during his travels. I expected I would meet him someday soon.

The boat landed by Havnegade and we walked over to Kongens Nytorv, where my father always pointed out the statue of Ludvig Holberg, whose nose was often painted red.

"The students do that," he said.

I looked forward to being a student so I could paint that awful Karl X Gustav statue, on Stortorget in Malmö, black and white all over, just like Pierrot at Tivoli Gardens in Copenhagen.

I suddenly noticed that Laura was crying.

"What's the matter?"

"I was a student once. Happy and carefree."

I have to keep telling my story I thought.

"We walked down Strøget and turned in on Jorcks alley, where we visited second-hand bookstores and little antique shops. We always ended up at Sparrdahl's Art & Antiquities on Kultorvet where my father disappeared into a secluded room studying secret folders full of new and valuable acquisitions. Their negotiations had nothing to do with normal prices; Sparrdahl was always doing my father a favor. He gave my father a chance to add the very best finds to his collection. Their relationship was filled with a kind of tenderness, beyond the typical vendor and customer; there was some kind of magic in their sacred bond. I watched my father open his big wallet and count the few bills he had there, which quickly disappeared into Sparrdahl's big hand. After closing the deal my father was satisfied and happy. When we were back out on the market square again, he would show me the sketch or the lithograph and speak highly of its value. There was no money for ice cream now, but it didn't matter, I knew we would soon be millionaires."

"I think your father knew a lot about darkness. What did you do after that?"

"'Let's go to the Hirschsprung Collection!' my father said with an exhilaration in his voice that I would have expressed if we'd been going to the Tivoli. The tobacco manufacturer Hirschprung collected ninteenth century Danish art, and his greatest passion was, just like my father's, the Skagen Painters. We visited the museum every time we were in Copenhagen.

"Not because of the sweetness of Krøyer," my father said, "but to admire the true down to earth Anna Ancher. She's the real genius. Time has proved that."

Anna Ancher was the wife of Michael Ancher; during the turn of the twentieth century no one took her paintings seriously. It was her husband's paintings of fishermen that sold the most. But I frankly didn't understand how time could show that boring interiors of everyday kitchen life could surpass the goddess-like beauty of Marie Krøyer. Children are romantics and have a taste for everything that is sweet, and I was at least as much in love with Marie as the painter himself —and desperately enraged when I found out from my father that the Swedish composer Hugo Alfvén had taken her away from her husband, and that everybody had been very unhappy for the rest of their lives after that. Perhaps that's when I formed my ideas about love. My childish mind was tormented by the idea of losing, or betraying Marie by giving up the love I had for her.

That night Laura asked me if I believed that the body's atrophied feelings can come back to life again. I didn't know how to answer.

"You can reach a point that resembles emptiness, but it may not be the end," I answered.

"Maybe a collector, like your father, could hide his sadness in the collections; he could overcome something very unpleasant when he looked at things like that."

Reason betrays us when it stands alone.

I thought about the binders in the cellar. Had he overcome his troubles that way? Is that why he was able to put them down there? Was he released from his yoke? Had he categorized away his sorrows? Perhaps it wasn't a failure?

We always slept on opposite sides of the hotel room in two separate single beds—an open arrangement that had led to a natural harmony between us.

We were moving toward a difficult physical intimacy, at least in our conversations.

"I thought about what you said regarding losing Marie. It was so compelling. But she was your fantasy woman, right?"

"She had been alive but didn't exist anymore. She had been painted and idealized, and I absorbed her picture into my dreams. Sometimes dreams can help me, as long as I don't compare them to reality. A dream can help you stay true to perfection. Then you can block that unscrupulous beast from entering into your soul."

"Were there other women on the walls of the Hirschsprung Collection?"

I paused; my secret love for Marie could be viewed from a perspective that would belittle the experience of her as an anecdote of puberty.

"Don't you want to answer?"

"Sometimes you have to protect your dream images."

"Forget it then!" Laura said and bit her lip.

"My heart always skipped a beat towards the end of the Hirschsprung's, when my father went over to look at the nineteenth century painter Kristian Zahrtmann's soldiers. He had purchased a preliminary study, a detail of a soldier with a golden helmet, at an auction. I snuck over to the side hall to catch a glimpse of the Italian girl and her naked bosom. I imagined the heat in this sundrenched landscape, studied her skin and the melancholy in her eyes. And I looked at her beautiful breasts, without having to listen to my father clearing his throat—because he was at the other side of the museum. It was as if that Italian girl knew she would never belong to the world of the artists. She would only cook food, do dishes, wipe the mouths of children, and in the end be too tired to smile. If only I could stand there with her in the sunshine and take her hand! Put my head on her shoulder. She would be my Marie, my secret love.

For a long time I could only love at a distance, just like at the Hirschsprung's Collection. All the living girls as well as the artistically represented figures belonged together in their own distinctive ways. The living were given energy from the beauty of the painted and vice versa. The Italian girl in the gallery was no less real than the girls in my classroom I most desired to be with. I learned to love the figures of the past just as much as those of the present over there at the Hirschsprung's Collection. It didn't matter that they were intangible; there was an intimacy in the art that defied both time and emptiness."

That night Laura came over to my bed and put her hand on my shoulder. I didn't dare move. She sat there on the edge of the bed and looked at me. A moment that defies description. The feeling of wild and unreasonable love is like a wave carrying laughing children far up onto the beach where they are caught by goodhearted mothers and fathers and pressed against their shielding bodies.

"Do you think we can stay out of the way long enough to eventually find a place that is peaceful and quiet—where we can be safe and secure; where the cold grip of death doesn't exist?"

"No," I answered, "but what's wrong with this kind of insecurity?"

That's when she said she wanted to stay with me.

Everything I had learned from Baudelaire fell into place, and I felt the criminality of modern times had just received its worst enemy in me: a loving passer-by in the crowd, so tense.

I let go of eternity in order to protect my love.

Thereby celebrating the breaking up of genres.

Morals are not static, they are a continous
seeking, a renewal, a scent, a creative
action and an awakening.

"ARGUMENTATIO PROVOCAT"
Ulf Hallberg, black notebook.

11. The M/S *Gripsholm*

"Einar Bager told me about the M/S *Gripsholm* this morning!" my father said while we were sitting by our cereal bowls in Pyttebo.

"Who did you say?" my mother shouted.

"Einar Bager!" I answered.

"Oh yes, uncle Kin," Eva said, "Did he have any fish?"

Uncle Kin, Henrik Bager's grandfather, went out cod fishing from his small sail boat every morning; later on he went around in Mölle and gave away his catch of the day to people who, in one way or another, represented his cultural ideals. My father saw it as an honor to be one of the admitted—one of the chosen —into this fellowship of art amateurs. At the same time it was a major problem since the gift stirred up the worst memories from his childhood. His father Victor's tyranny of forcing my

241

father to eat fish came to mind at the very sight of that innocent and healthy cod, which caused gag reflexes inside my father's guts, even if it had been Einar Bager who had taken the fish off the hook and handed it over, with its shiny scales, in a most courteous manner.

"Life is not furthered by fish!" my father said in Pyttebo, "fish is harmful to both body and soul. Roy Emerson never eats fish."

"What about Janne Lundquist?" I asked.

"Are you crazy," said my father, "it would ruin his forehand."

My mother realized that her summers would be full of beef stew, Wiener Schnitzel, and a lot of plain country food of meat and vegetables, but no fish, since Rod Laver probably didn't eat fish either.

We assumed that father had thrown Uncle Kin's cods in the bin behind the corner of the house. My sister and I quickly verified that we were right. "The cod fish had Victor's dead eyes and stiff posture," my sister said, "Dad says so, too."

When we sat down by the table again, and Lena and I winked at him, my father continued, "Anyway, returning to the more important issues—Friday, January 25th, 1929, was the day when Einar Bager's parents Harald and Ellen were on the train that pulled out of Malmö station going towards Göteborg."

"Calm down now," my mother said. "What was the question?"

"The seamstress Mrs. Liedholm had been sewing clothes for months before. It was a circumnavigation of the World shortly before the Kreuger crash: Göteborg—Halifax—New York—Haiti—Jamaica—Nassau—

New York—Jamaica—Colón—Panama—Colon—Havana,"

"What happened?" Eva asked.

"Nothing special except that 'The Society of the Seven Stars' finalized their statutes about the nature of things, and that Ellen Bager, in the midst of her seasickness, found an explanation as to why the world of men is so helplessly petrified."

"What did you say, Dad?"

"Did they travel to America?"

"The Statue of Liberty is also petrified, right Dad?"

"I don't think you should have thrown away that fish."

"I'm sorry Eva, but you have to understand that my childhood was frightening in a way that not even Sigmund Freud could have imagined."

"I thought Victor was quite chivalrous."

"Chivalrous?"

"What's chivalrous, Dad?"

"I don't know," my father said, "I seem to recall that the expression is used in America when someone attempts to roll out red carpets for the wrong people."

"Someone like Victor, right Dad?"

Ellen saw the M/S *Gripsholm* for the first time anchored next to the "American" Concrete Shed in Göteborg harbor. Its gigantic white sides with two chimneys seemed to her bigger than any machine she had ever seen before. She shivered at the thought of spending twelve days inside this horrible monster's oily guts, and in addition, on a stormy ocean. A few quick steps toward the stairs leading to the gangplank, and the reality of her journey to America became clear. Among swarming crowds of elegant fur coats and simple ulsters, modern travel hats and one or two drooping sixpence hats, trunks the size of small houses and bags of the cheapest kind, the flow of people siphoned her up the gangplank.

Ellen and Harald had a comfortable four-bed cabin, which they left quickly in order to look at the flow of people boarding the ship. First, second, and third class passengers had, little by little, embarked when a cheerful second-class passenger proudly ran across the gangplank yelling: "I'm the last one aboard," just before the gangplank, slowly and majestically, was swung over and onto the quay. They were separated from land, music was playing, streamers swaying in the wind, hundreds of people stood on the quay when that colossal monster of a boat slowly pulled off from the mainland. Neither those who remained on shore nor those who were leaving on the ship tired of waving at each other and searching out each other's eyes. Ellen followed a mother, who from the quay was looking for her son on the deck. She could see the son's somber expression and how he struggled against those fragile emotions with manly strength.

People who read a book and then want to meet the author, are like people eating goose liver and then wanting to meet the goose.

They were free. The tugboat wasn't needed anymore. As the M/S *Gripsholm* took off, lines of streamers came off the ship and blew down into to the water. Ellen thought the ship looked like a giant toy, dressed in paper ornamentations with a variety of flowers waving in the air.

"Fit for an Atlantic giant," she said to Harald.

"Just like Mrs. Liedholm's cuts on your clothes," he answered proudly.

When they passed Vinga, Harald said:

"Last chance to send off a written note to your family!" and Ellen suddenly felt a lump in her throat.

They were out on the ocean, the ship's horn sounded, and down in the majestic, yet welcoming dining area, people were arriving for lunch. They sat there as if in an elegant dining hall in a luxurious hotel, glancing around in surprise.

"The last thing I think about here is that we are on a steamer," Harald said.

"Isn't that Ernst Kruse?" Ellen called.

"Where?"

She pointed towards the third table astern, and he noticed Kruse, surrounded by beautiful ladies carrying on a pleasant conversation. That rascal!

"Young Ernst!" Harald yelled across the entire hall, so everybody would notice them. This was terribly embarrassing for Ellen. His voice was way too loud.

The Society of the Seven Stars was established as an offshoot of The Old Sweden League, an association founded by six young men for the purpose of being able to look back at their youth's good resolutions with satisfaction and pride when they reached a ripe old age. Harald's brother Ernst was number seven to join the league. Harald Bager was already a member, as was Ernst Kruse's father Axel.

"It is important to memorize article six and seven!" Carl von Geijer said. "Article 6. One shall behave with chivalry and respect toward the fair sex." "Article 7. Each consequence, including tardiness, will be fined at ten öre per occurrence."

The chief steward announced gravely that at three o' clock in the afternoon all aboard must be on deck wearing the lifebelts accessible to them in their cabins, reporting to the lifeboat number posted on the wall of their cabins. Up on deck it was impossible to keep from laughing at the sight of all those people with big pillows on their chests and back. An officer of the decks spoke in a stern voice.

"In an emergency, the lifeboats will be pulled down from the top deck on to the B-deck. Passengers from the second and third class will be embarking from the B-deck as well. We are a total of fifteen hundred persons on this ship. Most important for all passengers during an emergency situation: Remain calm! Wait for a crewmember's instructions."

Ellen thought about the different classes with a certain amount of dread, but concluded that things would probably work out okay—deep down inside all people are kind.

The first dinner was wonderful. It was an evening with a full moon and bright stars.

Her Harald was in deep conversations with Lieutenant-Colonel Lundström, Baron Klingspor, Master-Builder Monsén and Ernst Kruse.

"What is the purpose of your fellowship?" Lundström

asked. "It sounds like you are against any kind of pleasure? What does it mean when you state that you want to 'eliminate and attempt to prevent those bad habits that are so likely to gain footing among young men'?"

"We are against gossiping, breaching of promises, dishonesty, bad language, disorderly ways of living, discourteousness, effeminacy, boorishness, and lack of punctuality," Harald answered.

"What do you approve of then?" Monsén asked, "Do you want to murder all desires?"

Ellen had had enough. Men had their discussions, and women had theirs.

She left the dining hall towards the front of the deck. There was some snow there, and she could observe the open vault of the sky. She had a hard time obeying her husband or thinking about getting some rest.

After they passed the Orkney Islands, the ocean grew more turbulent, and the ship as well. Everything started to spin for Ellen while Harald was as alert and cheerful as ever. He talked, laughed, made acquaintances, told stories, played shuffleboard, and was at peace with the world. Ellen dreamed of dry land and longed for her lovely home on South Tullgatan in Malmö, which never shook, swayed, twisted or turned. The spacious apartment gave her fresh air without having to get up onto its roof. She felt nauseated no matter where she was on the ship. The dining hall was the worst. There sat the men, always so contented. She could hear Harald's voice above a murmur of voices. "He thrives on projecting a varnished, shiny image of himself to others," she thought. "He enjoys making a spectacle of himself. But I love him in spite of it all. Tomorrow I'll tell him not to talk so loudly, though."

Ellen was comfortable lying on her lounge chair on deck until long into the night, and the friendly deck steward wrapped her over and over again in more warm blankets, as the air got colder. She took Barbital and slept relatively well all night, and continued to doze off until one day she woke up and noticed that the nausea had vanished. She could finally eat again, play shuffleboard, and talk.

Ernst Kruse stopped by her lounge chair and congratulated her on her new found well-being:

"Thank you Herr Kruse! I feel so much better. I think I'll be able to eat again tonight."

"Well, I look forward to seeing you at the table again, Mrs. Bager!"

During dinner the men were talking about the magic of being engaged in collecting things. Harald detailed his most expensive daguerreotypes, one Nadar and two Carjat. Lieutenant Colonel Lundström referred to his most valuable medals, which none of the others seemed to appreciate the significance of. Baron Klingspor enlightened the gathering about the sixteen prize cups his race horses' performances had garnered for him, and wondered if you could consider that a collection. Master Builder Monsén mentioned his beer bottles from five continents and thirty-two nations, while Ernst Kruse appeared to be self-absorbed.

"Don't you collect anything, Kruse?"

"I have great respect for all the things you have mentioned here, but I don't collect anything material— I collect experiences."

"Can you describe them for us?"

"You never know how they look," answered Kruse with a light sigh. "Experiences change all the time, they are subjected to the same wear and tear as we humans are."

"Do you sort them into subcategories?" Harald spurred on.

"Emotion and intellect, sometimes more plainly called the internal and the external, followed by time intervals of tens of years, marking off periods within a life span."

Ellen listened in awe, then took leave and went back to her pleasant cabin, her true resort on this difficult journey. She was already looking forward to the homeward voyage. The idea of sitting in that comfortable drawing room on South Tullgatan talking about their journey and all that they'd seen filled her with warmth.

"Bager" was written in gilded letters on the cabin door, a pleasant welcoming. Each cabin had a dressing table with a washbasin—she had noticed that—and decent beds with sheets and blankets. The same cleanliness and orderliness everywhere, only a bit simpler in the other classes— here in First Class you had the most refined luxuries. "Everybody is okay," she thought and lay down on her bed. She was awake for a long time and thought about Ernst Kruse's words. She and Harald lived in different decades; he was twenty-years-older. And that he was the type that

Freedom is the notion of courses of events within us. Slavery is the notion of courses of events outside us.

projects his experiences outward was easy to see. Here she was, lying on the bed, still a bit seasick and physically uncomfortable, getting the feeling that she never dared to act according to her own inward observations. "I'm too conscientious," she thought. "I should stop trying to please everyone. I have to start taking myself seriously."

"What an elegant man," Ernst Kruse told Ellen the next day while they stood next to each other watching the pancake-making demonstration in the kitchen of the M/S *Gripsholm*. Ellen didn't know how to respond "Amazingly skillful!" she quickly said.

The chef worked six iron pans at once, buttering and pouring the batter, grabbing a pan, giving it a quick jerk and flipping the pancake in the air to be cooked on the other side; then the next pan with the same speed and agility while the pile of finished pancakes kept growing.

"We will cook one thousand, five hundred pancakes today," the chef proudly declared.

It was a Thursday; the peas, pork and sausages looked very appetizing.

"The chef's a war baby," Ernst Kruse said, "and half of him is an artist. He carved the ten ornately lighted ice sculptures that stood on the tables when the waiters, all dressed in white, came out to serve ice cream last Sunday."

How did Kruse know everything? It seemed as if he kept a sharp eye on every corner of every domain. Did it have something to do with his unique collection of experiences?

"You surely are in the know," she said, and straightened out the starched dress that suddenly bothered her.

"That dress is very becoming on you," Kruse said.
"Mrs. Liedholm should take the credit for that,"
Ellen said, "an excellent seamstress with her own ideas
and advanced feel for elegance."

"I would rather say that it has to do with you,"
Ernst Kruse said and smiled.

Ellen wasn't used to such compliments; she
desperately started to look around for Harald. Where
could he be?

Ellen, Ernst Kruse, and about twenty other passengers
were given a tour of the storage room: milk and cream,
butter and cheese, conserves and fruit, meat and fish.
Everything so well kept that the cream and the milk
lasted for ten days. Ellen admired the amazing system
and the fantastic amount of produce. She realized at
once that a housewife might not be indispensable in an
area where she considered herself a natural ruler. Here
on the ship men ruled even over this realm. Unusual.
She became irritated by the thought that Harald would
rather play shuffleboard than care to absorb these details
of their existence. She had wanted to discuss with him
questions about the worlds of men and women based on
the kitchen and the storage rooms on the M/S *Gripsholm.*

"Your husband isn't very interested in the domains of
the kitchen?" Kruse said as if he could read her thoughts.

"Harald needs to relax," Ellen said. "He is always
so hard-working. Before we left, he worked day and
night putting together albums containing photographs
of activities from the summer and the fall."

"Your husband is an extremely talented artist," Ernst
Kruse said. "When he looks at us through the camera

lens I get the feeling that he does so with a tenderness he might not be able to express in any other way."

"You collectors have a feeling of being something special," Forester Ödman said, "myself, I'm just an ordinary person."

"But you're a hunter," Harald said, "that should tell you something about us."

"There's a porcelain collector on the boat," Master Builder Monsén said, "one Count von Rosen. It is said that his most expensive find was purchased in one of the most remote provinces of China."

"I think all collectors are dreaming of a better world, in the past as well as for the future," Ernst Kruse said thoughtfully. "They simply hope for the existence of characters that are better than us." Cigars were lit now and then, thick clouds of smoke formed in the room, an attempt to dispel all judgments and assertions about the world, here on this jovial and secluded cruise liner the M/S *Gripsholm,* destined for America.

"I am my own example," Harald said, "but that's hardly ever enough to put me in a good mood. When I look at other people through my camera lens I feel much better."

"Bravo Socrates!" Master Builder Monsén called out, giving Kruse, whom he didn't like, a look of disapproval: "I think we all need some refreshing punch after this discussion about our collected experiences."

After eight and a half days the ship's machinery finally came to a halt. Ellen stood on the gunwale and saw hundreds of lights. It was Halifax. Harald and Ellen observed the lights with a special interest.

"We are in America for the first time!"

The passengers stepped ashore, dressed in their finest clothing for their promenade in the New World.

Ellen pressed closer to Harald's arm and whispered: "It is so amazing to be here in the New World!"

She examined her heart and found that she really didn't think so; the walk might have been enough in itself. A speedy return to the firm grounds of South Tullgatan, without odd interruptions, provocative remarks and the continuous feeling of being seasick in a foreign land, was all she asked for. They had been to America now. In spite of all that, she did not dare mention her homesickness to Harald. And there was something about Kruse that worried her. Harald, who had brought his box camera and a bag full of Kodak film, kept asking her to stop so he could create a detailed documentation of America.

The large, snow-covered woods and hills sloping towards the ocean made it feel as if they were standing on a pier in Norrland.

"The houses, and the huge warehouses, appear American, though," Harald commented, and quickly unfolded the lens bellow.

She heard the familiar shutter sound, and enjoyed the thought of her husband adding all of these to his collection.

The next day, as they approached New York, Captain Lundmarck and the Head Steward Andersson came up to the First Class deck and briefed the passengers on the rules for entrance into the United States, customs rules, et cetera. It was relatively simple for those who were only staying for a couple of days, like Ellen and Harald; they didn't need to carry any official documents. Ernst Kruse, on the other hand, who planned on staying for an unspecified amount of time, had plenty to do. When Ellen looked at him, she felt sad that she had to see him go away forever. So many of the questions about occurrences and adventures she had yearned to pose had not been allowed to pass through her lips.

During the last lunch in the dining hall before arrival in New York City, Count von Rosen walked up to their table with his wife, the Countess, their engineer friend Percy Tamm and his wife and asked if they could have a seat.

"I have heard about The Society of the Seven Stars," he said, "and would greatly appreciate further information about their statutes. As a collector of porcelain I intend to build a society for the preservation of the enchantment that is inherent in these objects. I entertain the hopes that an association of this kind could give new energy to humanity during a historical moment, when the economy appears to be heading for a crash and at the same time dragging humanity down with it into depression and destitution."

"There's nothing wrong with the economy," Master Builder Monsén said, "without it the individual is mainly at its service. With money comes freedom."

"But also the constraints are very depressing," Ernst Kruse said, "and those constraints are in the form of machinery that tear apart the human soul. I have given my father Axel a proposal to suggest to The Society of the Seven Stars, that every member also 'search for his soul beyond the magic charms of finance'."

"We are four to three in favor of Axel's, that is, young Ernst's suggestion! Harald said.

"I am not against it," Otto Östberg said, "I only said that our credits and disbursements must be handled with the same accuracy as before."

"Recently I traveled around in China," Count von Rosen continued with a nobleman's lack of interest for complaints that divert from his own intentions, "and gave an account there for a Chinese merchant about Pope Bonifacius VIII's ban, during the fourteenth century, on removing the entrails from the human body after death. Bonifacius' edict was aimed at the collecting of holy relics, the crusader's bones. By boiling a corpse and removing the bones the relics could be taken home. What's remarkable about it is that the ban rather increased the anatomists' curiosity for the human body, and it escalated the bargaining of relics. My point there in China being that the collecting of things is based on a rational moment and that even the merchants of the church, its travelers, missionaries, and priests contributed to a demystification of the world. As a porcelain collector I actually devote myself to recreate a form of magic that is lost. My vases restore a lack of holiness, and in connection with this I feel, based on how the world deteriorates, that it is time to form an association, and therefore I am interested in your statutes."

"There's also an economic cost estimate with possibilities for investment," engineer Tamm added, and took out an elegant black leather folder containing papers that looked like stocks and bonds on which there were some Chinese characters written as well.

Ellen stood alone on deck when Ernst Kruse came to say good-bye. He was elegantly dressed with a silk scarf around his neck; she felt regretful for not having changed clothes herself yet.

"But we'll meet at Columbus Circle, according to the plans you made with my husband," Ellen said when Kruse took her hand and pressed it.

This was the moment she had waited for, to ask her questions. But how could she, still so relatively young and inexperienced, with an older, dominating, though witty husband, and without being pigeonholed, ask Ernst Kruse what he knew about that longing for someone or something. How should the question, about those strong feelings she still experienced inside herself, be formulated? A desire to grow instead of always doing the same chores, a desire that actually had come from all those thoughts out at sea, from the starry sky above her, with Jupiter as the lonely observer. A desire that had completely imbued her when the alert and friendly nurse on the quarter-deck handed out the powder and only with her fresh personality made Ellen feel better when the heavy ground-swells had bothered her.

"What are you thinking about?" Kruse asked.

"I'm thinking about everything you're going to do in these foreign lands, all the new experiences waiting for you down those avenues."

"And you continuing on to Haiti, Jamaica, and Nassau on the M/S *Gripsholm*," Ernst Kruse said, "insouciantly swimming in the pool on board, wrapping yourself in an elegant terry towel from the department store Nordiska Kompaniet in Stockholm, suppressing all that nonsense about experience that I probably would never have been able to cope with."

"Don't be so hard on yourself," Ellen said with her best smile. At that moment Ernst Kruse gave her a kiss on the cheek, which she would remember for the rest of her life; at her deathbed she would hold it in recollection as one of the most enigmatic experiences of her life. Two years after the cruise, living on South Tullgatan, she started her secret journal based on her travel notes, she wrote: "I'm happy to once have experienced the feeling of freedom. Perhaps that freedom is connected to something unfinished and impossible to carry out." She thought about how beautiful Ernst Kruse had been, in his youthful insecurity, at Columbus Circle, where Harald had taken a photograph of him.

Sometimes during cold winter nights, when Harald was away at his meetings with The Society of the Seven Stars, or at a board assembly for the steamboat company, Ellen sat, alone, by her writing desk looking at the photo of her and Ernst Kruse hurrying across Columbus Circle. At the border Harald, using his finest handwriting, had written: "Ellen, dragging the somewhat noticeably anxious Ernst along."

Ellen could be honest with herself when she was alone with her black notebook; she wrote about Kruse's pose, his arms extended, wearing a beautiful ulster, dragging along behind her like a fugitive, and not like a hunter. It made her think of how ridiculously little we know about the world, how deep every moment is embedded in the complexities of emotions, the veils of illusion, and how tightly twined together it all is in every day's bonds and constraints. "Sometimes the collectors stare themselves blind at their objects," Ellen thought, "and have no idea what goes on beyond the spells they use to protect themselves against all vulnerabilities."

At the very bottom of Ellen's secret drawer in her writing desk, in the apartment on South Tullgatan, was Ernst Kruse's letter from America where he explained, in three pages, the advantages of California over Södergatan and Stortorget. He also gave an account of all the details about John Gilbert's hopeless love affair with Greta Garbo. For example, when she heard about the wedding of John Gilbert to Ina Claire, that would take place on May 9th, 1929, Garbo went over to Gilbert's agent and best man Harry Edington, and with tears in her eyes, asked them to stop the wedding immediately. Towards the end of the letter Ernst Kruse announced his engagement to one Caroline Ullman with the addition: "I will never forget the moment when I mustered up enough courage, as a collector of experiences, to what I never ever had been able to approach: the mystery of emotion, when it's at its greatest. With peaceful melancholy and thankful for the photographs that Harald sent to me here in California, I shall always remain Yours, most faithful, Ernst."

"Who are you?" the grandchildren asked Ellen frequently when they played a game of "Personages in the Port of Paris," while Harald recklessly climbed the cliffs of Kullaberg in order to find the best camera angles.

One time, in 1937, she answered:

"I am Greta Garbo, the loneliest woman in the world."

"No, you are not, grandmother!" hollered Märta, with a swim ring around her waist.

"All women have some Greta Garbo in them," Ellen said mysteriously, as she set the table with the finest set of Rörstrand porcelain, and a variety of delicacies.

"I'm starving," Harald called out, while Ellen looked at the reflections of the children in the water, and the play of the shadows when someone moved behind the sunshade made of sailcloth that had been stretched out against the horizon.

A passenger liner was heading north out there, making its way through Kattegat. With a pang of sadness, Ellen felt herself nodding off on a lounge chair on the M/S *Gripsholm,* in another era that already seemed to her as belonging to prehistory, and with a man other than her husband in the lounge chair next to hers. This was a man whose relative uncertainty and melancholy curiosity of something he called experience, on a voyage to America, that, for her had been filled with anguish, still ignited risk-taking moments of life, lighting up her soul with collective energy.

When asked how he was able to create
David, Michelangelo replied: "He was
trapped inside the rock, all I had to
do was to chisel him out."

"ANNOTATIONS & INTELLECTUAL BEAUTY"
Ulf Hallberg, black notebook

12. The Renaissance Man

During dinner parties my father talked very often about the Renaissance. It was his dearest subject of conversation. I quoted him many times when I wanted to impress people and make them think that I was a universal genius. Over time I have realized that we all know less than we think, but that only makes quotations more essential.

He agreed with the German cultural historian Jacob Burckhardt's thesis that the lack of culture is the New Barbarism.

"Burckhardt zeroes out the present and lets it fill up with the past," my father said. "The reference to the Renaissance is an encouragement: our times need to be re-born."

"Burckhardt writes about cultural history as opposed to official historiography," my father said to anyone who would listen, "by and for those excluded from power."

"When Burckhardt, referring to the Renaissance, disapproves of modernity, he turns cultural history into a science of opposition," my father said. "He was interested in creativity, he wanted to give an account of sensations, perceptions, experiences, and the effect they have on the understanding of our world. He provides the historian with a communicative relationship to the past and its texts. Burckhardt writes: 'I'm standing at the world's end, extending my arms toward the source of everything.' That's what I do too," my father said. "It's a little bit like reaching out in flight to hit a forehand volley."

I am at the end of a story, my arms reaching out towards a father who is lost to view. Every day I wish I could take his hand, hear the tone of his voice, and meet his eyes. I don't have anyone who can give me advice on my footwork any more. When life stops, and a father only belongs to the past, the important things are thrown forward like the shelved luggage on a train crashing into another train head on. The future and the past become entangled. My father was the only one who held my little hand with a strong grip in order to cut my nails, thoroughly and carefully, as if they were jewels taken to the jewelry store to be polished. My father was the only one to tie my shoes quickly, while my boyish legs were already heading out the door again. My father was the only one who transferred half of his meager pension to Berlin so his son could survive the first hard years there; my father was the only one who sent envelopes of newspaper clippings to me abroad in hopes that his son wouldn't lose contact with his fatherland. He is the only one who read his son's book as if it emanated from his own soul. Yes, my father is the only one who's waited for his son to arrive at one-thirty in the morning, with freshly brewed coffee, and sixteen scones in the oven, to discuss the conditions of existence, before that same son the next morning, at eight o'clock, went off to work. But one day a son must say farewell to his father, and when that father leaves this earthly life, the son must go back home to an abandoned apartment with a small Istanbul lamp in his hand, without knowing what will become of all those things, as well as of himself. That is when the sky is the darkest, the streets silent and deserted. But when a son enters the apartment of his deceased father, the Trash begins to speak in a new language that resembles the view from a cliff over a stormy sea, or a quiet song from a pier along the Bosporus. Each and every object, which seemed lifeless before, now has its own special vibrating tone. The vase from China, the wooden figure from Africa, or the bronze elephant from India suddenly speak with a father's voice, and when a son touches a map that belonged to his father it's as if the father's voice naturally continues to relay the world of the Renaissance:

Arcadia is never complete.

"The World Citizenship of the exiled Dante is the highest form of individualism. Dante finds a new home in the Italian language and its culture. Dante goes even further, he says: 'The World itself is my fatherland.' Burckhardt finds the highest degree of political self-esteem and the most highly developed creative forms in Florence. He calls Florence the world's first modern state, the home base for political doctrines, theories, experiments and developmental surges, and the home of historical representation in the modern world."

That's the situation when a son becomes dependent on the European Trash.

A son does not want to let go of his father's Trash, no matter what people expose him to, or what they might imagine. A son can perceive his own life in that Trash. He simply continues to hear his father's voice:

"Rome's history is written in Florence. Dante's exiled model-emperor is a righteous, philanthropic, supreme judge, answering only to God, heir to the Roman Empire, sanctioned by nature and by God's counsel."

"But aren't you forgetting about those in power, now?" a son says, since he thrives on raising objections, and knows that the trash has powerful enemies.

If anything, my father's thinking did not disregard authority. All his ideas and projects were somehow derived from the negation of authority: economical, political, international, religious, individual. Since he was mainly a theorist, his analysis of authority never quite encompassed those who were oppressed by authority; he had managed to acquire his dignity without the intervention of authority. It had its price (our household budget), but most of the time he disregarded the real strength of those in power. That his analysis of authority was tainted by idealism became evident in 1988 when he said to my life's great love, who at the time lived in East Germany, "Come and spend the summer with us in Skagen!" He was aware

Now, on a hot day in June, with great difficulty I managed to carve my name into an icecube.

of the Wall, but authority would never be able to suppress and control his feelings.

"Dante is the visionary counterpart to authority. Then you have Machiavelli. His main contribution to historiography is something else. His political objectivity is terribly frank, but it came about in a time of utmost difficulty and danger, when people no longer believed in righteousness or expected justice. Machiavelli's analysis of authority is based on a societal condition not unlike our own. Just think about my collection! I can't get rid of any part of it. How could I voluntarily give up that painfully gained totality? Why should I dispense with all these important things and set off all this energy. Today, people carelessly and disrespectfully throw away that small piece of unity they managed to create, and replace it with new illusions, new freedoms, and that is why so much of their inner lives lie within the realm of emptiness. Their chances for growth disappear, they destroy their seeds, burn their brittle bridges. Spiritual freedom and objectivity come to life in Florentine historiography," my father said. "If you ever write down a person's history, you must refer to them," he said.

"The Florence that gave us Dante and Machiavelli is, according to Jacob Burckhardt, the most important workshop for the European spirit."

My father said that the reasons for his own collection were intimately connected with the Renaissance man's demands to reach toward totality without representing it.

"The Renaissance man is not a totalitarian," he said, "his will-power is more like an attitude leaning towards confusion."

I listened carefully, but my father noticed that I had an objection, which he assumed had something to do with the shady sides of systems and totality.

"The unity I'm talking about has nothing to do with totalitarianism," he said. "That is a terrible misunderstanding used as an assault by the advocates of abstraction and diffusion. It is vital to differentiate between unity from above and from the outside, which often is negative and suppressing, and the struggle for unity coming from within. That is the creative being's manner of coming to grips with the chaos of existence, and growing collections of disorganized matter. My collection represents, with the help of sensations, the human urge to counter a feeling of the void. The Renaissance man noticed that the soul's endeavor to reach unity meant fighting darkness and blind intentions."

"But when darkness takes over, what happens then?" I asked.

My father's apartment was a cabinet of curiosities constructed to represent our family's history. I can remember the two sabers hanging over the entrance to the dining hall when Fammi was alive. Later on my father hung up the icons there. My childhood was guarded by the Samurai on the piano, with a drawn sword, and the sickly sweet Madonna with the infant Jesus. Tyko Sallinen's large charcoal drawing of gruff tailors sitting on a large worktable with their legs crossed marked the hallway and the entrance to my father's world. They expressed the impact of hard and serious work. And between the paintings were crucifixes and other mementos, cushions filled with insignia and badges of obscure organizations. The spaces under the beds were storage places for paintings, boxes and music records. His closets were archives for collections of photographs and hand painted post cards. A black and white decal from Paris with the text "On verra bien" was hanging over the mirror in the bathroom. Fasse lived in the same apartment building, and when she was in a bad mood, because my father didn't open his door fast enough in spite of her fiery gestures, she yelled: "There's my damned brother, cataloging the Trash again, and no time to chat with his dear sister."

The greatest sorrow has no language.

After my father's death I discovered everything that I thought had been lost, even the 16 mm film from 1967, which I starred in, wrote the script for, and directed. Up in the attic I found several bags of our saved summer items. On each was a note detailing everything the bag contained: Julian's beach ball, Peter's second-racket, Lenny's gym shoes, Jana's books, one boomerang, seven tennis balls (three Dunlop, four Tretorn). Each year had separate bags with a precise label of its contents. In various desk drawers and bureaus I found all of his life's documents, every statement and official letter, including my father's written proposal to the *Skånska Daily News* requesting that the paper take over the 1700 crowns per year payment for, and the care of the cemetery plot belonging to my father's grandfather Rudolph Asp and his family. He had loyally paid the fees and cared for the plot for many years, but now felt he was beginning to lack the strength as well as the financial means to continue his duty. In the same drawer I also found the rejection letter to my father's proposal. As a matter of principle the *Skånska Daily News* could not, unfortunately, take on the founder's cemetery plot.

"Burckhardt's short overview of the Papal state is a wonderful sample of his style and his disposition," my father said. "A different set of dangers threatened the Church-State during the fifteenth century, Burckhardt says, the lesser of these dangers coming from the outside, or from the people, having its source in the mindset of the Popes themselves. If the papacy had been threatened by extinction, neither France under Louis XI, England at the onset of the War of the Roses, the almost dissolved Spanish empire, nor Germany—cheated at the church meeting in Basel—would have been of any help. Italy itself had a number of educated, as well as uneducated, individuals who found some kind of national pride in being the country of the papacy. The Republic of Venice was the principal exception, proud and independent."

If Fammi and Fasse had any unique characteristics it was independence. Fammi's apartment after her husband Victor's death had all the signs of a strong woman's clarity of style. Fasse lived in a room which after our relocation from Ryttmästare Street became mine, later my parents' and eventually, towards the end of his life, my father's bedroom. For as long as Fasse lived on the first floor with her mother they always quarreled. Fammi would lean over towards me and say:

"She just yells and yells, Peter."

"But she's so funny, Fammi."

I grew up in Fasse and Fammi's old-fashioned drawing-room world of drama, draperies and story telling. That's where I felt most at home, with Fammi and Fasse, in a different time. The big candy bowl always waiting for me, the madness in Fasse's room, and sizing each other up in the bathroom. "Who is tallest? Why aren't you growing? Aren't you going to out-grow me soon?" I loved all those paradoxes, that strong belief in survival by overcoming formality. Turning one's weaknesses and greatest sorrows into one's strength. I loved Fasse's contempt for conformity.

"Our place is like the Carnival of Venice," Fasse said, and dressed me up in Fammi's most lavish silk dress, silk stockings, and black high-heeled shoes. She painted my lips with a deep red lipstick, and showed me how to charmingly pucker up. When I looked at myself in the mirror I saw an irresistible young Venetian girl. Fasse took me, dressed like that, to the dinner table where the rest of the family was seated.

I understand now that he was one of those unique individuals who had found a personal philosophy, and whose life was devoted to making it real.

"Take off those clothes at once!" my father said.

"My brother has no sense of humor," Fasse said.

I tried in vain to keep my balance on those high-heels.

Later on, my father told me about his arrival in Venice:

"Upon arrival at the central station, Santa Lucia, of the Venetian Lagoon, stairs outside the terminal led directly to the Grand Canal. The first thing we heard was the din of the vaporettos and the waves lapping. When you first get there it is hard to keep from laughing. The joy in that laughter suggests that the unexpected and the paradoxical have a much greater attraction to our souls, so worn out by routine, than the affirmation of anything permanent. In Venice everything is afloat: especially the gondolas, but also ideas and moral precepts. Venice is a city where the water mirrors everything, a place for introspection. We realized, sitting in the vaporetto, how beauty is strengthened by distance, movement, the nuances of color on the water surface, and the breeze from the Adriatic Sea."

> Saudade = in Brazil an expression that is very difficult to translate. It is a sorrowful but yet joyful longing, Saudade. It is the feeling that sends one's heart into one's boots when hearing a favorite song, or when missing somebody very much.

I asked him to pause for a moment before continuing with the story I knew so well. Maybe I just wanted to enjoy his facial expressions.

"We had ended up in the Odyssey, and when our eyes met the stuccowork of the Palaces we wanted to keep on sailing, at least to a pleasant hotel. The vaporetto, with its mixture of arrogant signori, powdered beauties, and a heavy ballast of tourists, made it clear to us quickly that the visit to Venice would make an impression on us, both in our present and on our future. We realized, from the price we had to pay, that Venice is part of an international financial conspiracy against the individual, but we decided to take a break from the harsh reality of our private economy and instead trade in the air and water business: art and enjoyment. We needed to reconsider, and with the lack of cars the entire modern civilization vanished with its unnecessary technical acquisitions. It was replaced by something indefinitely classical, which it was our task to explore. Canals and narrow alleyways, where the sky was seldom seen, reflected our unprotected lives, and we felt connected with something unbelievable: to walk on water and to get lost in that city. Fasse was right when it came to Venice. She must have seen herself among everything here, which seems to be floating and self-forgetting."

He continued, in a low voice: "In Venice you are what you look at. No other city can make a tourist forget everything he or she believes in. The tourist is subdued upon arrival, but is raised to nobility immediately after. Here you become exalted, the city has made a living on this phenomenon since medieval times. The privileges of commerce, the republic, the doges, the stone façades, the administration of justice, and tourism; it all seems to have grown out of some nearby primordial force within the sea, its powerful waves fatefully hitting against the foundation that was created by man. That is why the tourist, especially in Venice, understands that not only the excursion but also life has an end. Venice is the place of residence for the existentialist and it reforms the visitor. Venice is the location of Casanova's sexual licentiousness, as well as the symbol of the vows taken in marriage. Two sides of the same coin, both responding to one threat symbolized by Venice. After all we mostly consist of water, and in Venice we come to understand that—the same way looking at the clock's movements connect us to our allotted time. In other cities we look at tourist attractions, but in Venice the palaces, canals, and the works of art are observing us. Venice forces the traveler to write or think beyond every day practicalities. The streets are full o water; what do you do? As the Grand Canal slithers around like an eel, Venice pretends there's no other side to it than the pink seashell of tourism. But beyond the glass pearls and the masks are the depths. Like the sea, it is unfathomably dark and glistening blue-green, a reflection in history's cold water-mirror of the tourist's life. When the allied forces recaptured Venice from the Germans towards the end of World War II, all fuel had been used up. The American commander-in-chief secretly contacted the gondoliers and occupied Venice with a fleet of gondolas. It must have evoked the same smile seen on the tourist standing on the stairs of the train station feeling like being on the promenade deck of a steamer, or like Napoleon, beholding 'the most beautiful living room in Europe,' floating on water. You can't believe your eyes, and that is the meaning of great art: the unbelievable."

I remember filming all the rooms in my father's apartment after he died because I could not imagine a world without solid evidence of the collector's brilliance, as well as the rooms' atmosphere of concentration and creative reflection. But I never wanted to study these farewell images. When I stood in his apartment I couldn't stop looking at all that Trash, but when I, little by little, had to drive some of it to the Spillepengens landfill site, instead of the Malmö museum, my childhood came to an end. At that moment I realized that we never get older, time progresses, our faces and bodies change, but we are aged children. That time has influenced all of our lives; eventually the reckless forward movement of time and the Trash overwhelms us. One fine day everything we looked forward to is part of a broken-down past, and our practical arrangements are basically about sorting out primary sources. I could see that my father realized this early, and that his collection, for this reason, had a more distinguished cosmopolitan context. He had traveled all over the world in his room; by that he had avoided all the petty hypocrisies of Malmö. The passion he had for his task led to the European Trash penetrating into every dark corner of the deepest closet.

"The Renaissance Man hopes for the highest development possible of his personality, versatile growth and education, an aspiration towards *l'uomo universale,* the Universal Man. The fifteenth century is the century of the versatile man. All biographies of that time portray multi-talented personages. This is all based on notoriety of course, but if the Renaissance Man can find pleasure in the thought of a posterity that will remember him, he declines any praise from his contemporaries."

My father completely avoided effects and attributes. His endeavors were genuine and devoid of others' opinions and judgments. He might have had an old wound from his school years of failing, not being good enough. During the last two years of high school he was moved to Spyken in Lund, where the writer John Karlzén was his teacher. It might have been due to his poor grades. In issues about tangible achievements, grades, and examinations he remained unclear. He didn't care about what others took seriously or tried to achieve. He held Karlzén in very high regard during his time at Spyken. I identified with that writer as well. I wanted to travel to Uruguay, just like Karlzén—or at least to Udine. My father's prudent disposition was more likely to predestine him for Uddevalla or Unnarröd. But his point was that it didn't matter. As a traveler he encompassed everything anyway. The whole world was represented in his collection. From the bed in the bedroom to the writing desk in the living room he journeyed through all continents, epochs and belief systems.

"The transition from the Renaissance man's ideals, attitudes and desire for enlightenment to the modern man's indifference occurred at the time of Casanova in the eighteenth century. Casanova's failures put an end to the Renaissance man's struggle to overcome passions in his search for morality and beauty. Casanova consequently, becomes the first to act out modern man's comedy of life: a frantic race, without any loyalty to anything touching his life, towards an abyss."

Casanova collects those passionate escapades without being able to absorb them into his soul. He always feels a yearning for new women, slim, fat, young, old —it does not matter—what's important is to satisfy that uncontrollable hunger, the pure passion, the obsessive need to fondle new objects. Casanova is a coldhearted collector, just like Don Juan and all other individuals who are drawn to things that way. The magic of collecting things is a means to release tension and conflict deep down in one's own identity's deepest layers of unconsciousness. And all collectors, in their hunt for new objects, exhibit some part of Casanova's uncontrollable frenzy and visceral ingenuity. My father went one step further which became quite conclusive; he added the things into his family's dream world, he constructed intricate systems, binders and directories suggestive of some kind of universal history. He lifted us up to the riches of the world. Just like Strindberg, he tried to make gold. I am now convinced that he succeeded.

Richest is he who knows what he doesn't know.

"Casanova's escape from the lead chambers of the Doge's Palace is a great culmination of an adventure tale by an author who only speaks the truth, and never would sink so low as to write a romance novel. Casanova openly admits that he goes to the opera not in order to listen to music, but only to view the female singers. His blindness to other people's social realities makes him an observer, clearly and distinctly. Casanova is a frantic witness, pursued in Tempo Furioso by a confusion that is growing to a staggering size up to the present. Today the deification of the self is of olympic dimensions. But Casanova does not have a plan; his self-intimidation has Venetian dimensions. The twilight of Venice provokes insanity of the mind. It is as if Casanova experiments with temptation to see if he can keep himself alive. And when closing his book of memoirs it is clear that beyond lust, passion, and suffering there is a lonely and neglected victim in our world of indifference: love. That is the modern-day within Casanova; where restlessness and subjective frenzy come from. The one enjoying life is affected by the same melancholy as the tourist: 'What can I do with all this beauty?' Casanova surely knows, but it is his yearning that can't be satisfied. He is in love with his own blindness; he can only admire perspicacity. Casanova's humorous description of his visit to Voltaire contains the great, deeply self-ironic, warped final comment: 'I ought to have considered, aside from his sarcastic comments which on the third day made me despise him, that I had found him sublime in everything.'

The Frenchmen led by Napoleon in 1797 brought the Venetian empire, and its growing extravagance with 136 casinos and five thousand families holding salon every evening, to an end. Finally, while on the way back to the train station, my father decided to visit Palazzo Venier next to the Grand Canal in order to study Peggy Guggenheim's art collection. He stood in the garden looking at a sculpture with an irrigating penis by Marino Marini. In a world flooded with sexual undertones, it was refreshing to think of the Beat Generation poet from the 1950s who had stolen that penis during a visit to Peggy Guggenheim. Confronted with accusations of theft, according to my father, Gregory Corso replied:

"No, it was that fucking Austrian guy, Hundertwasser!"

He said that Peggy Guggenheim, who was the owner of the last private gondola, called on her suntanned gondolier. In Venice there are moments when the splashing of the waves in the sunset is the only answer. In a letter to Djurna Barnes she added, that twentieth century artist female Casanova: "I love sliding across water so immensely. I can't imagine anything more pleasant since I laid off sex—or more correctly—since it laid me off."

Fasse's love life was influenced by a fantasy image of Casanova as an honorary guest. I remember a photo of a dark-skinned handsome man on her bedside table. The subject was definitely taboo; because she had been lured into a partially financed house purchase in Skåne. In general it was considered unwise to bring up the subject of love to Fasse, as if she didn't belong to that circle of enlightenment.

"Who do you love, Fasse?"
Fasse loved us children, my sister and me, with a love that transformed us into gods. Fasse, the dwarf who people would call on the bus, had no respect whatsoever for all those adults with their overbearing offspring.

"Look at that small person!"
"Take a look at yourself, you look completely nuts!"
The confused adults accused her of being rough with their little poison darts.

Fasse knew that most adults had given up spontaneity and happiness for a uniformity that she considered stilted and dull.

Her smile had greater dignity in my eyes.

She grinned with a quickness and wit that signaled to us children that in the next instant something even more decisive would take place, at her command.

She smiled in an attempt to effect a more childish future, where small people with their ingenuity would limit the idiocy of the adults, and her eyes shined: "Let's do it now!"

Wit was something my father could analyze and enjoy, but Fasse was more effective with its use. He was inhibited by his discretion, his entire theoretical build: "During the pinnacle of the Renaissance quick-wittedness was theoretically analyzed and its practical use in the higher societies of life thoroughly established. Baldassarre Castiglione in *The Book of the Courtier* instructs the person of rank on how to deal with wit. Amusement by recounting fun and lovable stories in the third person is what he mainly suggests. This is how it might sound in Castiglione's theories of living: 'To give you an example you should take a look at Don Ippolito d'Este, cardinal of Ferrara, whose lineage so joyfully formed him that his personality, physical appearance, choice of words, and all his movements are done with such harmony and grace that he, in spite of his youth, among the older clergy has such authority that he seems fitted to instruct rather than in need to learn anything.'"

Sometimes it is good to hold reality at a distance in order to observe it in the light of an idea.

My father's need for new avenues of study was unlimited. The number of notebooks with descriptions of living persons, mythical characters, words and expressions are innumerable. He had an uninhibited enthusiasm for learning, an unsurpassed belief in the value of all knowledge, and was prepared to take the next step up the pyramid of knowledge. He embraced everything —Greece, Rome, Byzantium, Europe, the Orient, America—everything is colored and high lighted in his personality like some kind of wonder medicine, a way to improve the moment of contact, to hit a perfect cross shot and surprise those who are blinded by wealth or success.

"During the fifteenth century the ruins of Rome were given new meaning in connection with its enhancement. The carefully mapped out ancient monuments of the city's outskirts lead to a revitalization of antiquity. The popular fantasy pictures in the carnival parades of the time were the ancient Roman emperors triumphal processions."

"That was the mindset of people in Rome on the 19th of April, 1485, when stories were told about a well preserved corpse of an incredibly lovely Roman girl from antiquity that had been found on Via Appia. Some masons had dug out a marble sarcophagus with an inscription: Julia, daughter of Claudius. The body had been covered with a protective essence and looked just as fresh as a newly diseased, fifteen-year-old girl with living colors, eyes and mouth were half open. She was moved to the conservatory palace on Capitoline Hill, and a veritable pilgrimage of visitors interested in seeing her was started. People even came to paint her, for something so beautiful had never been seen. The most touching in all this, my father said, was the resolute, preconceived ideas that the body from antiquity was considered so much more beautiful than anything that was alive at the time."

Just like my father, Petrarch collected old Roman coins and medallions. For centuries after distinctions were made between discoveries by man and natural discoveries (*artificilia* and *naturalia*). Humanists sought knowledge of Greek, Roman, Arabian and Hebrew history. My father identified with the humanists' aspirations to look, distinguish, categorize, and compile. He looked at himself as a copyist and a preservationist:

"We can thank the Renaissance for our understanding of the authors from antiquity. Boccaccio ordered the first Latin translation of *The Iliad* and *The Odyssey*. Not until the fifteenth century were a great number of new discoveries made, the systematic foundation of libraries by copying and translating books. The scribes who understood Greek were called *scrittori* and were highly paid. The others, *copisti,* remained poor but well learned. The tired scribes—not those who made a living by copying, but all those who had to copy a book in order to have it—rejoiced when the printing press was invented."

Once on a Christmas Eve, my father—reacting to a story Fasse had told about a man at the County Government Office who seemed to use the word "sense" all the time, denying that "sense" is a public matter—said:

"It's different with Jacob Burckhardt."

As soon as we heard the name, Jacob Burckhardt, we held our breaths.

The herring had been served and it was time for

meatballs. Preferably, they should be served warm. It was my father's job to do that and to serve them.

"Burckhardt doesn't primarily want to explain occurrences," my father said, "Instead he compares different epochs to relate images. He represents reason in aesthetic forms. It's not a matter of comparing facts," he said and nodded at Fasse. "That's different from the County Government. Burckhardt tries to filter out the things that may be interesting to humanity."

"What is of highest interest for us right now is whether you can filter out some meatballs or not," Fasse said, "before our epoch comes to an end."

My father replied to such comments with an eloquence that impressed Fasse, who had not spent more time than necessary with homework and books.

"It is refreshing, in today's dismantled and helpless view on educational ideals, to read Burckhardt's wording of his 'attempt to understand the timeframe of the Renaissance man in all of its powerful uniqueness.'"

"Well, you almost had your B.A. in Law yourself," she answered quickly. "And now you're the CEO of the European Trash."

Travel books have always stimulated the collector's appetite for foreign objects and distant treasures.

"As the Marco Polo of Malmö, I've always preferred Copenhagen over Asia," my father said. He had a very keen sense of his financial limits. But he viewed every reader and writer as a "Homer in the moonlight," an excessive amount of travel was always to his liking, though he himself was satisfied with destinations close to home.

"Burckhardt writes, in his introduction to the cultural history of Greece, that he is backed up by facts which reveal actual links to our souls. It is a likeness with Odyssey's voyage to Ithaca. The voyage becomes an essential part of the Renaissance man's education. With respect, one turns toward Columbus, the Genoese, the first one who dared to say: *Il mondo é poco*—the world is not as big as one thinks. That is the mindset of the Argonauts. In Greek mythology the Argonauts were heroes who, with their leader Jason, sailed to Colchis by the Black Sea to fetch the Golden Fleece."

"The day I became acquainted with Claudio Magris he talked about the sea," I said to my father. "I look at him as a real Renaissance man of the twenty-first century. He gave me the insight that the ocean is larger than all of us, it mirrors every detail of our lives."

My father smiled and seemed interested.

In order to keep his attention I quoted a sentence from Claudio Magris' work. I wanted to point out its particular beauty and connection to the Renaissance man. I picked the author's regeneration of the character Carlo, born Mickelstädter, from *A Different Sea*. I wanted my father to listen to the drift in some of the sentences I thought were describing him as a collector, "Carlo had told him that just at the time when the boat departs he would climb up into the attic room where he could look through the window in the roof and turn his eyes toward Trieste as the sun set, where he, Enrico right then would board the ship, as if his eyes could penetrate the darkness and liberate all things from obscurity, he who had taught that philosophy, a love for all wisdom, aims to see things far away as if they were close, and eliminate the desire to capture them, since they simply exist, in the great stillness of existence."

"To see distant things as if they were close," my father said.

"Isn't that what you are doing?" I asked.

"I will never be able to entirely erase my longing to capture them," he answered.

Towards the end of Fasse's life, gaps appeared in her façade and her stories ruptured. It was hard for her to walk; she would collapse on the street or fall while traveling by bus. She became dependent on others for help. That broke her spirit. She knew the world around her had its limits, but now she had nothing to set against it. She was down on the ground, legs like lifeless jelly, incontinent. Strong and sound people leaned over her and said. "What happened to the little lady? Get up, you poor thing!" I think it was the chatter and the lack of fellow feeling that was hard for her. "But she's just lying there, that little person!" Her otherwise quick tongue failed her; she couldn't find the right words, she had no cogency. More frequently she ended up falling to the ground or on the floor. My mother cared for her on the second floor of the apartment after she came home from her work at school. My father, meanwhile, sat by his desk and analyzed the important circumstances of existence. Fasse was put in a convalescent home with a roommate

The power with which Art is perceived is the beatuy of Art.

and a small garden patch—but after a few days there she ran back home where the situation became unbearable. Finally she was accommodated at "The Last Gasp" in the Värnhem District, where we often came to visit her. My father visited her once a week. Fasse troubled him with strange questions and expressions regarding their mutual past; frequently bringing up his education.

"Did you manage the test?" Or, "Could you handle all the questions?" "Will you take your exam, do you think?" As if she, in her unclear conscience, only had the reminder of a wound and the knife that poked into it. But, in her most poisonous comments there was still a peevish tenderness that hinted to me about her life's deepest love belonging to my father. In spite of that she had only reached him with her jokes a few times over all these years, and he had rarely reached her with his knowledge, which she did admire immensely. We children were messengers between the two of them, and my own life has always balanced on that tension.

The greatest helpers: those who've had to save themselves.

Fasse really wanted to be part of the collection, but being a sharp-tongued dwarf she was predestined to be the foremost court jester of the European Trash. Just like my father she only wanted to be seen.

She had a crucial influence on my ideas of the European Trash and its pretentious governors and authorities:

"The Trash is worthless if you can't laugh at it!" she said.

My father smiled when she said it. That made Fasse

so happy she patted his head and called him "Ulfapulfa."
He had protected her against all evil during her childhood.

I told my father about the Maccastorna castle on the
plains along the Po River, a hundred kilometers south of
Milan. During the fourteenth century Ghibellini built
a castle in the marshlands between the Adda and the Po
rivers, a well-calculated location. Every city along the
plains of the Po was independently
ruled, the adjacent city Cremona
was not under the rule of Milan
but, just as Vicenza and Lodi, was
autonomous. Not until the end of
the fourteenth century did Milan's
royal house of Visconti begin to
take over the rule of Vicenza, Lodi, Cremona, and
Piacenza. Germany's emperor wanted to attack Milan
and attempted to ally himself with the small cities. The
city of Lodi allied with Germany during this period.

Man is blind,
dreaming in
order to see.

"Dissenters were tortured in the dungeons of
Maccastorna castle during an age when war initially was
viewed as a work of art, and its consequences as part of its
artistic movement. At the time it was next to impossible
to get at those well guarded tyrant rulers, other than at
some ceremonial church visit. It was especially difficult
to get at a whole royal family at any other time. In the
beginning of the fifteenth century Cabrino Fondulo ruled
over Maccastorna. During the fourteenth century the
smaller cities were seeking help from the larger ones.
Every city and castle had a *capitano di ventura,* a chosen
leader, who kept a small army. As Cabrino Fondulo was
very ambitious he invited his adversaries from Cremona

to his castle in Maccastorna—and killed them all. Most likely while seated at the dining table after his guests had taken off their swords and daggers."

"It sounds like *Macbeth*," my father said. "Blood calling for blood."

"Seven hundred years later I stood in those dark dungeon caverns with the castle's master Paolo Biancardi. It quickly became clear to me that spiritual development, education and schooling, emanated from such bloodguilt," I continued, "like a renunciation, a denial of egotistic tyranny."

My father laughed, "Like your childhood on Ryttmästaregatan, full of medieval jousts!"

"Let me continue! During the Middle Ages both sides of the conscious mind, the observation of the outside world and introspection, were in a half-dream state, or an obscure stupor. Race, people, parties, alliances or families were impenetrable veils surrounding the individual. Insight and development didn't make it on to the program; survival, violence and power had absolute sway."

The most important part of rasing children is fostering their ability to love as their foremost objective.

"I have succeeded in filling you up with Baudelaire!"

"When Paolo Biancardi locked up the dungeon cell he said that the Maccastorna castle is haunted by those who were murdered there. 'Living in one of the rooms in the guest wing I should expect soundless footsteps from phantoms as thin as air, waving their blood stained clothing and emitting half-stifled screams,' he said. But, at night, I preferred to hear the lord of the castle's own story. Towards the end of the eighteenth century his ancestors built up an empire as cheese-merchants of the famous Parmesan cheese Grana Padana. The Biancardi dynasty bought the Maccastorna castle at the end of the nineteenth century. During the first year of Paolo's life the castle had lords, soldiers, shoemakers, and tailors. That was the last year of Word War II."

"How was he educated?"

"After his education in Paris Paolo Biancardi worked at the Boston Consulting Group for thirty years, which had two offices and sixty employees when he started, and sixty offices world wide, with over four thousand employees when he retired. Upon his retirement, at fifty-five, this man had ten thousand trees planted in the marshes next to the Maccastorna castle, and was devoting his time to the telephone hotline for psychiatric emergencies in Milan. During a ten year period he gave artists from Europe and the United States commissions to create installations on site in the castle's halls, on the hills by the marshlands, and by the little lake at the nearby woods. The castle is a living art museum. He is a collector just like you. At night he takes care of his trees."

My father gave me an imploring look to continue, a conclusion that would encompass us.

"The Renaissance man's life has to do with advancement. Erland Josephson's father comes to mind, he lost his sight as he got older and was unable to read; he was given the advice to enjoy the sunshine. When he was asked if he enjoyed it, he replied, 'Sure, I like it, but it's not formative.'"

"Don't forget Burckhardt's conclusion!"

I knew my father wanted his hero to have the last word.

"Which conclusion do you have in mind?"

"Towards the end of the nineteenth century he claimed that the belief in Progress, Science, and financial power caused individual desires and the subjective nature of man to be rejected for the advantages of unbridled selfishness."

"So what can we find to stand up against that?"

There are two kinds of great talents:
those who can see clearly what is only
obscure to others, and those who can
vaguely see what others can't see at all.

"PRIVATE SELF-CONTRADICTIONS"
Ulf Hallberg, black notebook

13. Prague Pietà

I visited Prague together with my father right after the fall of the Berlin Wall. We stayed with Eli Solakova, who, inside her stove, burned old worn-out shoes she had found in the street. She was always waiting for us in the kitchen when we returned from the antiquary and used book stores. Eli told us about her life, while my father listened, wide-eyed, there in that kitchen in Prague. She didn't hesitate to tell all the worst tales that I knew backwards and forwards from all my visits, but I naturally wanted my father to find out about those times.

Eli turned to him and said:

"Now listen here: then *my* Dad took Werner's daughter as his mistress! Can you imagine? She was thirty-five and he was fifty. I was supposed to keep an eye out at the entrance to the mistress's place. I called home and said: 'Mommy, I don't see anything, and I'm freezing to death.' That's what you have to do, isn't that right, Peter? Aren't I right? I *am* right. Mommy just said:

'Stay where you are!' Then she arrived in a taxi with two girl friends, and they pushed their way into the inn. It caused a big uproar."

After a pause, she turned to me.

"Does your Dad understand?"

I heard him mumble, "I understand."

But I noticed that he wasn't getting it at all, and that he had trouble grasping those East European experiences. This calm, timid man, who loved his wife above all others in the world, sat in Eli Solakova's kitchen, and nodded as if he understood when she said:

"When I saw my first husband walking around in the garden, poking about, like the lazy dog he was, I had a sudden urge to put a bomb right under him. I wanted to blow him apart. You understand, don't you? Aren't I right? Yes, I am always right, aren't I, Peter?"

Eli is the closest I've come to finding someone like Fasse, my aunt, after her death in 1988. Eli had been sitting there in the kitchen, with her sewing machine on the kitchen table and her bed in one corner next to the oven, following those crucial changes in my life. And now she was meeting my father at last.

He turned to Eli as if he was replying to her descriptions from marriage Hell, and said:

"Now you listen to me. You have had one of the greatest artists in the world living here in Prague, Endre Nemes, and for many years I had a watercolor, *The Machine Man,* by him on my wall at home in Malmö. Nemes came from Hungary but lived in Prague during the 1930s, and I must tell you, Eli, that for me it is a great honor to sit here in your kitchen in this city of high culture, as if I were visiting Nemes and talking with his friend Jakub Bauernfreund. There's something very odd about Time. You know that."

"Bauerfreund! He must have been a relative of my cousins! And about Time being strange, that is something deeply ingrained into little old me. My God, all that political crap going on."

"It's so corrupt!"

"Corrupt? It's bankrupt. I didn't believe in National Socialism, I didn't believe in Socialism, and I don't even believe in Capitalism! If we can't find a solution soon, I think humanity is doomed. Everyone just thinks about himself. Aren't I right, Peter? I am right."

"You must have faith in art, Eli!" my father said.

"Then explain why."

My father managed to convince Eli that she was part of a cultural milieu that was indestructible. We were sitting a stone's throw away from Karl's Bridge, and my father was talking about Endre Nemes' painting, *Prague Pietà*.

"The Madonna sits enclosed in a box which is standing on what looks like your own kitchen table, Eli. The metal mechanic nearby is winding himself up with a crank. That's me and all my chatter. The Christ Child looks like an astonished Peter here who is staring at the cathedrals and pillared vaults from his place on the Madonna's knee. Only Peter's notebook is missing. We belong here in this room with you, Eli. History exists right here. And we are the only ones to carry it forward."

Stocastic = influenced by an accidental element of chance.

Eli, who during her entire life had schlepped things

here and there, listened with deep respect. Yes, yes, you must always be carrying something. She certainly had run often enough carrying things through the streets of Prague. But a Madonna in Prague, that she was not, oh no! Instead of paintings and cathedrals she spoke of her work as a seamstress in the good old days. In the thirties she had sewn costumes for performances at the National Theatre and been a part of the ebullient world of art.

"That was when Thomas Mann was here with his daughter, Erika," my father said, "and Kokoschka stood in the room in Frau Tauber's tower and painted two dozen landscape paintings—most of them views of Karl's Bridge from various perspectives. The philosopher Theodor Lessing was here as well. But he was shot dead while he sat by an open window reading a book."

"Art is dangerous," Eli said, "You can't depend on artists. They run up and down hallways and play footsy with one another. They drink too much, act histrionic, and sleep until late in the morning. You can't depend upon an artist the way you can depend on a seamstress."

The Aryan heresy = the idea of the completeness of God as a conceptual necessity leads to the Son being created and of a different being than the Father.

Then she described difficult cross-stitches and appliqués, sleeves sewn on the inside, cuffs and collars, silk and velvet. My Dad nodded approvingly. Thanks to his intense interest in the experiences of people he liked, he managed to convince Eli that he had at least a theoretical expertise of sewing—he who never mended a sock or threaded a needle. But he did warm up needles to remove splinters from my feet.

"People search for Beauty because it vaguely reminds them of the Good. Art embraces virtues that are otherwise threatened with extinction," he said.

"I'm a loose woman who hasn't understood a damned thing about Art before now," Eli said, serving the sandwiches.

"You guys want coffee? Right again, right?"

She didn't drink coffee that late at night but occupied herself with knitting, looking at us sideways with furtive glances. Every now and then she stirred the wood stove. When we stood up and offered her our thanks, she said: "Mommy always said *In uns selbst liegen die Sterne des Glücks.*

And then she looked and gave him a wink.

After my father's death, in one of the closets on Rönneholmsvägen in Malmö I found, behind the archive boxes, billiard balls and more miscellaneous European Trash, a sixteen-millimeter film roll that captured my parents' attempted voyage to Africa in 1951. The trip only got as far as Spain because their RV, *Jumbo,* showed its first evidence of mechanical failure—signs of its incapacity to traverse the entire European continent.

My parents were traveling with two close friends, Harriet and Bosse. The four of them had managed to cross France into Spain. They sent reports to the Malmö Evening Post from, among other places, Paris, Bordeaux, Zaragoza, Pamplona, Barcelona, and Marseilles. My mother and Bo Nordlund sang and played music in the streets and squares. It usually began with Bosse employing a spoon to start the beat, and then Eva would follow with the song. The local Spaniards were so impressed with those songbirds from Malmö that they invited the whole quartet home. Harriet wrote it all down with her travel typewriter. They slept in the RV and bathed in the local streams. They prepared their food on a camping stove. Daringly exciting footage of my father exists where he appears to expose the Spanish landscape to an acute risk of incendiary fire with the incredible ability of his fingers to become all thumbs when it came to anything mechanical. In the film my father also demonstrates his idiosyncratic way of washing his underarms with a washrag, without soap and water and with his shirt on. His sleeves, though, were rolled up. But, then everything was hypothetical like that in his life.

The driver, Bo Nordlund, was in the process of unscrewing the entire RV down to its last bolt—something he had proved he could do for the previous owner, Gösta Nyberg, before departing. Gösta Nyberg owned a furniture store on Lantmanna Street. Back in Höllviken, Nyberg had gaped in wonder at that interior design which included windows cut out of metal and hubcaps refashioned into seats. In some of the photos from their trip—one even printed in the *Evening Post*—my father can be seen poking a large monkey wrench into the inner depths of the engine, with the deftness of a little child dipping its fingers into a bowl of pancake batter.

My father considered mechanical things to be an enemy both of himself and of humanity at large. He didn't understand them, couldn't get interested in them, and was on a short fuse when it came to blowing up over them. He just knew they would fall apart at the wrong moment. If something malfunctioned, it was a conspiracy. When the radio or the television set broke down, he took it as an evil plot, a personal betrayal of himself, culture, and concentration. A flat tire or a car accident was an assault from Hell with my father as the target. When I was growing up in Malmö, my hero was my father's best friend, Jan Brandt, a carpenter.

> Mahler considered the symphony to be like the world, encompassing everything. Sibelius, however, admired the rigor and style of the symphony and the deep logic that creates an inner connection among all the motifs.

On one occasion, after our melancholy drive home from spending the summer in Mölle, we were waiting for the oncoming traffic at Limhamnsvägen in Malmö to pass by. My father was about to make a left turn onto Erikstorpsgatan. Being the very cautious driver that he was, he preferred to yield so he could make his own turn in peace. Toward the end of his life I had to ask him to give up driving altogether because he consistently yielded to all traffic to the point of stopping completely inside roundabouts. Someone has called that a *circulus vitiosus,* the Devil's vicious circle, without this being a comment on my father, but on his belief about the nature of technology. I think it was Nietzsche. For us in the family, my father's confrontation with technical things was the Eternal Return of the Same.

When we were stranded on Limhamnsvägen waiting—his engine in first gear, his foot on the clutch—as the lines of cars behind us grew longer and longer, we overheard our father mumbling to himself and coming to a boil about technology and humanity, life's frightful events, the decline of moral values—everything tainted— humanity's war on Nature and its reckless idea of Progress. Then, resolutely, he released the clutch in complete panic and with great accuracy collided head on with the next passing car. "My point exactly!" he yelled, "What did I tell you? It was to be expected."

> The poet is a person who deliberately prolongs his or her childhood.

Shocked passengers came stumbling out of the other car. My father made no attempt to diffuse the situation. He kept us focused on his analysis in that crucial moment. "Banality! Always this incredible technical banality! If you had only been quiet back there, it never would have happened."

Technology, in my father's worldview, was an evil demon out to crush all our chances, limit our freedoms, and interrupt our attempts at collection and recollection. Technology was the archenemy of the European Trash, and he identified it to a certain degree with Endre Nemes' watercolor, *The Machine Man,* which he had found in a pile of trash at an auction hall in Copenhagen, where no one seemed to know who that Hungarian-born artist was, though he was well-known in the rest of Scandinavia.

He explained to me at length, before I could comprehend exactly what he was saying: "Nemes' *The Machine Man* proves everything I've been saying about the corrosive effect of modern technology. How can any person be behind by two games to five in the final set and still win the match? That only works if you have an outlook that unites body and soul, and you train your psyche to overcome your opponents' sly maneuvers. *The Machine Man* threatens us with its sense of false limitations, its ugly angularity. His mechanical maw only reiterates the most stupid clichés and is doomed to rust. I turn my back on this monster but celebrate Endre Nemes who captured it all and, in doing so, focused the problem as a confrontation of the Baroque with the Renaissance."

My father's purchase of *The Machine Man* was made only a few days before they embarked on the trip to Africa and contributed further to the extreme tightness of their travel budget and to the odds against their ever reaching that distant continent.

When I view the photographs and film from the African Trip, I see something rarely accessible to a son: my parents' youth, the nuances in their innocent eyes, their hopeful faces as they brush their teeth in a stream. Eva's happy smile as she kneels by the roadside in Spain. Ulf's proud and boyish essence, the *savoir-faire* he brought with him from Fammi and Rudolf Asp's world.

"The Trip to Africa," that ten-minute color-film, preserved among all the other European Trash, portrays that period in every person's life when he or she is full of laughter, careless of all of life's predicaments and responsibilities, perilous chances, and rolls of the dice. In those innocent smiles an immense strength can be found. Both Eva and Eli developed brain tumors in later life, and both overcame their hardships. Perhaps that kind of carefree, rebellious energy so visible in the film taken in Pamplona, Zaragoza, Barcelona, and Paris survived throughout their lives. I understand all that a lot better now, like a kind of chronicler or historian. I have turned it into part of my own life. That's the advantage of age: the ability to understand. You grow nearer both to the living and the dead, in a modest attempt to define your own identity in others' destinies.

> It is a classical problem how to be able to sit in a corner and think, without being the object of repression.

"It was *fiesta* time in Pamplona, and to the Spaniards this meant a time for dancing, wine drinking, and bullfighting." Harriet wrote in her report from the Jumbo-Expedition, the trip to Africa: "Imagine five hundred solid citizens from Malmö leaping about on Södergatan, their arms waving in the air" she continued, "everyone of them singing with more or less the vocal resources God so generously equipped them with. Now, in your mind, dress these people in white pajamas with a red apron around their waists and wide-brimmed sombreros on their heads, and that would be our introduction to the siesta."

These travelers on their way to Africa went to the bullfights. The film camera pans over the waving, excited crowd, and in the arena, the matador brings down the bull. In that old-film technology, without a zoom lens, the action seems distant and mechanical. I stare at the details in the background. A face appears. Could it be Eva's? Ulf's profile, with its sideways, glittering glance, is barely visible.

When they return, their car won't start. Bosse raises the hood and reaches down into the entrails of the engine. Eva and Harriet sit down on the grass. My father picks up tools and passes them to Bosse—usually the wrong ones.

"Sit down and tell us a story instead, Ulf. You and car engines, that's two separate continents. Do you think we'll ever make it to Africa?"

"Africa begins just south of the Pyrenees."

"That's what Harriet is writing about, but I'm getting tired of engine troubles."

"A car engine is not like us. It has no soul. Yet so many people are in awe of precision mechanics."

"Not you!"

"Why should I?"

"No, you are an arts' accountant, or whatever. That watercolor you bought in Copenhagen, is it really worth what you say it is?"

"It's priceless."

"But you don't have the money to buy Eva a new blouse."

"I don't want a new blouse, Bosse."

"She actually does."

"Art prevents you from living, Ulf!" Bosse said.

All of them turned their eyes toward Ulf. He was the aristocrat of that travel tour. He often slept late, his practical skills were few, and when problems arose, he never was the one to solve them. Yet everyone had respect for him. He was serious and they all knew they could trust him. Eva had been attracted to men of shifty values, some who suddenly disclosed that they had wives and kids. To her Ulf was someone quite unusual. She thought he looked like that refined Francesco d'Este, the Duke of Modena, in the Velazquez painting, and she knew that a life at his side would be dedicated to art, not just to that down-to-earth practicality she had been brought up with in Bårarp. She aimed at a union of two glowing energies.

"Haven't you ever heard about Rudolf the Second?" my father said while Bosse loosened the carburetor and cleaned out a beautiful mess of European Trash cluttering the insides, while Harriet and Eva were lighting the camper stove to begin cooking the meal.

The others took Ulf's allusion to Rudolf the Second as a sort of tipping of the hat to his family traditions, having a connection with the fact that in repeating confessions in the evening they had asked him which area of the law he would specialize in. And he would answer: "Law isn't for me!"

"But isn't that what you're studying?" Harriet asked.

Then a silence would fall. The others had finished their inquiry and gone back to work. All three of them were teachers. They never could forget that the limits of their journey were marked by the end of summer vacation and their return to classes.

Now they wondered if Ulf was ready to do an about-face, fulfilling his grandfather's mission to inform the farmers of Skåne of the world outside Hönsinge. Perhaps he hoped to be the new Rudolf Asp, Rudolf the Second and devote himself to cultural columns in that world of journalism, the *Skånska Daily News.*

"Rudolf the Second," my father added, "was the Emperor of the Holy Roman Empire, centered in Prague. Like any other Habsburg following his family's traditions, he had an extensive education in the field of art collecting. He was obsessed with it and surrounded himself with scientists, painters, sculptors, instrument makers, and alchemists—all in his service. Appropriately, as a Renaissance man, he was especially interested in advances in Science and Education. He hired Tycho Brahe as a mathematician at his court in Prague and set aside an entire castle at the astronomer's disposal. As the Thirty Years War's military machine grounded down to a stalemate, skilled clock makers built some rare clocks and instruments for Rudolf. The search for more items to add to his collections absorbed all his time. That's why he hired agents who could be sent out to acquire paintings, minerals, clocks, fossils, exotic animals and other rarities. His collections expanded, but his governmental apparatus withered away. His ministers waited in vain for an audience with him while he was deep into alchemistic experimentation or Cabbalistic rituals. He wanted to encompass all Nature into his collection."

Art does not reflect what we see, rather it enables us to see.

"He surely was a madman!" Bosse said.

"Did he ever marry?" Harriet asked.

My father shook his head no.

"He never had time for that."

"But we managed to get married!" my mother said.

"Rudolf the Second was deeply depressed," my father said, "but he found a way to overcome his melancholy."

In the evening at Eli's in Prague when we had finished

our discussion with her about art, my father expressed his thanks in a short speech with references to Eli and their common belief in Art and the importance of Prague to the citizens of Malmö. My father had a way of rising to the occasion when it came to something really important.

After that, when we went to the bedroom with the large double bed made of oak and the old fashioned radio on the table by the window where you could look out over the roof tops in the Old City of Prague, my father could unwrap the day's finds. He immediately sat down on the corner of the bed and took out one object after another from his canvas bag. Then he spread out books, lithographs, photographs, small statuettes, and other curiosities onto the bed—all purchased on his tight budget—which in other people's eyes were next to worthless. As he raised each item up in his hands, he would turn my way and, with boyish excitement, describe that European Trash:

"A Hrabal original, a little shabby, with spots here and there, but what a beautiful volume it is, and look at this lithograph! Do you see how the artist was able to catch those emotions in the facial expressions? And look here: the greatest find of all!"

He inspected the watercolor minutely.

"This must be by an unknown artist who was a contemporary with Nemes. He uses the same color scheme. Do you see the similarities? It looks like a human figure on its way to eternity."

His hands were shaking as he uttered his incantations.

"This is totally priceless."

My father held the European Trash towards me in a persuasive gesture, reminding me of a person praying, with those same arms that used to hug me so often when I was a boy.

And I could see that he was happy, and so, I believed his every word.

To realize that, is spite of the futile
results from the search, the struggle
has its own rewards.

"LA TERRE EST SI BELLE"
Ulf Hallberg, black notebook.

14. Heaven's Gate

When St. Peter first caught sight of the bewildered Hungarian-born painter, Endre Nemes, attempting to peek through the huge iron gate in hopes of getting a glimpse of what might lie beyond in Heaven, he said: "People like you aren't allowed in here."

"Why not?" asked Nemes timidly.

"You simply don't belong."

"How do you know?"

"When you died, God put that chair out there," St. Peter said—and Endre Nemes noticed in amazement a true-to-life chair, designed precisely as he had once painted it—"But you can't sit down on it. What nonsense!"

"I simply painted it; I don't have a knack for carpentry."

"More nonsense," St. Peter said.

And so he looked at Endre Nemes, who simultaneously concluded that St. Peter was a rather shabby fellow, quite ailing and doubled over, a little like the old waiter at the Café Boulevard in Prague. But the old man's penetrating glance made the painter squirm. He felt anything other than in a pleasant mood. What now? His eternal reward? Just another gate keeper. And with bad breath to top it off.

> I believe in the meaninglessness of the whole and the unintentional meaningfullness of every detail.

"I should get a chance to sit down once in a while," St. Peter said.

"It's not a real chair," Endre Nemes added.

"It doesn't help to be a smart ass. Do you call it 'unrealistic' to ask for some rest and comfort, at least every once in a while, as the starry heavens spread out above me and I stand guard forever?" asked St. Peter. The saliva at the corner of his mouth and the tremor in his hands proved that he meant business now. "Shall I stand here like Horatio and wait for ghosts, with a chair right next to me with knives sticking up out of it, and where you fall backwards into the Baroque era with all its paradoxes and antitheses? Do you think that is normal? That chair is downright uncomfortable."

"People would like to have everything as comfortable as possible in life, but that doesn't help them at all. It only spoils them. Those knives may be a reminder of that. Or they are just there like any other dangers in life."

"But up here ya ain't part of life anymore," St. Peter said.

"I don't think we're quite ready to cast off *all* the

polite formalities," Endre Nemes said, and declared thereby, in an obviously Central European manner, his independence—even though he was a wandering, tormented soul. "You can't explain the unexplainable. Not even here. But formalities must be upheld."

"Yeah, yeah, I know," answered the old one. "But Time's pendulum is cutting into something very concrete: my back. Not to mention those knives," he went on, and began rubbing his buttocks.

Nemes fiddled anxiously with his tie and put one hand into his coat pocket, which he found stuffed with scribbled notes and several dollar bills. His own scratchy handwriting on those notes clearly indicated what he had failed to complete during his lifetime, both on a human and a professional level. There was something written down about Helene and his first daughter, Catherine; about the flippant, yet successful woman writer who treated him like a toy; his lover Anna Sebastian; about how boorishly he had responded to the negativity of his colleagues' attacks. Here his sins and shortcomings were exposed, but not a word about that general distrust of émigrés, about the decades of contempt—during the hard years—where they blackballed him as a copy cat and a dabbler in eclecticism, called him "The Stale Surrealist," "The Effete Esthete"—an interloper in Swedish art. Not a word about his good sides, of his amicability, about his second wife and daughter—not a word about his art, that sign language he devoted is life to.

"Not much to go on here," St. Peter said with a snide grin.

"I have adjusted to the fact that the artist is the hunter and the hunted at the same time," Nemes said, "but I still demand, anyway, that my work be shown respect."

"I suppose that that's why God set that chair out there," St. Peter replied and laughed scornfully.

It appeared St. Peter hadn't enjoyed a square meal for quite some time. There was something Eastern European about him, Nemes thought: cheap shoes from some Bata boutique. And weren't those tattered overalls he was wearing with fading yellow stripes and, to top it off, instead of a regular belt, a length of thick twine to tie together his coat? But, to offer him, quite simply, a little money might be taken as an attempt at bribery.

"Are you by any chance from Prague?" Nemes asked tentatively, to gain a bit more time. "There's something familiar about you."

"Don't try to change the subject," St. Peter replied. "If I set my tired, old feet down on that annoying excuse for a chair, a Melancholy Lady will jump out and scream: 'Don't interrupt my vacant gaze! Death lurks everywhere.' As if I didn't know that already! This damn chair business already reeks of dead fish. Nope, God is devilishly unfair when he exposes me to this baroque chair. His demands on me have gone too far."

"In there," St. Peter said, pointing beyond the closed iron gate, "they sit in black-leather, auto-adjustable chairs with a plasma TV screen on a sliding shelf and with an MP3 player built into the arm rest. They even adjust their back—and leg—rests with their remote controls. Why should I—who am constantly at work—have to sit on this *thing?*" St. Peter gave the baroque chair a swift kick. "I would also prefer to be sitting in a black-leather reclining chair. Don't stare at me like that," he muttered irritably.

"I'm only trying to imagine what you did before you arrived here," Nemes said.

"It was even harder work back then," St. Peter said. "For a time I was obliged to go walking with God on his endless excursions, but do you really think we ever found anyone who qualified to be allowed entrance through the gate? No, you must be kidding. That's when God started this whole system of documents—and the necessity of carrying a resident's permit. And that's something you obviously don't have!"

"No, I guess I don't," Nemes said. "I did, in fact, acquire Swedish citizenship in 1948, but I never really felt like I had a 'resident's permit.' I was an alien. And probably it's just the same here."

"God declared that your chair is full of heathen symbols and corrosive allusions to an existence without hope."

"No," Nemes said, "it isn't so."

"What's that there for example?" St. Peter asked, pointing at a clock. "It doesn't even work. Those fish look like they've been poisoned, and what is she doing there?" St. Peter said and pointed at the Melancholy Lady. "Is that a deposed queen or only an abandoned woman?"

"She's enclosed by the frame," Nemes said, "for her, time has stopped in the shape she fills. She doesn't move anymore. She doesn't react, either to a bolt of lightning or to the glance from your eyes. It's just what it is by itself and can't be explained."

"Nonsense!" St. Peter screamed. "God isn't interested in artsy-fartsy clichés. He demands the facts. And obedience."

"She represents my deepest insights and uncompromising belief in art," Nemes replied. "Nobody can see into her eyes."

"Don't give me that *Sturm und Drang* angst." St. Peter shouted. "Otherwise, I will have to give you a thorough thrashing."

Right at that moment it looked like St. Peter was about to attack Endre Nemes, just the way artists over time have come to blows with one another while trying to resolve controversies, even though St. Peter couldn't be classified as an artist, really. But he was certainly as pissed off as artists often can get. And Nemes felt the same kind of threat that, during his hard life, he felt from the Artistic Establishment in Sweden: no holds barred, especially when it came to covetousness and backbiting. Because Endre Nemes had been forced to understand that he himself came to symbolize an "incomprehensible nobody" who franticly wants to get in somewhere where nobody really wants him. Everything is placed in its proper hierarchies and comfortable structures, which don't wish to be disturbed by threats from outsiders.

"At least I had a Swedish passport," Endre Nemes said defensively.

St. Peter looked both surprised and suspicious. But then he calmed himself down and said: "If that's true, it eventually could turn out to be a more favorable case."

Then Endre Nemes turned sour.

"The Swedes travel the world like privileged, first-class passengers with shiny passports and smooth-skinned faces," he said. "They impose this privileged condition and their naivete without letting the locals disturb their good-natured, sentimental self image. They expect to be well liked and to have everything go their way. They don't know what it means to be a foreigner. Their sense of belonging and mutual understanding isolate them, in a way, from the rest of the world. I always felt like I had a phony passport, and many customs officers, after staring into my face, suspected it was falsified."

"Now don't badmouth people who have helped you during life," St. Peter said. "Perhaps you are one of those who can never feel at home anywhere, a Wandering Jew. Your friend, Peter Weiss told me, before God turned him invisible and sent him back to Berlin, about that Max Berndorf fellow who always longed for some other place. In Oslo he spoke of Prague; in Prague he praised Barcelona; and in the end, as he lay in his hotel room in New York, he could only think of Europe. Those who can't feel at home anywhere only have themselves to blame."

It is said that the Gothic cathedrals in Europe can convert us by virtue of their pure existence.

"Home can be viewed in at least two ways," Nemes said, "both my Prague and my Stockholm are long gone. It all appears to be a lost world. And, the question is, are we really better off when we feel at home? We lose our instinct for the unexpected in life. We forget to take responsibility for the most important thing: the past's influence on the present."

"Is that why you painted that good-for-nothing chair?" St. Peter asked. "Because you fancied that we are not making any progress; that we will get bogged down in your musty old habitat, always remaining outsiders everywhere we go."

"To speak honestly," Nemes said, "I believe that

everything inside me and everything I created in some way expresses my link to Central Europe. But I'm not certain that Sweden wants to belong to Europe."

"And what would that be, your enigmatic Central Europe?" St. Peter asked.

Now Endre Nemes thought the guardian at Heaven's Gate reminded him more of the head guard at Göteborg's Municipal Art Museum, a man who had appeared in one of Nemes' dreams and asked which hall the artist preferred to sleep in. And then he scrambled away with his huge ring of keys and pointed down a long hallway.

"Maybe it's just my belief that we really can save the dead. A dream of a different existence, where different languages, arts and music would, for once, all play in unison, with the lightness of a dream."

"Yes, of course," St. Peter said, "but have you ever, quite concretely, been down to earth before you died? Or have you been living your entire 'life of art' on Cloud Twenty-Three? And everything else revolved around that—what ordinary people had to occupy their lives with—while you sprang around up there in layers of thin air."

"Art isn't an airy cloud. It's not like it is up here. It's a way to pry into the human condition. The motion goes from the outside into the soul. You first sacrifice your sense of community. No one can pry into art without being able to bear solitude and one's own limitations. To dare to push yourself to the limit of your talents gives you self-awareness."

St. Peter appeared not to know what to make of this drivel.

"But, after all, it seems you made out pretty well

from what I've heard," St. Peter said agreeably, in an effort to avoid an impasse, which otherwise might force him to come to grips, ever so slightly, with his inner self. "Though I eventually was successful, I continued to feel like an outsider. It was in my blood. My guardian Virgin Mary was the creative energy derived from being an outsider. That crude impulse to observe my own truth was the only thing I had, the fleeting image of a likeness to an inner vision that suddenly burst into flames, laden with despair, but brightly colored—as when the sky turns deep red on a summer night after a thundercloud passes by or there's a shower of rain."

St. Peter hung his head. Apparently he couldn't find anything similar in his own existence: no true faith, no real drive, no dedication such as Nemes was describing in his painting of a picture that seemed to burn in front of his inner eye. The gate keeper's dejection made Nemes nervous. People can collapse and die right in front of you if you don't watch out, Nemes thought. Nobody can go free without some illusions. The sad part was that the man Endre Nemes stood in front of now was worse off than he himself had ever been during his worst days, because Nemes, even when he wasn't clean, still had the ability to be, if not elegant, at least tidy. He preferred a simple suit and tie, an almost bureaucratic, grayish-brown costume that made him look compact and highly competent despite his short height. Yes, that's how he always looked, and that's how his worried spirit looked as well. But this St. Peter came

It is important not to be blunted by the powers of others, and lastly not by the lack of power in one's personal reign.

315

directly from the barren regions of the tundra or from a filthy back alley in one of the suburbs of Prague. He looked as though he had never had a chance to come into his own—just like the insignificant and the weak, those other Jews and refugees, all those who didn't get away, those who for lack of insight and possibilities, with a tight grip on a few minimal hopes, went under; all those in that forgotten world who were gone forever, all those pale faces and worried hands behind the dark curtains of the past, which Nemes tried to capture in an image, in shapes and colors, attached to a canvass beyond the effects of time.

Quickly the storm chases our years.

"The blue streetcars of Stockholm are long gone," Endre Nemes said, "and so is the house on Master Samuel's Street where I had my studio, all that life in the Klara District. No more Bohemians there either, and all those stories come to an end. No one listens anymore. And most of old Prague has vanished. It's only in the gloomy mansions and the baroque vaulted ceilings where you can still get a taste in the present of times passed. Fewer and fewer want to know about it. They'd prefer to sit instead in the most comfortable chair at the head of a big corporation—something that would have horrified Kafka—and he had seen a lot."

"I just want a regular chair," St. Peter said, "preferably of leather."

"What do you expect to gain from that?"

"Enjoyment. Because I have to relax."

"And then what?"

"Then what what?"

"Yes, because time is endlessly long," Endre Nemes

said. "What will you do with your time when you have relaxed?"

"Then I will pick up my ax and shatter your damned chair to pieces and burn it up . . . But before I do that, I'll grab you like this . . . "

And then that old one, with surprising force, grabbed that short, frightened painter and lifted him up by his shirt collar so that Nemes was swinging in the air like a pendulum.

"If you can make me believe that there's a reason to paint or put together uncomfortable chairs, then I will allow you to enter Heaven. Otherwise you will have to fashion glowing spears and spokes for wheels down in Hell for eternity. Amen."

And then St. Peter had a hearty laugh.

All of the above made Endre Nemes realize that only one thing could save him now: a story. So he told the story about the leg of the table.

"When I was two-years-old we lived in Nova Ves in the Slavic portion of the former Austro-Hungarian Empire, and my mother had an inn. Every evening she tied me to the leg of the table so that I wouldn't run away or get under her feet. From there I noticed the legs of the guests, their dirty boots next to the carved table legs. I saw that several of the farmers carried coarse, thick knives, tucked into their leather belts. I observed their non-descript ruddy faces and ran away as far as the rope would let me when somebody scared me. Then I saw the candlestick on the table, the burning flame, and heard the clock ticking on the wall. I was trapped there under the table, listening to the clinking of glasses, the whispering of voices, and the raw laughter. And perhaps

I already had an inkling then of the ice-cold answer that might follow such gaiety and enthusiasm, especially if a mother could tie a child to the leg of a table like some bothersome mutt. Nobody in that antiquated world wanted to see what was going on. Emotions were allowed total license and intellect was ridiculed. Children were treated like animals or like adults. There's a photo of my brother and me from 1915, a half year into the First World War. I am five-years-old and Lajos is a little over six. We are standing in our Austro-Hungarian uniforms with corporal stripes and swords in hand. Our clothing portrays everything about our parents' view of the world. Nationalism's power of attraction was just a release from the instability that weighs down every sense of identity," Endre Nemes said and peeked at St. Peter who nodded, if a bit skeptically.

About myself: It could not be done better, only differently (this goes for Peter and Lena as well).

"When I left Prague in the fall of 1938, I stored my paintings with my friend, Jarmila Haasova, who was married for a while to Willy Haas, publisher of the German-speaking periodical, *The Literary World*. Jarmila was a dyed-in-the-wool Stalinist. On the 14th of March 1939, she sent me a telegram: "Return! All's well!" The very next morning Hitler's storm troopers marched into Prague.

Endre Nemes added with emphasis that, thank God, he had managed to get himself to Helsinki, through which he came to Stockholm via Oslo.

"The light in Helsinki and the cold white snow gave me a feeling of consolation even at my lowest point. Nature constantly sends out messages to us. A friend of mine, the painter Eugene Nevan, sent the stored paintings by freight ship to Helsinki via Stettin. Yes, that's the way it was at that time."

Both remained silent for a moment.

"When I think of Stockholm, I sense that if there was anything sacred that I discovered in Sweden, it was Nature," Nemes said then, "Perhaps Nature gives to the best ones, yes, to the ordinary people, a message about something important, so that they develop a kind of seriousness and a naïve openness I came to like in the countries of the North."

St. Peter stood completely still and pondered Nemes' words. Even if he still felt righteously and totally critical of Endre Nemes' horrible chair and everything that artsy-fartsy fool called art, there was something in that painter's insistence, yes, something attractive in all his stories about the old Eastern Europe, and even something rather disturbing in his view of Sweden that St. Peter couldn't deflect.

So he slowly opened the big, heavy iron gate, and that is how the Hungarian-born painter, Endre Nemes, actually managed to sneak into Heaven (even though he wasn't really a Swede) by an ungodly and unusual logic.

The baroque chair sat there under the skies of Heaven, and the only thing audible besides St. Peter's shuffling foot steps through meaningless, cold airy spaces was God's holy maledictions. But when the next morning St. Peter tried to turn the baroque chair into firewood with his ax, the figures in the chair whimpered and screamed. Those suffering and ill-starred *Figures,* walking out of eighteenth century palaces, the reclining female forms and the Melancholy Lady were splattered with blood and excrement. The fish tails writhed. But no matter how hard the old gate keeper hacked away, these things stood up to their opponent, and when St. Peter returned the next morning on the same errand, the chair stood there again, whole and undamaged, and the figures had resumed their positions as if they never could be destroyed, neither by fate nor by St. Peter's shiny ax.

Then the rusty iron gate swung open and out bolted Endre Nemes from Heaven with eyes bulging. St. Peter felt complete disappointment in his breast—the battle was lost. He had suspected this from the start. That little, unreliable Central European ghost should have been sent packing immediately. How much trouble can a lone artist make— in a small country

"Black holes = If you are flying towards a black hole gravitation gets so strong that time comes to a standstill. You can look back and then you see the history of the Universe roll by until it comes to its end, because time out there passes incredibly quickly in comparison to one's own lifetime. On the verge of the black hole you can see the Universe fade away and disappear.

or up in the wide Heavens? A thunderclap in the background, and lightning flashes like some chintzy, melodramatic B-film from Hollywood.

"No one gets away with saying that Heaven is a bore without being punished," God bellowed. "We'll see what you do now while suffering for eternity."

"I'd rather have that . . ." Endre Nemes called out.
And while he was running, he felt how much he
longed for the atmosphere of the Café Boulevard in
Prague, where the waiter, without the blink of an eye,
could greet a man who had been gone for ten or twenty
years—who had survived trench warfare and two equally
blitz-krieg marriages—with the words: "Good day,
Publisher Reichmann, will you have a cappuccino with
mineral water and the newspaper, *Bohemia,* as usual?"
And he thought about his good friend in New York, the
old Jew Isaac Verständig, who survived the concentration
camps in Eastern Europe and every morning for sixty
years, while shaving, greeted his image in the mirror
with a joyful, triumphant "Heil Hitler, Meschugge!" in
order to emphasize that without a good sense of humor
you can't even survive prosperity.

Now he understood why everything is topsy-
turvy—and why every situation or conclusion by itself
includes its own contradictions. At least he fancied that
he understood what was happening at that moment,
running along, out of breath, looking for difficulties.
Peace and quiet aren't to be found; comfort is just escape
and betrayal. The whole activity involved in his work
as a painter, the struggle with the easel and with life,
everything he had never been able to find words for and
was forced to paint—all that was clear to him now as
the blackness of the night sky, and he believed that in
the flames of the Inferno he would at least—against all
odds—paint his final, most radical work: *The Advantages
of Hell: The Anatomy of the Riddles of Life.*

"Only survivors and the truly independent can bear
witness to the fact that everything in life has a dual

existence," Endre Nemes was saying just as the Devil pointed out to him the well-known hook in the ceiling, on which one hangs one's self.

And the Devil allowed him, thanks to that witty one-liner, to lay out his paint brushes and set up his easel.

So he continued painting his sense of loss, in tempera and red ochre, and enjoyed being able to work in Hell.

The author wishes to thank Henrik Bager. Without his attentive reading of the manuscript and good advice this book would never have taken its present form. His tireless interest in the nuances of the text has been a great gift, similar to the inspiration derived from his paintings. For concrete details in portions of "The Messenger" I am indebted to Jean-Francois Steiner's *Treblinka*, and in "The Lonely One," to Barry Paris' wonderful biography, *Garbo*. A special thanks goes to my American editor Dwayne Hayes, for his deep devotion to European literature, present in the magazine *Absinthe* for nearly a decade.

For Jana, Julian and Lenny, always.

Translators' Notes

The translators wish to thank the author, Ulf Peter Hallberg, and his Italian translator, Massimo Ciaravolo, for helping to direct us to standard translations in English for pieces by Walter Benjamin. We relied on *The Arcades Project,* translated by Howard Eiland and Kevin McLaughlin, Belknap Press, Harvard University, 1999, and *Illuminations,* translated by Harry Zohn, Schocken Books, 1968. As for fragments of poetry from Baudelaire, the translators relied on their own versions from the French.

Editor's Note

In 2009 I published an excerpt from Ulf Peter Hallberg's work *European Trash* in our eleventh issue of *Absinthe*, a journal focused on European literature and the arts. Little did I know that four years later I would be involved in the English-language publication of this novel.

Erland Anderson, Hallberg's translator, invited me to meet him and Ulf Peter in Chicago for the conference of the Society for the Advancement of Scandinavian Study at the end of April in 2011. Ulf Peter and I immediately bonded over a mutual appreciation for European literature and culture (including admiration for Ingmar Bergman and the fine Swedish actor Erland Josephson) and also over our roles as fathers and our commitment to our children. I made two short videos for the *Absinthe* blog where Ulf Peter discusses *European Trash* and his relationship with his father. These videos can also be viewed on YouTube.

Several weeks later we decided that we should collaborate on the publication of a book. I was initially drawn to Ulf Peter's co-authored novel with the actor Erland Josephson and we proceeded with plans to publish that work, *The Meaning of Life and Other Troubles*. After a few months we separately came to the conclusion that we wanted to start with *European Trash*, because that was the bond between us, our mutual fascination with certain values. We viewed this decision, made thousands of miles apart, as serendipitous and began plans to work with Erland Anderson to have the novel translated.

I noted that we came to a decision to "start" with *European Trash* and I fully expect and hope that English-speaking readers will have the opportunity to read Ulf Peter's other books, including *The Meaning of Life and Other Troubles* and his widely-acclaimed new novel *Strindberg's Shadow in the Paris of the North,* which has been called a sort-of sequel to *European Trash*.

As you know by now, *European Trash* is subtitled *Fourteen Ways to Remember a Father* and I was immediately struck by Ulf Peter's movingly elegiac prose as he describes his father's room, his desk, and his father's system of cutting out articles, quotes, images, and other items of the European Trash that he collected. Through his father the collector, in *European Trash,* Hallberg explores the role of art, not only in the wider context of society, but on a more intimate level: how art penetrates and influences the soul. Ulf Peter learned the value of art and culture from his father and has been handing down those same lessons and values to his sons, Lenny and Julian. So this book is not just a book about the values inherent in European art, literature, and culture. It is a novel of a son's love for his father and that same son's love for his children.

In 2010 *European Trash* was awarded the Albert Bonnier Award. The jury's statement captures the essence of the work and what I love about it in jurist and acclaimed Swedish writer Lars Andersson's summation: "It all reverberates like the light of dawn. Even as we are led through feelings of nothingness or despair. They, too, are enveloped in the light of dawn. It is a book to warm yourself by. The light gets into your eyes. 'Are there fragments', he asks, 'in every human being's past that can save him – if he takes them seriously?' It feels like that's exactly the way it is."

Dwayne D. Hayes
editor, *Absinthe: New European Writing*

ULF PETER HALLBERG, a Swedish writer born in Malmö, has lived in Berlin since 1983. He is the author of many books, includin *The Glance of the Flâneur* (1996; translated into German and Italian) *Grand Tour* (2005) *Legends & Lies* (2007), *European Trash* (2009), and *The Meaning of Life and Other Worries* (with Erland Josephson, 2010). Hallberg has also translated Shakespeare, Molière, Walter Benjamin, Schiller, Büchner, Wedekind and Brecht into Swedish. For twenty years he was one of the co-editors of Res Publica, a cultural and literary quarterly.

ERLAND ANDERSON has published several books in translation, including *Between Darkness and Darkness: Selected Poems by Rolf Aggestam*, (with Lars Nordstrom, 1989) and *Views from a Tuft of Grass by Harry Martinson* (2005). While working on the Martinson book in Sweden in 2003 he met Ulf Peter Hallberg and began translating his work. Anderson lives in Los Angeles, CA.

INGRID CASSADY is from Stockholm, Sweden, and currently lives in California.